
Edmund: The skinny hitman's father had been a jazz player, his brother a graduate of MIT. When Salvatore Pescatore, aka Sally Fish, called him for a double bang, it was the beginning of a mad dash into a private hell . . .

Dr. Karen Winterman: A brilliant psychiatrist, she didn't believe in coincidence. But when her charming patient Arnie turned up dead, she was pulled into an unlucky streak—of violence . . .

Arnie Feinstein: The pampered grandson of Holocaust survivors, Arnie was having an affair with his shrink and playing a dangerous game with hip Sally Fish—until Sally Fish wanted him dead . . .

Vinnie Crow: The hulking, bald-headed cop had long ago turned bad—and brought his partner in with him. His last living act was to whisper in Benson's ear, and hand him the key to half a million dollars . . .

William Benson: Billy the Kid had muscles like steel, a crush on his partner's wife, and the key to a locker at the Port Authority. But the cops were waiting for him to make a move—and the wiseguys were hunting him down . . .

Sally Fish: He told his Uncle Frankie, "I'm a master criminal. I do things with flair." But bootlegging Pierre Cardin suits led him to one crime too many—and now he was in over his head . . .

Books by Heywood Gould

Cocktail
Double Bang

Published by POCKET BOOKS

Double Bang

Heywood Gould

POCKET BOOKS

New York   London   Toronto   Sydney   Tokyo

POCKET BOOKS, a division of Simon & Schuster Inc.
1230 Avenue of the Americas, New York, NY 10020

Copyright © 1988 by Heywood Gould
Cover photo copyright © 1989 Mort Engel Studio

Library of Congress Catalog Card Number: 87-26558

ISBN: 0-671-67835-3

First Pocket Books printing May 1989

10 9 8 7 6 5 4 3 2 1

POCKET and colophon are trademarks of Simon & Schuster Inc.

Printed in the U.S.A.

To Pattie

Double Bang

ONE

HE'S ON THE SPOT

A little after two in the morning the phone began ringing. Edmund was wide awake, watching the numbers flip on the digital clock—2:08, 2:09. Raymond and the redhead were at war in the bathroom. They'd been in there since 1:06. "I'm gonna desecrate you, bitch," Raymond yelled. The chick yelped. There was a "thwap" like somebody slamming a wet fish against the wall.

The phone rang until 2:12. It stopped, then started at 2:13.

Edmund leaned over and put the ringing phone against the ear of the brown girl next to him. She didn't flinch. She had coked herself into a coma. Like traveling so far south you end up freezing. She was sleeping on one arm, while the other hung over the bed. One eye was half open, the sightless pupil gleaming from behind the lashes. Her lips had a gray rind around them, her nose looked like it was stuffed with plaster of paris. She'd be out for hours, and when she finally woke up it would take another gram to get her out of bed.

At 2:20 the phone stopped ringing, but Edmund knew it would start again. He knew who it was, and he knew what the guy was doing—standing in a phone booth somewhere, checking the number in that little blue phone book of his. Getting madder and madder because he knew what Edmund was doing to him.

Ring! This time Edmund picked it up right away.

"Who's this?"

"Mr. Feinstein, who the fuck do you think it is?"

"What's up?"

"The guy's on the spot."

"For when?"

"Now, man. Why do you think I'm callin', for Washington's Birthday?"

"It's late," Edmund said.

"I just got the thing set up."

Edmund struck a match and flipped it on the brown girl's back.

"You noddin' out or what, Edmund?"

"I'm here." The girl moaned in her sleep. Edmund flicked the burning match off her back.

"He's in room three thirteen at the River Royale. His name's Vinnie Crow. He's a big white dude with a big, square, ugly fuckin' head. You can't miss him. He'll be the only guy in the room."

"Then what?"

"There's a chick in there. She's with me. She's gonna wait ten minutes and split. She'll leave the door open. The guy's on the bed passed out."

"How do you know?"

4

"Look, the guy's a juicehead. He's already on his third quart."

"How do you know he's passed out?"

"He'll be passed out by the time you get there."

"The chick has to call you when he's passed out. Then you call me."

"What do you think I'm runnin', a fuckin' telethon over here?"

"You said he was passed out, so now he's gotta be passed out," Edmund said. "Call the chick back."

"I can't call the room, man. What if the guy answers?"

"If he's on his third quart he won't be answering telephones."

"Okay, okay." Mr. Feinstein hung up.

Edmund shook the brown chick. She moaned and licked her sandpaper lips. He lifted her free arm and let it drop knuckle first onto the bed table. Nothing. He got up and knocked softly on the bathroom door.

"I'm busy," Raymond said through the door.

Edmund opened the door. "You gotta go, man."

Raymond had the redhead kneeling in the bathtub, her breasts hanging over the side. He had her by the ears, her head pulled all the way back. One side of her face was blue and blotchy. There was a trail of bite marks from her neck down to her breasts.

"Can't get it up," Raymond said hoarsely.

Edmund remembered the old man on Manhattan Avenue. "Cocaine's about always goin' someplace and never gettin' there."

"I got some people coming over," Edmund said. "You understand. . . ."

Raymond snarled, "I've got to desecrate this bitch."

The phone rang in the bedroom. "I ain't got time for this," Edmund said. He kicked Raymond's legs out from under him. Raymond grabbed at air and knocked the glass shelf off the top of the sink. He went down hard, hitting his head against the toilet bowl.

Edmund went back into the bedroom and picked up the phone.

"Okay, he's out. Room three thirteen. The chick's gonna split in fifteen minutes. The door'll be open. . . ."

The redhead staggered out of the bathroom and leaned against the wall, breathing hard. Raymond wobbled out after her, holding a bloodsoaked towel to his arm.

"I got some people coming over," Edmund said.

"Yeah, yeah, sure, I understand. Uh . . . can I . . . ?" He pointed out into the living room.

"Help yourself."

Raymond grabbed the redhead by the back of the neck. "C'mon, slave."

The redhead giggled and looked at Edmund. "Everybody's naked."

Raymond shoved her into the living room. "Get in there."

Edmund turned toward the brown girl, but she was already up, sitting on the edge of the bed, her eyes wide open.

"Can I take a shower?"

"Yeah."

The girl padded obediently into the bathroom.

"Watch out for the broken glass," Edmund said.

In the living room the redhead was bending over a line of coke, her hand trembling so much she could hardly keep the straw in her nose. Edmund stood in the doorway until Raymond noticed him. "C'mon, hurry up and get dressed," Raymond said, shoving the redhead. "My man's got some people comin' over."

"Take your time," Edmund said.

In fifteen minutes they were gone. He opened all the windows. Their odors faded, and it was like nobody had been there.

"Always show something a little cleaner than what you are," the old man on Manhattan Avenue had told him. "If you're a burglar, then you show booster, if you're peddling reefer you show numbers. You ain't never gonna get people to believe you're straight what with hangin' around all hours, what with your wardrobe and your wheels. But if you can get them acceptin' you're something you're not, then you're cool because they'll always be lookin' to catch you doin' something you ain't never gonna do."

So Edmund showed coke dealer, which was something cleaner than what he was. He worked up the outfit, the black leather pants, African gold bracelet lying smooth on his brown wrist, top-of-the-line Rolex. The white boys in the elevator whispered about him when he got off. The potbellied Puerto Rican super gave him a wink when he paid his rent in cash. The old Jewish ladies in the laundry room pursed their lips and looked away when he came in.

It was a good front, but it had its problems, and

Raymond was one of them. Raymond had grown up on the block, 107th and Manhattan Avenue, and he had hung out in Cathedral Park with Edmund and the other guys in their crew, the Jokers.

But unlike the others, Raymond had stayed out of trouble and concentrated on basketball. He had gotten a scholarship to Duke. Now he was hooked into a Wall Street investment firm. He wore three-piece suits and Johnston and Murphy shoes. He was smart and ambitious, but his nose still came around the block five minutes before his head showed up. So when he heard Edmund was dealing blow he began knocking on the door at all hours. Edmund had to let him in. He had to keep enough of the goods around to make it look like he was a "shonuf" gram dealer. He had to hang out with Raymond. That was the worst part. Edmund didn't like hanging out with anybody.

The doorman knew Raymond so well he didn't bother calling up when he came. There was just a knock, and there was Raymond in the fisheye of the peephole, giggling and waving money. He had a fistful of hundred-dollar bills and smelled of sour wine. "Hey, bro, can you tighten me up?"

Edmund had been waiting all day for Sally's call, but he had to deal with Raymond. Raymond marched in and set up his gram scale and his "Tiffany kit," as he called it, which consisted of a stone, gold-plated razor, straw and mirror, in a leather bag. Edmund couldn't stand cocaine. It made him sick watching Raymond woof on it, starting out up and happy, then after an hour getting that mean look and nonstop rapping about politics and women and white people and whatnot. A little of this powder and he thought he

8

knew everything and could do everything. And Edmund had to put up with it because he had to maintain the front.

But this night had been a little easier. Raymond got restless after a couple of toots. "Let's go out and get some pussy, man," he said.

They went to the Crossroads, a bar across the street from Edmund's building on Seventy-second Street. "It's convenient, livin' on the West Side, man," Raymond said, looking around at all the loose women. "I've got to get out of the Village. Too many faggots."

After a few drinks Raymond forgot about women. "What do you do with your bread, anyway, Edmund? I mean, you're in a cash business. . . ."

"I give it to the United Negro College Fund," Edmund said.

"Bearer bonds," Raymond said. "It's like they were invented for dudes like you. No name, no way to trace ownership, and no tax. All you do is clip the coupons. I can hook you into some gilt-edged motherfuckers, too. . . ."

Then the chicks appeared in the mirror behind them, talking real loud to the bartender about could he get them two seats because they had been standing all day. Working girls on their night off looking to get as high as possible without paying for it. The brown chick was dressed down in a red ribbed sweater and jeans real tight in the crotch. The redhead had on black silk pants and a sheer white blouse that showed her nipples.

Raymond gripped Edmund's knee. "You ladies can have our seats," he said, getting up.

"Thanks."

"That is if you let us buy you a round."

The redhead giggled and looked from Raymond to Edmund. They were just what she had come out for. "That's no hardship to me."

The redhead's name was Eloise. The brown chick's name was Arlene. She was short and trim with a cat's oval face and slightly bulging eyes. Eloise was all made up, rouge and lipstick and a beauty mark under one eye. Arlene was wearing black lipstick.

Raymond flipped a coin, and Edmund called "heads." It ended up heads and Edmund moved next to Arlene. "What are you drinkin'?" Eloise didn't know what had happened, but Arlene knew Edmund had chosen her, and it cheered her up to know she had beaten out a white chick.

They said they worked for the telephone company "in personnel." Edmund said he owned a shoestore in Brooklyn. Raymond was the only one who told the truth about what he did, and they didn't believe him either. After a few trips to the bathroom, and the promise of a lot more, they went back to Edmund's apartment.

Eloise settled herself on the couch right next to Raymond and his Tiffany set, but Arlene walked around the living room looking behind the chairs as if she expected to find a dead body.

"This a sublet?" she asked Edmund.

"Why do you say that?"

She pointed to the books in the bookcase. "You read all of these?"

"They're all hollow," Raymond said from the couch. "He keeps his money in them."

"Raymond thinks he's the only nigger in the world

can read," Edmund said. "Actually, they're my brother Thomas's books."

"What's he do?"

"He was an electrophysicist working on the space program."

"He committed suicide, didn't he, Edmund?" Raymond said.

Edmund ignored him. It was either that or throw him out, and he just couldn't do that . . . yet. "If you're lookin' for the stash—" he said to Arlene.

She pointed to the photos on the wall. "Who's that?"

"My father. He had a septet that played around New York in the thirties and forties."

"Is that him with the saxophone?"

"Yeah."

"Looks like you."

Gotta speed this shit up, Edmund thought, suddenly remembering the call. "Let's try it out," he said.

Arlene's hand was soft. He liked the docile way she followed him into the bedroom. Liked the way she stood quietly while he took her clothes off, slipped the sweater over her head, eased her back on the bed, slid off the soft suede boots, pulled the jeans over her knees.

But then she dove between his legs before he had time to get into bed, and started in on him like a windup doll, and he realized she was doing what she thought was expected of her, that she was really in a hurry to get back to the drugs. Nobody's a whore by accident.

So he lay in bed a few hours later, after she had

knocked herself out, and watched the clock—one minute less, one minute less—and then Raymond came in dragging the redhead by the hair, and slammed the bathroom door.

One minute less . . . one minute less.

And then the phone rang.

GOING THROUGH THE MOTIONS

*E*dmund put on his "subway best." The blue warm-up jacket with the hood up over his head. Yankee cap over the hood, Sergio jeans and Nikes, laces loose. Anybody on the subway who saw him would immediately turn away. Anybody on the street would hurry by. He was showing chain snatcher, push-in man, purse grabber. When he hit Times Square he blended right in. He didn't get a second look.

The River Royale Hotel sprawled over almost the whole square block of Forty-fourth and Tenth. The lobby was gloomy, the square-badge security cop made believe he was sleeping so he wouldn't have to deal with deadbeats, and the desk clerks weren't about to hassle anybody unless there were some bucks in it. But Edmund had a foolproof way of getting in without being seen by anybody. On the street side there was a little cocktail lounge. They kept the place pitch-dark, except for the flickering bulb over the cash register. A guy in a dark blue sweatshirt could move invisible as the breeze past the booths where people sat whispering right to the door that led to the rear lobby behind the desk. From there it was a short hop to the stairway, which was always empty, there being signs in the elevator advising guests to "refrain from using the stairwells unless in an emergency."

Edmund took the steps three at a time to the third floor. The corridor was empty. He slid the snub-nosed Charter Arms .44 Bulldog out of his pocket and cradled it in the palm of his hand. No silencer: you couldn't trust them at anything more than point-blank range, and besides, there was nothing like the sound of a shot to keep people in their rooms. Especially in this hotel, where everybody knew what a shot sounded like.

A slit of light gleamed from the room where the door had been left open. Three nineteen, three seventeen, three fifteen, three thirteen—there it was. No hesitating, no looking around to see if anyone was there, just go through the door from the blind side, and look left for the bed. He raised the gun shoulder-high and pushed the door gently.

The first thing he saw was a little PR chick, stark naked, cowering in a corner. Alarm tightened in his chest. He would have turned and run, but the door kept swinging, and there was the big white guy on the bed with a piece pointing right at him.

The white guy screamed, "You cunt!" He swiveled around and shot the naked girl, the big gun booming twice. The girl twitched twice. Little squeals came out of her like air going out of a balloon. Then the dude swiveled toward Edmund. Edmund dropped and squeezed fast—once, twice—aiming for the dude's

14

throat. A bullet splintered the door frame behind him. Edmund rolled out into the corridor as another bullet slammed into the wall. There was a roar of pain from inside the room. Edmund rolled up onto his feet as two guys came out of the room across the hall, one of them fumbling with an ankle holster. Edmund turned and threw a shot in their direction without aiming. One guy ran back into the room; the other turned completely around as if he had lost his way, and slammed into the wall.

Down the hall, a door opened. Edmund shot again, and heard a man shriek and curse as he headed for the stairs.

He jumped from landing to landing. At ground level he landed a step short and twisted his ankle. A guy with a walkie-talkie was running through the lobby toward him. Edmund shot. The guy dove behind a chair.

He made it to the revolving door. Bullets slapped like raindrops into the glass behind him. He took off into the darkness, down Forty-fourth, under the highway, heading for the railroad yard. There were voices behind him. Then they stopped, and it was quiet except for the sound of his sobbing breaths. The pain from his ankle shot in a jagged line up to the small of his back. The old Penn Railroad yard was up ahead, but didn't seem to be getting any closer.

Cars whooshed by on the way to the highway. Edmund stepped into the darkness of the yard. A bunch of derelicts flapped their rags over a fire in a trash can. Two men were kissing behind a shed. Above him the highway creaked with upstate traffic, the hum of tires. At the end there was a narrow path that opened onto Riverside Park, where the scene changed suddenly. There was a long promenade along the Hudson River. The lights of the houseboats in the Seventy-ninth Street Marina twinkled peacefully. The great dark shapes of the trees loomed out at him, the leaves hissing in the ebb and flow of the breeze. Lovers sat on the benches. A lone jogger circled the track. A brother with a Walkman and a Doberman watched Edmund warily.

Edmund clenched his teeth against the pain and walked with a normal stride toward an isolated spot. He leaned over the rail and dropped the pistol into the Hudson. The wind rose and covered the sound of the splash. Then it was quiet again.

A nerve in his neck was pulsing violently, but otherwise he was okay. On Riverside Drive a bag lady was going through a garbage can. She turned and shook her fist. "Sonofabitch bastard, Jesus Christ."

"That's me, baby," Edmund said.

"Sonofabitch bastard don't raise your voice to me."

She was talking to a son or a husband. He was right there next to her. The streets were full of people you never saw. Edmund calmed himself with these thoughts: *You're the man who doesn't care if he lives or dies. You're the man who's just going through the motions.*

The doorman was sitting on a car with a can of beer. Edmund slipped right by him. Up in his apartment he moved in the dark. He wrapped some ice in a towel and piled the pillows on the bed.

He raised his leg onto the pillows and applied the ice. Then he lay back in the darkness and watched the digits flip on the radium dial while he waited for Sally Fish to call.

END OF THE LINE

Detective William Benson woke up with the phone in his hand and no idea who he was talking to. It had been one of those nights where the four or five highballs after work hadn't seemed enough. ("If you make it off the highway alive you're not drunk enough," the old cop joke went.) So he'd continued through the evening with Grand Marnier, the only alcoholic beverage his wife, Doreen, allowed in the house, chasing the sugar off his teeth with cans of Bud. The last thing he remembered was aiming for the toilet and somehow splatting the shower curtain. The bedroom was pretty scuzzy, smelling of stale smoke and spilled booze. The test pattern flickered on the TV screen. Doreen was sprawled on her stomach across the unmade bed, a vial of pills overturned on the floor just under her outstretched fingers. His own bedroom, for Chrissake, and it looked like a crime scene.

"You're loaded, Benson," the voice on the phone said.

"No shit, Sherlock," Benson said. Doreen moaned and rubbed her eyes irritably. "Who are you talking to at this hour, for Godsakes?"

"Better sober up, Benson," the voice on the phone said. "Your partner's gone psycho."

Benson's head cleared quickly. The voice belonged to Inspector Duffy, commander of the Major Case Squad. Benson closed his eyes and took a deep breath.

"He's barricaded in a room at the River Royale. He's got a woman in there, an undercover officer in a narcotics unit. He's holding her hostage . . ."

Jesus, Vinnie, what kind of jackpot did you get yourself into?

"There was an attempt on his life about an hour ago. The perp shot two police officers on stakeout and got away. The officers both died . . ."

Vinnie, for Chrissake . . .

"Crow says he won't talk to anybody but you. Says he'll kill the girl and himself . . ."

"I'm on my way, Boss."

"Make it fast, Benson. I'm holding your shield over the toilet right now."

Good-byes seemed beside the point so Benson hung up and stumbled into the bathroom.

"What's the matter?" Doreen called after him.

"Vinnie's gone crazy."

"What do you mean 'gone'?"

Benson kept the light off as he ran cold water over his wrists and the back of his neck. They had always wondered how it would end. Their names in the paper—"Detective Vincent Crow, 46, and his partner,

Detective William Benson, 44, of the Police Department's elite Safe, Loft and Truck Squad, were accused today of taking payoffs from a burglary ring that operated in the garment district. . . .'' The wise looks from the neighbors. The friends who stopped calling. Guys on the job who all of a sudden didn't know you. Wives crying and nagging, What am I gonna do? What am I gonna do? The kids looking at you with hurt eyes, that would be the toughest part, having to deal with the kids. Because from the time they started on the pad they had known it was going to end some day. They had been cops too long, and were too good at the job, to think they could get away with it forever. Sooner or later some stool would drop their names. Or a wiseguy would get his nuts squeezed, and they'd go down along with a lot of other people. They had gotten loaded hundreds of times and decided it didn't matter. A couple of years in the can would be a vacation. The company would be good. They'd get a lot of reading done.

"What did you say?" Doreen called.

Benson walked out of the bathroom. "What?"

"You know I can't hear you when you're in there."

"Where the hell are my cigarettes?"

"You're the detective," she said, turning over on her stomach. Something crinkled under her thighs.

"Oh, shit, you're lying on them." Benson tried to turn her over.

"Billy," she squealed.

The Marlboros looked like they'd been flattened by a steam roller. He managed to salvage one only slightly bent.

"I'll have to buy the box if you keep gaining weight."

She pouted and flounced on to her stomach again. "Maybe if you weren't so soused you wouldn't leave them in the bed."

"Okay, okay, don't get your feelings hurt." He kissed her on the forehead. How long had it been, three weeks, a month? He'd been thinking about throwing her a hump—just for drill. But now, with the arrest and the lawyers and all the aggravation, the subject wouldn't even come up. What a life. He was about to be destroyed forever, and he was relieved that he wouldn't have to screw his wife!

On the steps, Benson lit up. The first cigarette always felt like someone was slitting his lungs with a steak knife. The next thirty or forty would go down easier.

The windows were wide open in the living room. It was freezing. He heard footsteps, frantic whispers. Then: "Dad, is that you?"

His fifteen-year-old Elizabeth came out of the kitchen, followed by Dominick, the altar boy with the sneaky look.

"I brought Dominick in for a sandwich, Dad."

Designer jeans, disco nails, this week it was a green streak in her hair. She looked like one of those runaways the Pussy Posse took off Eighth Avenue every night. And now she was smoking pot in the living room with this mutt.

Just for drill Benson asked, "How come you got all the windows open?"

"It got so stuffy in here."

"So why didn't you turn down the thermostat?"

"I didn't think of it. I'll do it now, right away."

The boy couldn't look him in the face, but little Betty, who he used to hold on his lap when they went to the movies, little Betty could lie like a junkie. Turn those bloodshot eyes on him and lie in her teeth, without blinking. Runs in the family, Benson thought. He was a good liar. He lied on the witness stand, lied to his prisoners, lied to the bosses, lied to his wife. You couldn't be a successful cop without being a good liar.

"Going to work, Dad?" Elizabeth asked.

"Just out for cigarettes."

It was a dumb lie, a real cop trick, but it would keep the little prick's pants on for a while until they realized he wasn't coming back. What else could he do? Couldn't smack the kid in the head and throw him out. Couldn't spank his daughter, stick her head under the faucet to wash the makeup off and keep her in the house for a month. Couldn't tell her, "Look, you little slut, you can shoot smack in here if you want, but I've got a hundred-and-seventeen-dollar-a-month oil bill, so turn the fuckin' thermostat down and then open the windows, I don't care if you freeze to death." He was a loser if he acted like a father. But if he acted like a cop, at least he knew they wouldn't smoke any more reefer.

Benson went out into the garage and got into the Seville without thinking. Only when he turned the key and heard that feeble Diesel snort and sputter like an outboard motor did he realize what he was doing. That's right, asshole, show up to your own suspension in a thirty-thousand-dollar Caddy—it'll be like a slap in the face to all those stool-pigeon cops. So he got out of the Seville and went around to Doreen's '76 Pinto with the body cancer and the cracked windshield.

Traffic was already starting to build on the Expressway. Four in the morning and commuters were trying to beat the morning rush.

He lit cigarette after cigarette. He'd have to play broke. Send Doreen back to work, which would be the best thing that ever happened to her. First thing, she'd trim down and start looking better. Next, some married guy at the office would start banging her. She'd get her self-esteem back on her knees in the Xerox room.

Dennis, his older boy, would be shook. The kid was in boot camp at Parris Island, doing everything the right way. It would destroy him that his old man, the hero cop, was a bum. What can you say? Welcome to the real world, son. It'll be easier to have something to live down, than something to live up to, you'll see.

Elizabeth would either straighten out or go right down the sewer, there was no way of telling. Funny, though, him getting busted like this would give them all options that they would never have had if he put in his thirty years and got out on a pension. They'd all stay straight because the old man turned crooked.

IT'S A TRAP!

*T*he River Royale was a jinxed joint. It had been built by a big motel chain in hopes of attracting the cheap tourist trade. They put it right off the highway. Threw in a heated pool, underground garage, little gin mill at street level where the hicks would sip their Manhattans and look across the street at the hookers and the dealers and the skells moving swag. A lot of entrances and exits, so you could get to your car. Plenty of room in the lobby, so the kids could run around. Great for the tourists? Yeah, but what they didn't know was that it was ideal for the grifters, too. The day they cut the ribbon, the mutts were standing on the line around the block, and they'd been there ever since. Anybody who needed a quick in and out—and that takes in every mutt that was ever born—came to the River Royale. The underground park-and-lock garage became a great place to leave anything from a bag of heroin to a cadaver. Hookers

wanted something within walking distance of Eighth
Avenue now that the side-street fleabags were going to
Welfare so the pimps talked to the clerks and a whole
floor was put on permanent reservation. Hustlers
needed a place for their bust-out crap games, dealers
wanted a room for an hour with no questions asked. It
had to be in midtown, but off the beaten path, acces-
sible to the highways, so you could be in Brooklyn,
the Bronx, or on I-95 on your way back to Miami in
fifteen minutes. Con artists wanted a respectable front
for their scams. A bar where they could entertain, a
room with a carpet and a color TV, a lot of entrances
and exits—you-wait-here-I'll-be-right-back type of
thing. It didn't take long for management to get into
the act. You got a desk clerk making a yard and a half
a week, and all of a sudden he's getting envelopes
stuffed with hundreds. And all he has to do is give out
a room key plus maybe a few little favors here and
there. Corporate Headquarters was in Cincinnati or
someplace like that so the bosses never knew what
was going on. Besides, the joint was booked solid
every day of the year. Doing better than the Waldorf.
And in cash.

So for a while everybody got what they wanted. In
a few years the place was notorious. There had been
over a dozen homicides on the premises. Whenever a
guy went on the lam the cops checked the River
Royale, and there he was, curled up in front of the TV
with a Big Mac and a nine mil, thinking he was safe as
a clam. And if you didn't find the guy, there would be
somebody at the bar who'd give up his hideout for a
twenty-dollar bill. On a given day there could be so

many wiretaps in the building that if you called Room Service six different waiters showed up.

But did that stop the mutts? No way. Now the place had prestige. They could say they'd been busted in a joint where the biggest had gone down. They washed up at the doors of the River Royale like Coney Island whitefish on a Sunday morning. Informers could make a living sitting in the lobby seeing who wandered in. Benson and Crow had made a big burglary collar in the hotel. The guy jumped bail and three weeks later they pinched him again in the same place. In the same room. It wasn't really a good place to do illegal business anymore. Lucky for the world the mutts weren't too smart—there would be nothing left if they were.

In the end the joint had suffered for its clientele. Nothing that could hold money—telephones, vending machines, stamp dispensers—was in working order. The rooms had been picked clean, carpets, TVs, even the plastic glasses. Now they were as bare as prison cells, and still the grifters kept coming. Maybe they liked it better that way. But Vinnie? Say anything you want, Vinnie Crow was a cop, and a cop goes first class all the way. For Vinnie it had always been class restaurants, Jake's Steak House, Il Forno, Beppo's in Little Italy. The high-ticket meals and the junkets to Vegas and Paradise Island were part of the pad. It doesn't take long to pass an envelope, why do it in a fleabag like the River Royale?

Benson had to park his car down the block from the hotel. The place was under siege. The Borough Emergency Team was milling around, thirty heroes with flak jackets and shotguns. Emergency Service guys were on the roof ready to rappel down. All these hooples just dying to make a major assault on one crooked cop, who'd finally cracked.

Benson picked his way unnoticed through the cops in the lobby, looking for a cigarette machine. Out of the corner of his eye he saw Lieutenant Shurz, his squad commander, coming toward him.

"Benson."

Twenty years out of uniform, and Shurz still rocked back and forth on his heels like a beat cop. He was a big guy with a white pompadour that probably kept Brylcreem in business and a gut that looked like Budweiser might send a mass card to his funeral. Benson inched downwind of his mouthwash.

"What's goin' on here?" Shurz asked.

"I don't know. You?"

"What do you mean, me?" Shurz said, trying to look indignant, but not quite making it.

Benson shrugged. He knew Shurz was on the pad. He knew Shurz got an envelope every time a move was made. Sally Fish had told him everything.

"What should I know about all this?" Shurz demanded. "What are you trying to say?"

"I thought somebody told you something, that's all."

Shurz shook his head bleakly. "No, nothin'. They get me out of bed, and then they treat me like a perp. Duffy won't talk to me. I ask him what's goin' on, he says you'll find out and walks away. What's the big fuckin' secret?"

He was talking like a co-conspirator. Sally Fish must have told him about their envelope as well.

"If they had something they would have locked us up already," Benson said. "He's just fishing."

Shurz got a sly look. He nodded, and moved in closer.

"Just fishing," Shurz repeated, and said it again as if the words gave him great comfort. "You think so?"

"Benson!" It was Sergeant McKinnon, Duffy's hatchet man, a squinty little bastard with sandpaper skin whose secret nickname was Tonto because he was always two steps behind the boss. "Duffy's looking for you."

"I just got here."

"He's on the third floor. C'mon."

McKinnon grabbed Benson under the arm like he was rousting a drunk. Benson pulled his arm free, slowly, so it wouldn't look like a provocative gesture to the hundred-odd guys in the lobby who were watching. Then he leaned in so only McKinnon could hear him. "Don't treat me like a collar, you little dirtbag, or I'll cut your heart out."

McKinnon backed off a step. "Third floor. He's waiting for you."

John Duffy was the youngest inspector on the job. The Department was his career. Didn't care about money or good times, he just wanted to be commissioner. He was a trim redheaded guy with a hangover squint and nicotine fingers. A cop just like the rest, only he didn't take money, and worked the full forty hours. That had been enough to make him the fair-haired boy.

He was pacing by the landing as Benson came out of the elevator.

"Where were you?"

"Downstairs talking to Lieutenant Shurz." Benson looked over Duffy's shoulder. The floor was jammed with brass. There were paramedics with stretchers and IVs, more Emergency Service guys with shotguns and vests.

There was an empty space in front of a room, obviously the one Vinnie was barricaded in. Guys on both sides of the door, but nobody standing in front of it.

"He wants you in there," Duffy said. "He says he'll only talk to you."

"What happened?"

"That's what we want you to find out. All we know is a black man was seen running out of the room. Four shots were fired. Two cops are dead, and Crow's got a Narcotics undercover in there with him and won't let her out. Evelyn Aponte, know her?"

Duffy used that old cop trick of looking you right in the eye to make you turn away guiltily. But old cop tricks don't work on old cops. Benson stared right back at him and shook his head.

"I don't know anyone named Evelyn Aponte," Benson said. It was true. He could say it with real conviction, and that helped because he was afraid to try a lie on Duffy.

Duffy waved Deutsch from Technical Services over. "We're gonna wire you, and don't give me any shit about not giving up your partner."

"I thought you wanted me to just get him out of there," Benson said.

"I do, but I want to hear how you do it."

Deutsch tapped him on the shoulder. "Drop your pants."

Benson stood there with his pants around his ankles while Deutsch strapped the recorder to his thigh. He saw Lieutenant Saldana, of Narcotics, a gray-haired PR in tight Calvins, his white silk shirt unbuttoned to his navel to show the gold chains, the birth signs. Some cops pick up the style of the people they're supposed to arrest. Saldana looked like a Cuban coke dealer. There were a lot of rumors about him. It was said that the people in his unit had nicknamed him Bustelo because he was supposed to have all his money buried in coffee cans. It was said he had as bad a coke jones as any gram dealer.

"Is this a Narcotics beef?" Benson asked.

Duffy just stared at him, then walked away, saying over his shoulder to Deutsch, "Call me when he's ready."

"They won't tell you anything," Deutsch said softly as he ran the wires up to Benson's shoulder. "They're going to ask you to take a polygraph and don't want you to have time to prepare your responses." He slapped Benson on the behind. "You can put your pants back on. You've got your own talk show now."

Duffy was flattened against the wall outside room 313 talking to Saldana. Benson moved through the crowd of cops; they jumped out of his way as if he were on fire. Guys he knew looked away. They didn't want the brass seeing them talking to him.

Duffy held out his hand. "Gimme your gun. Crow wants you in there unarmed."

"If he's really gone nuts I'll need something," Benson said.

"Don't negotiate with me, Benson, I'll get the wrong idea."

Benson handed over his off-duty pistol. What Duffy didn't want was him going in there with a gun because

29

he just might blow Vinnie away and say he did it in self-defense. That's what Duffy was afraid of.

Saldana grabbed Benson's arm and whispered vehemently, "Let it be understood that he's going in as a replacement hostage for my undercover."

"Won't work," Duffy said. "We already tried."

Saldana's shirt, dark with sweat, clung to him. "I want that girl out of there, Inspector. She's got a lot of information locked up in her head. I'd just as soon go through the door now. . . ."

Duffy gave Saldana a hard look. "I'm sure you would, but let's do what the man wants before we start with the heroics. Go ahead, Benson. Get him out of that room."

Benson reached over and knocked softly on the door. "Vinnie?"

"Billy . . . ?" It was Vinnie's binge croak. After he'd been drinking for three days he started rasping like a crocodile. Benson had to smile.

"I'm comin' in."

"Come in alone, Billy."

"I'm alone, Vinnie. I wouldn't bullshit you, you know that."

"Okay. The door's open. Come in and close it fast, Billy."

"Okay, Vinnie."

Benson opened the door as narrowly as possible, and eased into the room, closing the door behind him. Vinnie was kneeling over the bed, his upper body propped on a bloody pillow, his stakeout gun, the .357 Magnum, pointed at the door.

"You're in the line of fire, Billy," Vinnie croaked.

Benson stepped away from the door and almost

tripped over the body of a young woman. She was lying with her leg twisted under her, a pose only a corpse could maintain. The smell of gunpowder hung in the air.

"Billy?" Vinnie shouted as if Benson were across the street.

"I'm right here, Vinnie." Benson bent to check the girl's heart and got a handful of sticky blood. There was blood on the walls, the sheets were soaked with blood. Vinnie's huge, square head was dripping blood like a fun-house skull. He raised a trembling, bloody finger to silence Benson.

"I been sittin' here thinkin' about you, kid, for an hour. Thinkin' about the good times we had."

Benson dropped his pants and showed Vinnie the recorder. Vinnie nodded, and lay his shaggy head down on the pillow. "Smart guys," he said. "But not as smart as me, Billy. Not as smart as me."

Blood was flowing steadily out of a rip just above his collar bone. There seemed to be a lot of dark blood a little lower down on his chest, but Benson couldn't see where it was coming from.

"I wanted to tell you what it was, Billy," Vinnie said weakly.

Jesus, he's dying, Benson thought. "Vinnie, cut the shit and come out with me."

"Plenty of time to go outta this room, Billy the Kid. Plenty of time for that. I just wanted to tell you what happened. I want you to know because you're a good cop, and those smart guys out there are gonna think you had an end of this, so I want you to know what happened." He winked at Benson, a ghastly effort that involved his whole face. "So shut up and listen."

Benson pointed to his thigh. Vinnie tried the wink again. He loosened his grip on the Magnum and let it hang from his trigger finger before it plopped softly on the bed. "I know what I'm doing, Billy, so just listen, okay? You'll be fine, Billy. We'll all be fine. Except that cunt over there. She won't be fine. She's a fuckin' cop, Billy."

"I know she is."

"She set me up, Billy. It was a double bang. She had me comin' and goin'. She didn't need me. She had a case against the guy without me. She just brought me in for the fun of bangin' out a cop. . . ."

Benson nodded rapidly so Vinnie would know he understood. It was a Narcotics scam. Benson hadn't even known about it. Vinnie had stayed in that room, bleeding to death, to tell Benson he was clear, and not to let anyone shake him.

"I been shakin' down a big dealer, Billy," Vinnie said. "I know how you feel about that shit, Billy. Don't be mad at me, Billy, please."

He was putting on a show for the recorder and for all the guys with earphones listening outside the room. He was putting on a show to clear Benson.

Tears filled Benson's eyes. He touched Vinnie's hand. "Let's get you outta here, partner."

Vinnie shook his head. "No, I'm done. I'm finished. I just want you to know. I don't want you to find out from someone else. I met her at a bar, this rotten stool pigeon. This goes back eight months, Billy. I been wantin' to tell you all this time, but I know how you feel about drugs. I know you're an honest cop, y'see, and I was ashamed. . . ." Vinnie coughed. Blood ran out of the corners of his mouth. "But she drove me nuts, Billy. She led me around by the dick like I was a kid. She was an ounce dealer. She had me ridin' shotgun when she made deliveries. Then she hooked me up with this guy downtown who was doin' weight, and I started gettin' the envelope every week. And then she set up a meeting with this guy for tonight. For the fuckin' Royale, Billy. You'd think I'd know she was puttin' me on the spot, but since I met her I ain't been thinkin' straight. I let everything go to shit, Billy.''

''Who was this guy, Vinnie?'' Benson knew they were sitting outside with their headsets waiting for him to ask, even though he knew what the answer would be.

''Don't make no difference. Guy like that'll either be dead or in the can by the end of the year.''

Vinnie pulled himself up on his elbow, and beckoned with his head for Benson to come closer. With a groan Vinnie moved over until his mouth was right against Benson's ear.

''Sally Fish put me on the spot,'' Vinnie whispered. ''Sally's doin' big coke shipments in the Village. Evelyn was workin' for him. Didn't know she was a cop. Knew it was a setup when she left the door open. . . . Then this nigger came in and started blastin'. Light skin, Yankee cap, blue hooded sweatshirt. . . .''

A vein pulsed in Vinnie's forehead. Benson felt his cold breath. He tried to pull away, but Vinnie grabbed the back of his head with a huge, bloody hand and whispered fiercely, ''Locker at the Port Authority. . . .'' There was a locker key in a puddle of blood on the bed. Vinnie slid it across the sheets to Benson. ''Half is yours, partner. Take care of my boy. . . .''

Vinnie loosened his grip. Benson got up. Vinnie thrust the bloody key at him, breathing through his nose like a horse.

"Get lost. Nothin' you can do now. . . ."

Benson put the key in his inside pocket and went to the door.

"I'm comin' out," he said. He barely got the door open before the Emergency Service guys burst into the room.

Outside, Duffy backed Benson against a wall. "What was he whispering about? We couldn't pick it up."

"Told me to take care of his wife and kids," Benson said, looking Duffy straight in the eye, passing the old eye-detector test. "He couldn't talk. Too weak."

They wheeled the girl out, all crumpled up in a body bag. She was so tiny to be with a big hulk like Vinnie Crow.

Vinnie came out next, hooked up to an IV. His eyes had that faraway look. He was smiling and saying something. Benson knelt by the stretcher.

"Just a piece of ghetto ass," Vinnie whispered.

He was DOA at St. Clare's ten minutes later.

MR. FEINSTEIN'S ANALYST

I've made up my mind," Karen Winterman had written in her diary. "If Arnie doesn't come tonight it's over."

He hadn't come the night before, even though he had sworn on a stack of Bibles that he would. She kept dinner warm until eleven, then fell asleep in front of the TV. The smell of smoke in the kitchen woke her after midnight. The casserole was burnt black. In another minute the whole place might have gone up.

It's an omen, she thought. If I go on like this much longer he'll be the death of me.

But the next morning he called her at the office, full of that helpless little boy charm he used to such advantage. First, he tried the standard lame excuses: He had been hung up with a bunch of venture capital guys who were interested in developing some property the family owned in Brooklyn. Then he segued into half truth: He had meant to come, but lost track of time. And finally the pleading: She knew he had a problem. Who knew better than her? But he loved her, she knew that. And then the pleases—Pretty please, Pretty please, with sugar on top.

"Cut me loose now, and I'll be dead in a month, baby," he said.

"Stay with you, and I'll be dead, Arnie," she said.

"You? Never. You're indestructible."

In the end she gave in, as she always did, even though she knew she was in the grip of a walking suicide who would never get better but would drag her down with him. "I am his partner in this psychopathic dance," she had written. "If I break the embrace he *will* die, as he says. And meanwhile I am dying slowly. This is my first love affair, and I will not survive it."

A week after Arnie had become her lover the alarms had begun to go off. She had begun an affair with a patient, violating the cardinal rule of psychoanalysis. Arnold Feinstein was a sociopath, a criminal who needed help to function in the everyday world without hurting himself and others. This affair was a betrayal of herself, her patient, and her profession. Yet, up to this point she had been unwilling or unable to break it off.

It was then that she began the diary, remembering something old Professor Auerbach had said in his famous Psychology Before Freud class that had packed them in every semester at Yale. "Freud was not the first person to analyze himself. Those countless billions through history who kept scrupulous diaries, recording not only names and dates, but feelings, perceptions, even by cryptic notation frequency and intensity of sexual intercourse, were resorting to a form of primitive self-analysis."

Three months later she had filled three diary notebooks, the pocket-sized morocco-bound type with the gold lock. Every word was about Arnie, yet she felt she had hardly scratched the surface. And this night she had begun a new book, writing what she hoped would be the next-to-last entry. Because although he had called twice that morning, once in the afternoon, and had even left a pleading message on her answering machine, she knew he wouldn't come. It was the first week of the month. He had gotten the check from his grandmother. All the dealers, and the tramps, the spongers from the Village, who knew his schedule better than he did, would descend on him. At that moment, he was shooting up in a stretch limo with darkened windows. Or he was vomiting in some disco bathroom. Or he was in some strange woman's house trying to make love. Because that was Arnie—a real romantic, a true lover of women, although he exploited them, a beautiful soul, although incapable of truth. Contradiction into contradiction. Paradox into paradox.

"This indeed is the great romance I fantasized," she wrote. "This indeed are its consequences."

Arnie had been referred to her by a young graduate student working in a halfway house; a female (this hadn't seemed important at the time) who was overflowing with sympathy.

"He has an incredible story," she had told Karen. "His grandparents survived Buchenwald. His mother was hidden by Polish peasants. He's a cocaine abuser who lives off middle-aged women. Smart? He knows everything. Sexy? Just devastating, that's all. He fits your 'Charming Sociopath' type like you designed it with him in mind.''

The ''Charming Sociopath'' was a type that Karen had been among the first to identify. The middle-class white male, mid-twenties, late-thirties age range, handsome, intelligent, though poorly educated; no vocational skills but glib enough to make a case for himself. The type was addicted to petty crimes such as forgery, petty drug dealing, consumer rackets, shoplifting, and, in isolated cases, domestic violence against females. Karen was well ahead of the pack, having already treated a dozen young men on referrals from probation officers. She had submitted the first draft of a paper entitled ''The Charming Sociopath, Extending the Frontier of Psychoanalysis,'' to the *Journal of Clinical Practice,* and had received an enthusiastic acceptance.

Arnie showed up a few mornings later at her office in the hospital. He was very good-looking (no surprise, they all were), tall and dark, with the kind of thick virile beard that seemed painted on his skin—he was the type of man who had to shave twice a day. He had soft brown eyes (soft in a sad, almost feminine, way), long lashes that women would kill for. (Women loved men who had some feature—hair, lashes, eyes—that they coveted.) He dressed casually in baggy pleated trousers with a loose print shirt, not in the tight, flamboyant fashions this type usually favored. Karen noticed his hands. They were large and well shaped, thickly veined at the wrists, broad palms and long graceful fingers, the thumb arched backward slightly, an indication of aggressiveness and extreme sensuality. It was a warm day, the January thaw being upon them, and Karen allowed herself to float in and out of a vernal reverie as they spoke.

Arnie told her about his offense. "I learned her signature and wrote myself a couple of checks. I thought when the time came I would explain it away as I had done with so many women before, but she flipped out and called the cops. I was amazed. . . ."

Karen made a note. "The betrayer shocked at betrayal."

He told her about his grandparents. "My grandfather had a lumber yard in a little town in Poland. He got real paranoid about the Germans and tried to split, but it was too late. So he sold the lumber yard at a loss and tried to buy passports for my grandmother and my mother, but the guy ripped him off. People were being sent off to the camps by then. Zaydie knew his days were numbered. He gave half his money to a Pole who had worked for him to take care of my mother, who was nine years old. He buried the other half and promised to give it to him after the war. So they hid my mother in a grain cellar for two years and never let her out, even at night, because they were afraid one of the other peasants would inform on them to the Germans. . . ."

Karen made a note. "Research Holocaust children. How many have gone bad?" She looked up at Arnie. "Did your mother survive?"

"She didn't have me when she was nine, Doctor," Arnie said with a mocking smile.

Karen was flustered. "Of course, of course . . ."

"You're not paying attention, Doctor."

"No, no, I am."

"Not that I blame you. It's an old story by now."

"I think what I meant was, is your mother alive today? Because I see no mention of her . . ."

"She died when I was in high school. TB. She got it in that hole she hid in. . . ."

"Oh, because I see no mention . . ."

"I hated her, she embarrassed me. My father left when I was a little kid. He was an American kinda guy, smoked Old Golds, listened to the Yankee game on the boardwalk at Coney Island."

"Yes, I see he owns a butcher shop in that neighborhood."

"I couldn't stand my mother. Wouldn't walk on the same side of the street with her. She used to go in the bedroom and cough so I wouldn't be upset. Then she'd come out and touch me with those damp hands. . . ." He shuddered at the memory. "I was relieved when she died. Of course they never told me anything about the camps until a year later when they wanted me to come to the unveiling of her stone and I wouldn't go because I had a baseball game. So Bubby told me, 'Your mother suffered too much in her life.' So I went to the unveiling, but I was still pissed off because I had to miss the game, and a kid I hated was going to take my place. . . ." He broke off abruptly. "The important thing about Bubby and Zaydie was that they made a lot of money. They started in a candy store, kiting checks, juggling eviction notices, living three days ahead of the marshals. They would break the pipes and live with no water so they wouldn't have to pay the rent until the landlord made the repairs. . . ."

Karen made a note: "Obsessed with family saga . . ."

"They bought odd lots, little unclaimed parcels of land that go up for auction every year, brownstones in Bed Stuy, where they collected rents from pimps and dealers. Zaydie dropped dead lugging a washing machine out of a building on Neptune Avenue. You see, washing machines weren't allowed and he waited until Sunday morning to catch the lady doing her laundry. Bubby kept the business going. Only two things in the world don't sleep—sharks and Bubby. Now she owns every tenement and taxpayer in Coney Island. This old lady has got millions and they're all for me. I never have to work. I can do whatever I want, she doesn't care. As long as her little Arnie is happy. Is that sick?" And then, without changing inflection or expression, he said, "You're wondering what it would be like to be in bed with me."

Karen made a note: "The seduction attempt. No surprise." And tried to keep her expression neutral. "Afraid not."

"I don't expect you to admit it," Arnie said.

Karen put her pencil down. "I'd like to talk about your experience with drugs."

"I love drugs. I love cocaine. I use it to excess. I inject it. With clean works, of course. I'm a little rich boy and I can afford the best. I will always use drugs. Drugs will probably kill me. You have beautiful hair and you wear it long so everyone will notice it. You have beautiful breasts and you wear dark silk so they can stir around behind it like assassins hiding behind a curtain. . . ."

"Stop it," Karen said. They sat in silence for a very long time. Inside, the radiator knocked; outside, the typewriters clattered and the secretaries gossiped.

That night they made love in Karen's apartment. His body was strong and cool; she felt muscle wherever her fingers strayed. He didn't do anything that other men hadn't done. It just felt better. When he slept, a mist seemed to rise off his body. She stroked the hollows in the small of his back, shaped his buttocks with her fingers until he awoke with a drowsy smile. "The insatiable Doctor Winterman." In the morning she tried to piece together a chronology of the evening. How had they gotten from her office to her bed? She couldn't remember.

Later he asked her if she had found love. There was nothing smug in his tone. It was more of a sad joke. She lay back with the beginning of a headache behind her eyes. "This affair is not going to be good for me," she said.

"It won't last long enough to leave any scars," he said. "Anyway, you'll end up hating me. You'll be glad to see me go."

"No." She took his face between her hands. "We're going to break this cycle, Arnie. I have to help you now, Arnie. In my weakness, I've done you a terrible disservice. No jokes, please, I have. And I'm going to make it up to you."

"I'll make you hate me," Arnie said. "You'll be guilt-free when I leave."

In the weeks that followed he seemed determined to make his prophecy come true. There were nights she sat in restaurants or paced outside movie theaters until every creep in the neighborhood came on to her. He would show up three hours later. Or not at all. There were nights he was too wrecked to do anything but pass out in her arms, sweating and dribbling so much she would have to change the sheets in the morning. He had her on a roller coaster of rage and forgiveness, revulsion and ecstasy. He was turning all the stereotypes inside out. Good lover, bad lover, nice guy, evil guy, fulfilling, destructive: all the simple categories upon which she based her judgments suddenly seemed like false facades with nothing behind them.

Before Arnie, she had endured a succession of frivolous men offering themselves for anything from a weekend to a lifetime. She despised them all, but especially the ones who were easy and confident with her. The Adonises who would accept nothing less than slavish admiration for their perfect bodies; the tricksters who watched slyly as they put a woman through her paces; the animals who expected a round of applause because they had a few more inches of skin than the next guy. They were there to service her, and she knew enough about her body to let that process take place in a way that would leave them in humbled perplexity. But the paradox remained. Because any man she liked enough to go to bed with was a man who could inspire, in odd moments, such a wave of tender feeling, coming like a sudden sob from a reservoir of emotion she was hardly aware of, that she would have to steel herself against it, choke it off before he got a clue.

With Arnie, for the first time, the defense hadn't worked. She had been overwhelmed. She let herself go. And to whom? A man who specialized in making women love him. She had fallen for the same transparent tricks that had conquered scores of brainless, middle-aged ladies. With all she knew about him, she daydreamed about a future that included a home and children. With all he had confessed to her, she abandoned herself totally, she believed completely. On one hand she couldn't imagine life without him. On the other she knew somehow she had to get him out of her life.

A few weeks ago he had simply disappeared. No one was home at his apartment, his answering machine was turned off. She made herself sick with rage. Sleepless, feverish, she prowled her apartment plotting revenge. Then a letter came. He had gone off to Florida with his grandmother. It had been spur of the moment, which is why he couldn't call her (a feeble, contemptible excuse, not up to his usual smooth deceptions). He hadn't wanted to go, but she knew that he couldn't say no to Bubby. "How do you say no to a woman who spent two years buried under a pile of corpses at Buchenwald?"

What cheap, manipulative crap, she thought. How do you say no to someone who subsidizes your every perversion would be more like it. How do you say no to your meal ticket?

She threw the letter away in disgust. To think she would accept such an obvious excuse. The sheer arrogance of the man was unbelievable. The Arrogant Loser: that was a definite constellation in the cluster of satellite traits revolving around the sun of charming sociopathology.

She went around for days, the anger roiling inside of her. It was over now, over for good. She would write him a letter in West Palm. No, better to send a telegram. "It's over. Stop." No, better yet, she would await his return. She wanted to watch him pout and whimper and work his childish wiles. Finally, in the thrill of rejection, she would get some satisfaction out of this sick relationship.

In the meantime, several men hovered on the fringe of her life. There was Janowitz, the internist she worked with on the alcoholic ward at the Bronx VA. Thin and prematurely gray, with the slouch of a boy who had been ashamed of his height. Long, crooked fingers. Black hairs sprouting out of his nose. He was married, with the pictures of his sour wife and three chubby kids on his desk. One day, after a staff meeting, she was sliding her reports back in the folder and he was heading out of the door when he said, "What the hell," and came at her. The manila folder fell on the floor, and they bumped heads as she bent to retrieve it. It was before Arnie, and she could still laugh. "I want to have an affair with you, Karen," he said. "Please don't be offended."

He pressed her hand to his lips, and they sat under the conference table for a while. He tried to kiss her. He had terrible, stale breath. Karen thought of his wife. What must it be like to sleep with that stench? A married man with halitosis. How could anyone love him?

And then there was Frederick, whom she had known since girlhood up in Watertown where his father had been the town doctor, and he a fat, pink kid who had loved her forever. Now he was at New York Hospital, doing eye surgery with laser beams, a very celebrated guy, fatter now and bald, a pinkish tinge like an eternal blush of embarrassment suffusing his scalp. She and Frederick had been off and on for years, but after Arnie his presence became loathsome to her. Sitting in the movies one night he put his hand on her leg and kept it there until she felt its clammy warmth through her dress. Her attention was drawn to this appendage resting like a watchful reptile on her knee. And the more she looked at it, the less human and more repulsive it became. She wondered how those fingers could aim a laser beam with enough accuracy to kill a tiny tumor while leaving the healthy tissue unscathed. And she thought of Arnie's spatulate thumb, of his fingers, long and limber, sliding up her thighs, springing locks along the way. Of course Arnie could do nothing constructive for himself or humanity, if, that is, you measured social value in terms of impersonal skills that could be made to benefit people you didn't know. And she realized in that dark theater, with that lump of increasingly disgusting tissue resting on her knee, that she had to separate sexuality and social value in order to fully enjoy them both. She was doomed to spend her life on either side of that great divide, having one, yearning for the other.

When Arnie reappeared, trim and tan from his two weeks of total abstinence, Karen felt like a patient recuperating from a long illness, still shaky but on the road to recovery. She felt now that she could put their affair in some kind of perspective. So when Arnie warned her that he might be even more unreliable than usual ("After two weeks on the wagon, I feel a major binge coming on") she delivered her quavery ultimatum; "Stand me up one more time, Arnie, and it's over."

She had given him a second chance because everybody deserves a second chance, even Arnie Feinstein. And guess what? He had stood her up again.

So now it was really over. He would only prolong

the agony by a sudden appearance. "Stay away, Arnie," she said and then laughed in her silent bedroom at the thought of the next man who would slide between her sheets. The poor guy would slink away, a whipped dog, totally unable to fill the shoes of a sociopath he didn't even know existed.

And then the phone rang. Once, twice, three times. Suddenly she was terrified that he might hang up.

"Are you mad, baby?" Arnie's voice was blurred with heroin. She could always tell because when he shot cocaine he became shrill and cynical. On heroin he was soft, caressing; it always sounded as if he were calling long distance.

"You're high?" she said.

"Very high. Too high to deal with the streets." The voice went to a whisper, exhausted by the effort of two sentences. "Too high to be alone. Come take care of me, Karen."

"Not tonight, Arnie." It seemed so futile to issue an ultimatum to a man who only heard what he wanted to hear, stoned or straight, but she did it. "Not ever again."

Then came the ghostly chuckle. "I'm gonna curl up in bed and dream now, Karen. Hurry up. Bring your keys. I won't be up to answering the door."

"I'm not coming, Arnie."

"Better hurry, baby. I can't be alone too long."

"Why? You've been alone all night, haven't you? You were alone when you shot up. Why do you suddenly want company?" Stupid, stupid. She dug her nails into her leg. Bandying words with a drug addict. Having a little spat with a sociopath. Either go or don't go. And hang up.

"I need you, baby." Arnie's voice was getting fainter. There was static on the line. It sounded like winds were howling around him. Karen got out of bed, trembling, and went for her clothes. In the cab she realized she hadn't even hung up the phone.

Arnie lived in the penthouse of a luxury building on Sutton Place. It was paid for, not owned by his grandmother; Arnie confessed to a curious scruple about not living in a building his grandmother owned. "I wouldn't want to take the income away from her. This way I'm a tax loss, which means I'm not a total loss."

Karen got a wink from the night doorman. He was a young guy with the careful coif and trimmed mustache, the obscure points of pride of the post-teen proletariat. She was a familiar face to him. "He thinks you're one of my little coke chippies who comes around to get high," Arnie had once told her. "He told me he likes you the best. Don't get on the elevator with him when his eyes are red, you may never come down."

She ran out of the elevator on the penthouse floor and collided with a man. It was strange, feeling flesh, smelling sweat and whiskey breath for an instant. The man was dark and brawny, his white silk shirt unbuttoned across his chest, a gold chain glittering in the matted hairs. He stepped back to let her pass with a quick "Excuse me," but as she walked quickly down the hall she didn't hear the closing of the elevator doors and when she turned he was padding along behind her on the deep pile carpet.

"You goin' to see Arnie?" He had a thick Brooklyn accent. He licked flakes of dead skin off his lips. "I'm a friend of his, you know. I been knockin', but I couldn't get in. I don't think he's home.''

"He is, he just called me," Karen said.

"Well, he don't answer the door."

"I have a key."

An old man peeked out of the door of the penthouse down the hall. "What the hell's goin' on out here?" he asked in a surprisingly vigorous voice.

"Nothin', go back to sleep," the man said. Karen noticed his pinky ring, a big green stone. Couldn't be a real emerald, it would cost a fortune. He nudged her toward the door. "Okay," he said, dropping his voice, "I guess you can take care of it. I gotta go." He ran for the elevator, catching it just before the door closed. Karen thought she heard a thumping sound as if he were pounding the walls. The sound got fainter and fainter.

Arnie had four locks on his door. "Now you're a member of the janitor's club," he had joked when he gave Karen the keys. But only the top lock was engaged. Strange . . . Arnie was never in that much of a hurry to get high. He always locked his door.

All the lights were on in the living room. Arnie always turned off the lights when he left the room, a legacy from his grandparents. "You have stock in Con Edison?" they used to ask him. He told the story over and over, chuckling at their stinginess. But he always turned off the lights when he left the room.

The door to the terrace was open, the curtains blowing, the skyline poised beyond the terrace. Arnie never left the terrace doors open. He was afraid he'd fall off the terrace when he was high.

Turn around and get out, she told herself. Instead,

with her throat tightening, she walked toward Arnie's bedroom. She walked in a wide angle so she could see what was happening before she got there. The room seemed to be empty.

"Arnie," she called.

No answer. Maybe he had gone out, although he had sounded like he was in one of his oceanic semi-comas where he just wanted to be stroked and touched until he nodded out totally.

She walked into the bedroom with a bit more confidence. The blanket was bunched up in the middle of the bed. The bathroom door was shut; Karen had to put her shoulder against it to get it open. Arnie wasn't there.

On her way out she saw the outline of a leg under the blanket. She went back to the bed. Gingerly, she lifted the edge of the blanket and saw what was underneath.

Arnie was a big man, a six-footer, but he was curled in the fetal position so tight she hadn't seen him the first time she had looked. The side of his body pressed into the sheets was flushed deep purple, as if he had suffered a massive hemorrhage. Karen had never seen a corpse, and the first thing she thought of was the schoolgirl's tale that when a man died his penis became swollen. She lifted the blanket and there it was, bigger than in life. Thicker really, the length was the same. That proved he was dead, she wouldn't need a mirror; she wouldn't have to feel for a pulse.

Karen drew the blanket slowly over Arnie. That perfect body that had stayed trim and toned despite the massive insults he dealt it. That sculpted Hebrew profile, the pouting lips, the girlish eyelashes, the thick, clinging curls. "David, my David," she had called him once. "My name is Arnold," he had said. "Arnold Feinstein no Esquire."

Karen called for an ambulance. She had to clear her throat constantly to make herself audible, but that was the only symptom of unease. When the paramedics came they ushered her into the living room and closed the bedroom door. The police arrived a few minutes later. The sergeant she was speaking to kept looking around the apartment.

A paramedic came out of the bedroom and took the sergeant aside. Karen heard him say something about "track marks."

"Better not move him then," the sergeant said, then turned back to Karen. "What is your relationship to the deceased?"

"I'm his analyst," Karen said.

TWO

THE BITCH WAS A COP

*T*he phone began ringing again at 6:30 in the morning. By then Edmund knew he had broken his ankle. Ice hadn't reduced the swelling, Advil hadn't helped the pain, and Edmund never took anything stronger. So he lowered the shades and lay in the gloom, dozing until the pain or the phone woke him.

In early afternoon, with the phone ringing at half-hour intervals and the pain getting worse, Edmund caught the tail end of a "Special Report" on the killings. "Murder in Midtown will return in a moment," a nice-looking light-skinned anchor lady was saying.

There was a plain brick building with a white roof, and a Toyota in the driveway. Edmund heard the anchor lady: "Three generations of O'Keefes have lived in this modest two-family house in the Richmond Hill section of Staten Island. Another branch of the family lives two doors away. All told, seventeen

O'Keefes have served New York City as police officers. Today they gathered with friends and neighbors to mourn the loss of a young man who was the last in that long blue line—Detective Ronald O'Keefe. . . ."

Is this one of the guys I wasted? he wondered.

A bunch of big red-faced cops were crowded into a tiny living room. On the mantel were photos of the dead cop in high school, coming out of the Police Academy, with his wife on their honeymoon. And now the wife, a chunky blonde holding a bewildered little girl on her lap, was talking about how "he always wanted to be a cop like his father and his brothers. Getting his detective's shield was the happiest day of his life. . . ."

Now the picture switched to a tenement block somewhere. Some runty brothers were hanging out in front of the camera.

"One Hundred and Thirty-eighth Street and Lenox Avenue is a tough place to grow up," a reporter was saying. "Not many people make it off this block in one piece, but Lawrence Withers was one who did. Into the Marine Corps where he served with distinction in Vietnam and back to the Police Department where he rose to the rank of Lieutenant of Detectives. . . ." They showed Jenkins Bros. funeral parlor on Lenox Avenue. Edmund knew the place. It was the same place where they had buried his father. "Today," the reporter continued, "Lawrence Withers came home. . . ."

Back on the block a kid in a ski cap was saying, "Detective Withers was a real hero to everybody on the block. We figured if he could do it we could too. . . ."

The downstairs buzzer rang. Edmund hopped out into the living room, pressed the intercom and listened.

"Mr. Feinstein," said a staticky voice.

Edmund slipped the chain off the door, then hopped back to get the little .25 automatic out of the false panel in back of the oven where he kept all his pieces. "Never hide anything behind wood," the old man had told him. "Never hide anything in the wall or the floor." Edmund remembered how the old man kept a pot of red beans and rice on the stove all the time and had a .38 wrapped up in cellophane under the mess. And it was the first thing some cop went to when they busted him because, it turned out, that was where all Rastafarians hid their pieces, which was something the old man, who came from Louisiana, had never known.

The door flew open and slammed against the wall like it had been kicked. A shaft of light shot in from the hallway. There was a harsh laugh in the darkness. "Hey, kid, catch."

A newspaper flew through the darkness and landed on the bed. Sally Fish came striding into the bedroom after it, laughing and rapping a mile a minute like nothing had happened.

"You're a star, Edmund. This is a media event, you been watchin' the tube? I think you might need an agent if the shit keeps up like this. Mafia hit man tells how he went up against an elite unit of the Narcotics Task Force—isn't that what they're callin' these bums?"

"Slow down," Edmund said.

Sally felt along the wall for the light switch. "What are you, a fuckin' mole?" When the light came on,

Edmund could see that Sally had dressed Godfather for this encounter. He usually wore Sergios, Tony Lamas with extra high heels because he was uptight about his height, and some kind of pastel velour sweatshirt, which he hung over his pants to hide the gut. Today he was wearing a light beige Armani suit, cappuccino shirt, lemon tie, light brown Ballys. Could have a piece hidden on him, Edmund thought. Watch it if he goes to his pocket. Sally usually downplayed the jewelry. No point in wearing diamonds when you're trying to pay rhinestone prices. Today he was flaunting. The big emerald sparkled on his pinky, the gold tie clasp with the drooping diamond-crusted chain, the gold bracelet with inlaid emeralds on his right wrist, the big fat seventy-five-hundred-dollar Rolex. Dressing Godfather to the nines. Watch it if he wants to go out somewhere to eat. They get on the street, two guys come out of a car with shotguns. They drop a package of dope by his body and take off.

"You dressed to kill," Edmund said.

"Hey, you never know, somebody might want me for an interview. I played a supporting role in this little drama, you know."

He sat down on the bed. "Look at this." He laid the newspapers out and read the headline: "FOUR COPS KILLED IN MOTEL RAID. Four police officers, one of them a female undercover operative with the New York City Drug Task Force, were killed early today in a gun battle with an unknown number of assailants. . . ." He pounded the bed. "Unknown number? It was you, babe, you're the unknown number. You're a one-man army."

"I didn't shoot the chick."

"You don't know who you shot. You were shootin' and shittin' so fast you didn't know which end was up." He noticed Edmund's ankle. "What's this?"

"I got it jumping down the stairs."

"Well, I'm glad you got something. I mean, shit, you walk in and kill four cops and walk out without a scratch. I mean, what does that say about New York's Finest, you know what I mean? I gotta get an extra lock on my door with the kinda bums they're hirin' these days. . . . Wait a second, I got something here that'll really flip you out." He thumbed through one of the papers. "Here, listen to this: 'A slim black man in a Yankee cap and blue warm-up jacket was seen fleeing the building.' " Sally snorted. "A black dude in a Yankee cap is the best they can do. In the old days they would have made up ten black militants in fatigue jackets and berets carrying automatic weapons. Scare the shit outta the whole city and make themselves look like martyrs."

Sally looked over toward the bureau where Edmund kept his show coke. He's all cranked up and he wants some more, Edmund thought. He's getting edgy. Sally turned irritably toward the TV, where a young black minister was talking to a bunch of kids in the rectory. "Larry Withers was a soldier who died in the war against drugs and crime. . . ."

Sally snarled and jumped in front of the TV. "You believe this fuckin' propaganda? Look at that O'Keefe. A real Irish headbuster. First word he learned was 'nigger.' " Sally pointed to the close-cropped square-jawed photo in the paper. "Like to be pinched by this face? Beat the piss outta you, go through your pockets and then lock you up anyway 'cause this kinda mick cop's got no class. And as for the soul brother over there, well I don't have to tell you. He's on the same road as us only he's comin' from another direction. He got that shield 'cause he wanted a license to steal. How many bags of smack you think he moved a week? That's why those junkies on the block are cryin' over him.''

Sally paced restlessly. "Rat bastards! They shake you and shake you and then decide to pull the string on you. Dead, they're heroes. Alive, they're just two stool-pigeon cops waitin' to get busted." He rubbed his eyes with both hands like a little kid. "Gimme some of your stash," Sally said. "I'll make it up."

"It's got a two on it," Edmund said.

"So I'll do twice as much." Sally lunged for the drawer and took out a gram package. "Can tell you're not a dealer, you got too much in here by at least three tenths."

"It's all lactose."

"Don't matter. If they're paying for a gram you give 'em nine tenths, that's how it works." Sally folded the package into a cone, tilted his head back and let the coke slide into his left nostril. Then he did his right, and when the package was empty he stuck two knuckles in his nostrils and took an explosive snort.

"Drivin' that shit right into your brain," Edmund said.

"Where it does the most good."

Sally reached into his breast pocket.

"No," Edmund said. He took out the .25.

Sally smiled and took his hand away. "Payday, Edmund."

"Take off the jacket and throw it over here."

Sally took off the jacket, folded it neatly, and flipped it onto the bed. "Left inside pocket," he said.

There was a white unsealed envelope stuffed with hundreds. Edmund did a quick riffle count. Twenty-five added to the twenty-five he'd gotten as a down payment.

"Five grand for hittin' three cops," Edmund said, shaking his head.

"I only hired you to hit one," Sally said.

"And you didn't tell me he was a cop."

Sally shrugged. "You didn't ask. Anyway, I tell you he was a cop you want more bread. Or maybe you turn the job down and now I got a guy walkin' around who knows I want to hit a cop, so if I get somebody else to do it you know what went down you could trade the information if you get popped. *Capish?* That's how my mind works. There's a pack of Camels in the right inside low hip pocket."

Edmund threw him the cigarettes and a gold Dunhill lighter.

"This lighter could be a trick gun," Sally said, lighting his cigarette. "Anyway, I'm way ahead of you. Right inside pocket."

Edmund found another envelope. "I can't deal with the cigarette," he said.

Sally opened the window and flicked his ashes onto the sill. "Health-food hit man over here. Don't smoke, don't drink, don't do dope. Not much into the ladies, either. Did a little too much of that backwards pussy in the joint, huh?"

There were twenty-five more hundreds in the envelope. "Still ain't enough," Edmund said.

"So I'll make it up the next time."

"Ain't gonna be no next time."

Sally cracked his neck irritably. "How much money you made with me so far this year, Edmund?"

"You know."

"Forty grand you made with me and we're in September. How many hours you work?"

"I don't punch in."

"You work two hours all told? Three hours with traveling time? Huh?" Sally flipped his cigarette out of the window and slammed it shut. He's playing mad, Edmund thought. Why's he doing that?

"Being a banger is the easiest job in this business and you know it, Edmund," Sally said. "Especially when you work for me. I set it up so the guy never knows what's happening. I set up the spot, I set up the story. All you have to do is get there and do your little rat-a-tat-tat and then cut out. You wanna try somethin' hard, Edmund? Try standin' in a customs line with a fuckin' valise full of coke. Try movin' a fuckin' five-hundred-pound safe into a truck because the mechanic can't crack it. Try runnin' twenty numbers banks in Brooklyn where every banker is skimmin' and the boss, in this case, your uncle, who happens to be the baddest, absolute baddest, guy in the country, bar none, can tell you to a penny how short you are and then takes it out of your end. Try doin' things like that and you'll go runnin' back to bangin' out rats most of whom are stoned from the get anyway."

"If it's so easy why don't you do it?" Edmund said.

"I knew that was coming," Sally said. "You don't ask Donald Trump why he don't lay bricks. You don't ask Leonard Bernstein why he don't play the fuckin' tuba. I'm the boss. I put it all together. Without me you don't earn.''

"What do *you* do without *me?*" Edmund asked.

"I get somebody else. Maybe not as cold as you. Maybe colder.''

Edmund shifted his weight, but kept the pain off his face. Sally was watching him for the slightest sign of weakness.

"This nigger ain't dumb, my man," Edmund said softly. "You got a big name out there in Brooklyn 'cause they think you're doin' all this shootin' yourself. They don't know nothin' about me, so if I cut out you gonna have to fill your own contracts, boss, because you sure ain't gonna trust no *wallyo* to keep your secret like this nigger does.''

Sally stepped back and cocked his head as if he were looking at Edmund in a museum. "Where'd you learn *wallyo?* Where'd you learn that word?''

Edmund ignored the question. "As far as this gig bein' easy, it wasn't so easy last night.''

Sally stepped back to the window and lit another cigarette. "Last night was the first fuck-up of my life. These things happen, you gotta expect it.''

"I'd be dead today, if that cop hadn't turned around and shot your old lady when I came in.''

"She wasn't my old lady," Sally said. "That bitch was a cop.'' He looked over at the TV. "I read somewhere that black people are addicted to television. . . .''

"Turn it off," Edmund said.

Sally turned off the television. "Now you tell me if you start experiencing withdrawal symptoms. . . .''

Edmund pointed toward the stash drawer. "You want another package, go ahead.''

Sally beamed. He took another gram package out of the drawer and began loading up. "How'd you know?"

"Soon as you start talkin' about addiction and withdrawal you're talkin' about yourself," Edmund said.

Sally did the whole gram in two snorts. "This is garbage," he gasped, the tears rolling down his cheeks. He froze for a moment, grimacing, his fists jammed against his cheekbones. "I'm glad that chick is dead. I mean for the world's sake. You get a dynamite pussy and a conniving heart in the same body and the world ain't safe. I'm glad you killed her."

"I didn't kill her," Edmund said. "I told you that."

"I'll tell you how smart she was," Sally said. "She rode in on Sammy Pena, remember him?"

Edmund had shot Sammy Pena in the bathroom of an after-hours joint on Tremont Avenue in the Bronx a few months back. Sally had set up a buy. An eighth of a key. Edmund just went to the bar, showed the little fat guy the money, and followed him into the can to make the pass. Shot him in the back of the head with the little .25, shoved him into a stall and left him sitting there with his pants around his ankles. Next day Sally slid an envelope under his door. Twenty-five hundred plus the seventeen hundred he found in the guy's sock.

"I sent little Sammy on a trip to Peru," Sally said, pacing and gesturing wildly. "He came back with this little PR broad from the Lower East Side. Eldridge Street, right? I checked her out, everybody knew her. Sammy met her in a bar in Lima. She hooked him up because she's a piece of ass, one of them hot Spanish chicks, look like they got dick on their mind all the time and all they're ever really thinkin' about is money.''

Sally was moving fast. Jewels sparkling off his fingers, his black eyes burning out of his head, sweat glistening on his forehead. He was flashing like a video game.

"Slow down, man, you're givin' me a headache," Edmund said.

Sally laughed. "I can go from zero to sixty in a second. The Porsche Turbo of racketeers, and I have to be, I'm runnin' so many different scams at the same time. . . .'' Sally stopped for a breath and a deep drag on his cigarette. "So that's how I meet this broad, alright. She's already up to her eyeballs in my operation. And she checks out totally. So what am I supposed to do?''

Edmund tried his ankle. The pain shot up his leg so quickly that he couldn't hold back the groan. Sally looked sharply at him but kept talking as if he hadn't noticed anything. "Add to it that this Evelyn had the kind of pussy that walks and talks all by itself. That will cloud your judgment.''

"Bullshit," Edmund said. "You don't care nothin' about women.''

Sally raised his hands in mock surrender. "Okay, I'll go quietly. Truth is I got careless 'cause I knew I could use her. You're always lookin' for a good-lookin' evil broad. I mean real evil, not just sneaky and greedy like most of 'em. I mean most of 'em are whores in their hearts—except my mother . . . and yours, of course. But when you meet one that's vibrating evil, emanating evil, I mean you gotta put that chick to use.

I never even suspected she was a cop. Cops are cheap grifters, this chick was upscale. She had a Hoover like a tornado. She could stick the whole town of Cali up her nose, buildings and jeeps and all. You know she made about a half a mil off me before she decided to pull the string. Playin' both ends. Smart, Edmund. Cops ain't famous for brains, you know. And lady cops, I mean, you're lucky if they remember to sit down when they piss.

"To make a long story short, I put Evelyn on this cop, Vinnie Crow. I got a hard-on for this rat for a coupla years. Just waitin' for my shot to get even with him. The longer I wait, the better it is, because revenge is a dish best eaten cold, as my Uncle Frank likes to say. So first I get her next to him. No problem. In a heartbeat he's eatin' out of her hand, ready to leave his naggy wife and skanky kids, right? Big sacrifice, right? And I'm watchin' it and I'm diggin' it because I'm gonna nail this rat. So I tell her to put him on the spot. And that was when they decided to haul me in. They must have figured: If we nail this guinea now with a gun in his hand, we'll really have a case against him. Only instead of me you came boppin' down the hall and now they're trippin' all over their own dicks tryin' to figure out what happened." Sally clapped his hands. The sound cracked like a pistol shot in the empty room. He lunged at Edmund, his eyes bulging out of his head like a guy in a cartoon. He came so close Edmund could see the flakes of cocaine trapped in his nose hairs. "They came this close, Edmund," he rasped. "And now they're light years away, thanks to you." He licked pieces of dead skin off his lips.

"Don't try to sell me that," Edmund said. "That chick put you on the map and you know it."

"No way," Sally said, shaking his head even slower. "I never gave my right name and I did all my business out of some other guy's apartment. Evelyn knew me as Arnie Feinstein. That's who the cops are looking for right now."

"So the cops'll find this Feinstein and he'll give you up," Edmund said.

"They already found him—dead."

"From what?"

"Too much of a good thing. See, I used his apartment and his name. Paid him off in dope, he didn't need money. He overindulged a little tonight."

"With you doin' the cookin'."

"That guy was a good friend of mine," Sally protested. "I loved that guy, I swear on my mother's grave. I blame myself for his death. I'll never get over it. Because it was that cunt Evelyn. Arnie Feinstein would be alive today if she hadn't of gotten over on me, you understand what I'm saying?"

"Yeah. You used the guy's pad and his name. Then you gave him a hotshot so he wouldn't give you up to the cops."

"That's how you see it, huh? Yeah, well, niggers ain't very good at nuances."

The pain was constant now. Edmund just wanted Sally out of the apartment so he could get more ice. But he lay back and laughed like he had all the time in the world. "You're just a strung-out, lyin' motherfucker, Mr. Mafia. . . ."

"He was a kid I met in Rikers. What was I supposed to do, let him fuck up a five-million-dollar business?

Kid like that was gonna die anyway, it was just a matter of time.''

Edmund lay back, stifling a groan. When was this guy going to leave?

Sally pointed to his jacket. "Right-side pocket."

There was another envelope. Twenty-five more hundred-dollar bills. Edmund threw the envelope at him. "I'm not protectin' your five-million-dollar business anymore, man."

"This is a civilian, Edmund. Check out the photo."

There was a torn snapshot of a dark-haired woman standing on a beach. Her arms hung awkwardly at her sides and she was smiling shyly like she didn't get her picture taken too often. She was wearing a loose-fitting bathing suit, the kind you'd expect to see on an older woman. Even in the grainy photo you could see her breasts swelling under the suit.

"What did she do?" Edmund asked.

"I don't know, it's not my beef," Sally said. "It comes from the top and the guy's willing to go ten Gs, so she must have done something to somebody."

Sally tapped his foot nervously. He wants me to do this job real bad, Edmund thought.

Edmund held the picture out. "Here's your photo back."

Sally smiled grimly. "Something tells me I didn't play this right. Twenty-five. . . ."

"She under police protection?" Edmund asked.

"Nope."

"Is it about goin' through a hundred guns to get to her?"

"Nothin' like that, you got my word. Anyway,

you'll see for yourself when you case the broad. She's a straight broad, not hooked up with nobody."

"So?"

"I don't know," Sally said. "They're givin' me the contract and I'm passin' it on to you."

"How much sticks to your fingers?" Edmund asked.

Sally flashed his charming smile. "I take care of myself. You don't like your numbers, I'll get somebody else."

Edmund turned the photograph over. A business card was taped to the back. It read: "Karen Winterman, Ph.D."

FRANKENSTEIN AND BILLY THE KID

*T*hey sent Benson to the 14th Precinct to wait for Duffy. He sat around the squad for an hour. Nobody talked to him. Guys he had known for years walked by, their eyes lowered. Finally McKinnon strolled in.

"What are you doing here? You're supposed to be over at the One-Nine. Duffy's waiting for you."

So Benson took a cab across town to the East Side. It was six in the morning. Nobody at the One-Nine squad knew anything about Inspector Duffy setting up over there. Benson was about to leave when a call came through. Duffy was on his way.

Benson flopped on a horsehair couch in the corner, one of those broken-down jobs that the guys drag in off a pile of garbage in the street because the Department doesn't supply furniture long enough for anybody to stretch out on. He lit a cigarette and closed his eyes. They were moving him around and making him wait like you did with a fucking mutt. Playing cop tricks on a cop. Did they really think they were going to shake him? Benson put his feet up, finished his cigarette and went to sleep.

He dreamed he and Vinnie were in Beppo di Mare with Sally Fish. The table was piled high with food. Linguine in red sauce with shrimp and lobster, striped bass in brodo, a silver tray of cherrystones on a bed of crushed ice, side orders of escarole, potato croquettes, fried zucchini, three bottles of Corvo white sticking out of an ice bucket, a rum cake with strawberries, demitasse . . . In the dream he could smell the sauce, taste the cold, rubbery clams as they slid down his throat. Little fat Beppo hovered around them sweating blood. Did they want a little more of this? Or how about some bluefish, he just got some fresh today? In the dream Benson thought, *This greaseball would piss on three-day-old flounder if it was just Vinnie and me. But for Sally Fish, the big important wiseguy . . .*

Sally was wearing a dark suit with very faint pinstripes. He had gone conservative on the accessories, except, of course, for the big emerald on his pinky and the gold Rolex. He waved Beppo away and continued his story. ". . . So I knew that the guy knew that I knew, you know . . ." He looked from Benson to Crow, his black eyeballs spit-shined with cocaine, his perfect crowns ("this mouth cost me more money than you make in a year") bared in a savage grin. "So I told the guy to tell me next time anybody told him what to tell those guys, you know what I mean."

Suddenly, Benson couldn't stand it. How could he sit at the same table with the guy who had put his partner on the spot? He leaned across and grabbed Sally's swarthy throat. Sally's eyes bulged. His lips pursed and opened—he looked like a fish after all.

Then a hand came down in an iron grip on Benson's forearm. Vinnie was standing by the table in uniform. The numerals of the Seven-Three, the first precinct they had ever worked together, were on the tunic. Vinnie squeezed so hard Benson felt his brain bursting.

"First things first, Billy the Kid," Vinnie said, shaking his head. "First things first."

Benson woke up with his forehead throbbing. Billy the Kid for Chrissake, where did that come from? Billy the Kid had been his nickname in Brooklyn when he and Vinnie rode in a radio car. Vinnie they called Frankenstein. Frankenstein and Billy the Kid, that was what the cops called them. The skells in the ghetto called them the White Towers. Finnerty, their sergeant, called them the Dump Brothers because he had been working the night they had gotten drunk and tried to outshit each other on Livonia Avenue under the Elevated tracks. It was in the middle of a snowstorm. They just dropped their pants and started shitting in the snow. A bunch of Rastas came out of a bar and thought they were being mooned. Before it was over three Rastas were laid out in a drift, and somehow a lady Rasta had gotten her sweater ripped off and was running around with her tits bouncing, screaming for help. In the middle of all this Finnerty came up in the car and let them run around for a while with their pants around their knees. "Nice to see some talent on the job," he said. A few days later he kept them back after their tour had turned out. "How'd you guys like to donate your services to the Sergeants' Benevolent Fund?'' he asked.

So every Friday night Benson and Crow would pass a pleasant tour driving Finnerty around the sector to the various bookies, bootleggers, chop shops, fences and whorehouses that were "on the pad." Finnerty collected for the sergeants on the four to twelve—and for the captain. Benson and Crow were along just in case some mutt among the many who knew how much money Finnerty was carrying decided to hold him up. It seemed absolutely crazy to hold up a cop, but as Finnerty often said, "There's no telling what some mutt will do."

Finnerty must have been the same age Benson was now when they first met, but he always seemed so much older than everyone else. He was a skinny guy with smooth white hair and a basketball of a beer belly that Benson would pat for good luck. Broken blood vessels crisscrossed his cheeks and his fingers were brown with nicotine. He never missed a day's work and he didn't have an enemy in the world. Even mutts he had jacked in back of the car would cross the street to say hello, opening their mouths to show where he had knocked their teeth out.

But he had the deepest bags under his eyes. "That's where he keeps his money," the guys joked. "You last twenty years on this job and see if you can get a good night's sleep," he said. He lived in a two-family house in Bay Ridge with his wife and four kids. His brother-in-law, who was a fireman, rented the top floor from him. Finnerty never moved, never bought a nice car, never treated his wife to a nice vacation. Never even put all the pad money in a safe-deposit box, but buried it in the wall of his basement. When he got sick he went to a ward in a city hospital. He had Lou Gehrig's disease. Benson and Crow begged him to go out to the Coast where they had a new treatment for it, but they were asking over a hundred Gs and the treatment wasn't covered in the medical plan. "I'd have to dip into the pad," Finnerty said. "The shoo-flies would be on me like maggots on a dead man's eyes." So he died in a state nursing home a few months later. Toward the end he was so feeble that none of the guys could stand seeing him. The money stayed in the basement; it was probably still there.

Every year Benson and Crow would get drunk on his birthday. They'd close the bars and go after hours just drinking and telling the same Finnerty stories. Then they would end up at dawn sitting in the car a block away from his house debating whether or not to go and tell his wife about the money.

Now Benson would have two birthdays to celebrate, two sets of legends to retell. Only this time he'd do it alone. He'd drink by himself, remembering. Then he'd probably end up at dawn parked in front of Vinnie's house, debating whether or not to go in and straighten out his wiseass kid, Anthony. The kid had been Vinnie's favorite. He was the youngest, the only boy with three sisters, pampered by everybody in the family. He went to Holy Cross on a scholarship, was a starting quarterback in his sophomore year and an Honors student in math and chemistry. Vinnie bragged about him constantly, always adding, "And the kid hates my fucking guts." That was the thing he was most proud of. "He won't talk to me," Vinnie would say to anybody who'd listen. "He thinks I'm a drunk, an animal. He hates the way I treat his mother." He'd say it to anybody, even when he was sober. Vinnie's three daughters looked like him. "The Mung Sisters," he'd call them. "Six hundred pounds of shit in a wheelbarrow. Maybe I could get a three-time loser to marry one of them, but parole wouldn't be enough. I'd have to throw in a Presidential pardon." He felt guilty about his wife, but . . . "They want you to stop living, these broads," he would say about wives in general. "Come home after work and sit with her and the Clearasil All-Stars in front of the tube. You can't do that in this job, Billy. You can't bounce mutts off the wall ten hours a day and then come home for fuckin' *Dynasty*. But they don't understand that. Nobody really does but another cop."

The painful truth was that Vinnie left a lot of cops in the dust with some of the things he did. Career guys who wanted to make it on the job avoided him like the plague. Honest guys muttered about him but never dared complain openly. Vinnie was the first to admit that he wasn't too bright, but the one thing he claimed to know for sure was what being a cop was all about. "Terror," he used to say. "You gotta keep 'em terrorized, shittin' in their pants. You let up on 'em once, they'll be all over you." That was how he started the "first things first" routine.

It was a phrase Vinnie had made famous in Brownsville. Every time they had a tough collar, a mutt who put up a fight or cursed them in front of a crowd, they'd get him in the car and head for the "Inquisition Chamber," which was a burnt-out tenement on Saratoga Avenue. Most of the mutts knew the route to the house so they'd get nervous when Benson pulled off onto Saratoga. "Hey, man, this ain't the way to the precinct."

"First things first," Vinnie would say, turning to stare at the guy. And when Vinnie Crow stared . . . well, they didn't call him Frankenstein for nothing. He looked like he had been put together by a drunken bricklayer. His ears were so close to his head, if you looked at him from the front you'd swear he didn't have any. He had teeth like a horse. Three years of high school football, offense and defense on the line, two years of semipro every Saturday in Westchester, and he hadn't lost a tooth. His hands were so big and ugly you got scared looking at them. The nails were bitten down to the cuticle. He did it while he was driving, steering with one hand, gnawing with the other, then switching.

So Benson would pull around behind the building, tires crunching in the rubble. They'd drag the mutt out of the backseat, walk him down to the sub-basement and take off the cuffs. Then Vinnie would square off with him.

"C'mon, tough guy, you wanna fight? I won't file no extra charges. You win, you walk."

Vinnie would drop his holster and step away from it. "You want the gun? Come get it. I don't need a weapon to deal with a mutt like you."

The wise mutts would take one good look at Vinnie and apologize. But sometimes they got a guy who was big, or maybe had been in the ring, or maybe was so mean that he just wanted to get a few shots in and didn't care what happened to him.

Maybe the mutt would go into a karate crouch, or would snort and do an Ali shuffle; or come in throwing wild kicks and punches, hoping to get lucky. It didn't matter what the mutt did, Vinnie always did the same thing. First a quick jab to the bridge of the nose to get him off balance, then a few short crunching hooks to the ribs. If his knees buckled, Vinnie finished him with an uppercut under the chin, which would usually make him bite his tongue. The poor bastard who was still standing would get a straight right flush on the mouth, and he'd be spitting bloody teeth while they dragged him back to the car. The wiseguy who feinted toward Vinnie and lunged for the gun took a kick to the gut that lifted him three feet off the floor. It was such a sandbag job, Benson could almost feel sorry for the mutts, especially the big ones who had never been hurt. Vinnie Crow was the kind of freak who could knock you on your ass with a punch in the arm. Mutts who hadn't cried in the cradle dropped to their knees and sobbed. A lot of mutts discovered Christ in the Inquisition Chamber.

Vinnie was an animal, there was no way getting away from it. But so, in his way, was Benson. Vinnie had grown up terrorizing his neighborhood in Park Slope. Benson had done the same in Sunnyside. Benson had been All CHSAA halfback at Xavier, Vinnie All-City tackle at Manual Training, which gave him the edge, he always said, because he played for a public high school. Benson joined the police force three days ahead of his draft notice so he got an exemption. Vinnie Crow did the same.

Benson remembered seeing Vinnie in a gym class at the Academy. Of all the guys in the class he knew it would be between the two of them to see who was the toughest. So they never spoke, just watched each other warily.

Then after graduation he turned out for his first day at the Seven-Three, and there was Vinnie Crow at the end of the line. No sooner were they out of the house than they were fighting. They had to know who was tougher. Just like kids in the schoolyard, they had to settle it. So somebody said something and they were out of the car on Blake Avenue beating the piss out of each other. Benson had never been knocked down in his life. He was stunned when Vinnie did it. His whole world collapsed. He had to go back again and again, every day for three months, vacant lots, tenement basements, anywhere they could go at it for a few minutes without being interrupted. He got some vicious shots in, enough to get Vinnie to admit that Benson was the only guy outside of his old man to ever hurt him. He rocked Vinnie, but he never knocked him down. Finally he gave in. He was second-best.

And not only with his hands. There was another test of manhood—drinking. Benson didn't even come close on that. Vinnie had what alcoholic cops called "the fire." He drank like he was trying to put it out. His binges became famous in Brooklyn, and because Benson went along he got some reflected glory. Vinnie liked drinking in the black bars on Fulton Street, the bad ones where the only white man allowed was the wiseguy who took the quarters out of the jukebox. This was the mid-sixties, and Brooklyn was in the last stage of disintegration. The Jews had fled the entire Flatbush area. Downtown Brooklyn looked like an A-bomb had hit it. In Red Hook the Italians and Puerto

Ricans were killing each other across a line of demarcation on Fifth Avenue. In Bay Ridge the Norwegians were being pushed out. Desolation had come to Brownsville; they were burning down a house a night. Not a day went by when you didn't see black smoke billowing into the sky. The drug dealers, the car thieves, the pimps, the fences and the heist guys were settling in the abandoned neighborhoods. A guy on Meredith Avenue was cooking heroin in the wooden barrels they used to boil laundry, doing so much that a kid who worked for him made a fortune scraping the residue and selling it to college students upstate.

It was no time for a cop, white or black, to go drinking in those Bed-Stuy joints. So Vinnie went every night. He'd work his way from Brownsville down to Bed-Stuy, with Benson tagging along to watch his back. They'd always run into guys they had pinched, or guys they were shaking down. From Livonia Avenue to Fulton Street they never paid for a drink. And never even got a hello. Just silence. But Vinnie didn't care; he was putting out the fire.

Then there were those nights when Vinnie would get horny. There was another area where he left Benson in the dust. They'd cruise St. Mark's Avenue looking for hookers. Most of the girls had set up two or three to an apartment, but you could always find one or two stationed under a lamppost near a bus stop waiting to deal with college kids or businessmen on their way down Flatbush Avenue to the white neighborhoods.

When Vinnie spotted a hooker he'd pull over, reach around and open the back door. "Get in, baby." It didn't matter what they looked like, fat, skinny, young, old. Most of them were black, but there were a few washed-out white ones, bleached blondes with bad skin. Vinnie didn't care. "Get in the car, baby."

The old pros took a peek, read cop, took a deep breath and got in. The new ones who thought it had something to do with how sexy they were would strut around to the driver's side to talk terms. "I get twenty-five, lover. . . ."

"You get this, bitch." Vinnie would flash the tin with one hand, grab them by the throat with the other. If they fought back or tried to run away he'd get out of the car and smack them on the collarbone with a blackjack. Benson never understood why a guy who would fight any man with his bare hands had to jack one of those pathetic little bimbos. Vinnie would throw them in the backseat. "Once around the park, James," he would say and Benson would take the wheel, avoiding the rearview mirror. He would hear Vinnie tearing at the girl's clothes. He couldn't take the moans, the curses, the occasional gagging noise. Vinnie was hung like a billy club. "I'm part police horse," he used to say, dropping his pants to illustrate. Benson would imagine those pathetic junkie bitches wrestling with his brutal tool, and his bile would rise. By the time the broad was shoved retching out of the car he'd be ready to puke himself.

In the morning after one of their binges he would rush home and jump into the shower to wash off the stink of booze so his mother wouldn't smell it. His father had a Dugan's bakery delivery route and would be up making coffee when he came in. The old man had emphysema from drinking and smoking. He had been living through Billy's escapades since high school when he came to every football game and drove Benson crazy analyzing the other team and second-guessing the coach. Now that Benson was a cop, his father loved talking about what went on in the precinct, pretending to a knowledge of police work. He would jump in with the old routine about the niggers ruining the city. Drug addicts and pimps robbing from their own mothers. Look how they'd ruined the projects. And the goddamn Welfare. Make them go out and work for a living, maybe they'd respect property a little more.

Benson sat there, still living in the noise, the blood, the darkness of the night before. Still driving down spooky ruined streets, the smell of death, fire, piss, booze, everything, fuming in his nostrils. His father had the standard Irish line. Benson had been hearing it for years. It wasn't wrong, it wasn't right. It just didn't matter. You had to see a man in pain from a stab wound—the crying-praying sounds that would come out of him. You had to see a junkie so sick he couldn't stand up straight. Teenage girls nodding half-naked in doorways early in the morning. Or a woman with half her head blown off and blood all over the place. Or the kids crying in the precinct when both their parents had been pinched, or their mother was dead, or Welfare was taking them away because their parents were burning them with cigarettes. You had to ride around with a cop who was badder than anybody in the ghetto. Who committed assault every day and got away with rape once, sometimes twice, a week. And was considered a good cop. And was respected in a neighborhood of veteran cops and career criminals. After a while you just stopped using the words "nigger" and "spic." After a while you stopped making moral judgments and despised anyone who did.

For twenty years Benson lived in Vinnie's shadow. It was Vinnie who got married first. They took over Quigley's Bar, a cop hangout on Bergen Street, for his stag party. There had to be at least fifty guys, mostly cops and firemen, plus a few of Vinnie's buddies from the neighborhood. Vinnie got killed on vodka and Seven-Up. At one in the morning they brought in two hookers they had picked up from a guy on Forty-second Street who actually booked broads for these rackets—two skinny black chicks who went down a row of bar stools giving everybody head. Vinnie went crazy and took both of them in the bathroom. The chicks were stoned on grass and drooling drunk. Later, Vinnie ran out in the street and flagged down a PR in a gypsy cab. "You wanna blow job?" Turned out the guy had gotten out of Rikers two days before and was horny. He freaked when he saw the two broads and went down on one of them with everybody watching. It got so crazy that Benson couldn't take it and slipped out. Everybody was too drunk to notice, and the next morning at the church, all red-eyed and shaky, they were talking about how that was the wildest stag party they had ever been to and that Vinnie Crow was an animal like no other human being in captivity. And everybody got the giggles when they started playing "Here Comes the Bride" and Vinnie appeared at the back of the church by mistake.

Benson was the best man. He'd rented a gray morning coat and tails for the occasion, gray trousers with a black pinstripe, a gray tie over a white pleated shirt. He knew he looked good; he could feel the eyes of the

bride's friends on him, wondering "Who is this guy?"
He looked over the row of bridesmaids for someone
he could pluck. Then he saw the bride.

Carmela Intaglia was small and dark and scared like
she was being forced into this thing against her will
although Benson knew she and Vinnie had been engaged since high school. Benson had never met her
before this. Vinnie always joked about keeping him
away. "I got her convinced I'm the only man in the
world with a dick." The first thing he thought when he
saw her was how was a girl this small going to deal
with a hammer like Vinnie's. As she got closer he
could see the outline of her breasts behind all the lace
and tulle of the bridal gown. As she passed he could
hear the swishing of her thighs against the heavy silk.
She smiled at him and mouthed, "Hi, Billy." Someone
had pointed him out to her. She turned back to look at
him again. It was an incredible thing to do, turn back
instead of looking straight at your husband-to-be.

Benson was woozy and weak in the knees, but he
put that down to a hangover. Carmela's father was in
the rackets, and a lot of small-timers showed up at the
church. "Watch out you don't slip on the grease goin'
down the aisle," Vinnie's father had whispered to him,
pointing out the minor leaguers with their slicked hair
and cheap rings. Benson knelt behind the happy couple, thinking of the night before and hoping Vinnie
hadn't picked up a dose of clap from one of those
broads. He was paired with Doreen Cronin, the maid
of honor, Carmela's best friend. She knelt across from
him, her eyes primly on the priest. Maybe it was that
cock-teasing look, maybe it was because she was on
her knees, her face tilted up, lips parted. Maybe it was

his sudden confusion at seeing Carmela. Benson never knew. But suddenly he felt a violent passion for this chunky Irish girl. She was wearing a powder-blue dress, a veil over her decolletage. Benson couldn't keep his eyes off her cleavage. He could see she had big pillowy tits. She was a redhead, and Benson had always heard redheads had big nipples. Her little buck-toothed mouth drove him crazy. At the end of the ceremony she wet her lips when he bent down to kiss her. "Let's go out one night," he whispered in her ear.

For a few months after that he saw her every weekend. Took her everywhere, making small talk, sitting with his arm around her in the movies just dying to drop down a half inch to her boobs. And her staring straight ahead, pretending to watch the movie. They had frantic kissing bouts in the car outside her house, Doreen opening and closing her mouth like a goldfish. She had all these smooth moves for getting his hands off her tits without making it seem deliberate. And all the while she'd be moaning and kissing him so much his lips would get numb and soggy, signifying in a million ways that she wanted to go all the way. If only . . .

One night they doubled with Vinnie and Carmela. Carmela was pregnant then and just starting to show. Vinnie was kidding around with her in the back seat. "Once around the park, James, I'm gonna boff my wife." Benson looked in the rearview mirror. Vinnie had his hand way up Carmela's dress, so far he could see the tops of her stockings. Doreen saw it, too. That night they made love for the first time. Benson opened the passenger door and Doreen lay over the seat with her head almost touching the ground, gasping, "I think I'm havin' a heart attack." Two weeks later they were engaged. Vinnie was Benson's best man. He booked Quigley's for Benson's stag party and was going around telling everybody, "If you think mine was wild, wait'll you see what we do for Billy." Benson was afraid to find out, so he pretended to have the flu. Feigning chest pains he got the police surgeon to admit him to Kings County for observation the day of the party. On their wedding night, he got blitzed on champagne and Seven and Seven. He decided to force Doreen's head between his legs, but she was already pregnant with Dennis and he didn't have the heart.

Doreen never lost the weight she gained with Dennis. She let herself go after the first nauseous months of pregnancy, stuffing food in her mouth like it was the last meal she was going to get. "I'm eating for two," she said.

After Dennis came she got worse. He would catch her at one in the morning standing in front of an open refrigerator, eating out of cans and cartons.

"You're still eating for two," he said. "Only both of them are you."

"I have to get pleasure out of something for God's sake," she shrieked back. "I have no life. You're out with your friends all night long. . . ."

Benson stayed in shape. He still did the daily dozen from his football days and got out to play basketball with Dennis on his days off. You'd think Doreen would be happy that her husband hadn't turned into a blimp. But she wasn't. She took it as an insult. She'd watch him checking himself out in the mirror and sneer.

"Does your girlfriend like your big muscles?"

He was proud of his body, proud of his strength. As a kid he had been dubbed Pretty Boy Floyd by Brother

Benedict at Holy Name School for his baby face and
his fast fists. He was dumping guys bigger and older
than himself by the time he was twelve. His Uncle
Jack said he was the next Billy Conn. He had God-
given athletic talent, quickness, good hands, strength.
His senior year he was six one, one hundred ninety,
and perfect except for the neat little paunch, the "Irish
piggy bank" hanging over his belt, which came from
too many beers and Seven and Sevens on weekends.
When he got on the job it was a short walk from Pretty
Boy Floyd to Billy the Kid. Finnerty named him that,
really. His baby face was a little dented by then, but
he still had the curly dark hair, the apple cheeks, the
bright blue altar-boy eyes. He still had them twenty
years later, and with all the boozing he had only put
on eight pounds. He still liked to look at himself in the
mirror. There was plenty there a woman could appreciate.

"Think of a good one, Benson." McKinnon was
standing over him.

Benson came out of his reverie. "How long you
gonna keep me waiting here like a mutt?"

"Inspector's busy, he'll get to you." Then Mc-
Kinnon's look seemed to soften. "I feel sorry for you,
pal. You know how he gets when cops screw up. You'd
better have something good for him. Better get your
thoughts in order. He's lookin' to burn you, Benson."

Benson fingered his sleeve. "Asbestos." He lay
back with a contented sigh—he would never show fear
to this stool pigeon. But his mind was working. How
much could he give up? How much could he get away
with? Most of all, what had Vinnie been trying to tell
him in that dream?

THE REAL STORY

*T*o tell it right you'd have to go back ten years. Back to where the kids started growing up and that cop salary became a joke.

Vinnie's pride and joy, Anthony, was too old to share a room with his sister anymore, so there was pressure to move to a bigger house. Benson had moved out to Baldwin the year before. After six months he was dead broke and Doreen had to go back to work. She got a job typing for an insurance guy in town and complained bitterly about it. "I would have stayed single if I'd have known I'd have to work. So now I got two jobs and I don't see any profit on either of them."

"That's what I like about you, your loyalty," Benson replied. But deep down inside he was mortified that his wife had to go back to work to make ends meet.

So when Vinnie turned to him one day out of the

blue and said, "There's no future in tossin' skells, let's make some real money," it was like somebody had been reading his mind.

Vinnie used his old man's connections in the Emerald Society, the Irish policemens' lodge, and got the two of them assigned to Plainclothes in the Gambling Division. Then Serpico started giving people up, and the whole unit was disbanded.

Next they went into Narcotics. They worked backup for undercovers. It was mostly in Brooklyn, a little on the Lower East Side. Low-level dealers, no big money. But that turned out for the best when the SIU, the elite Narcotics unit, was dissolved because its members were taking payoffs from drug dealers and everybody started rushing to get immunity and testify against their partners. Most of the guys who had been nickel-and-diming the street dealers weren't implicated.

For three long years after that, they worked Homicide in Brooklyn. That was the glory detail. Everybody in the squad was into solving murders. It was like a TV show. Most of the cases they caught were easy enough. Family disputes that ended in murder, the husband going on the lam, so you file a fugitive report and it goes out all over the country. Nine times out of ten the guy goes back to his hometown, down South or in Puerto Rico. Or if he was born in the neighborhood you ask around a little and find him in some broad's apartment. Homicides in the course of a burglary or a robbery? The stools would be falling all over each other to tell you where the perp was. Drug-related homicides? Usually unsolvable, and nobody gave a shit anyway. One less mutt on the street. The lieutenant was a book cop named Mariano, who had no other ambition in life but to clear murder cases. He used Benson and Crow on interrogations to intimidate people with their size, and occasionally when no one was looking to give some mutt a couple of smacks to jar his memory. He used them on stakeouts. They'd sit in the car for hours, sometimes days, waiting for a suspect to appear, and then go out and grab him, which infuriated them because most of this work was done on other guys' cases and they never got the credit. When Mariano got a tip about a fugitive, he'd empty the office, calling everybody off their investigations to hit the location. But he always sent them in first. He had a million abusive nicknames for them, Abbott and Costello, Paine and Webber, Nixon and Agnew. "Prick stays up nights making them up," Vinnie grumbled. Mariano knew they were grifters and hated them for it, but wouldn't transfer them out and easily countered all Vinnie's wire-pulling. "I need you guys around here," he told them. "You're the brawn, the rest of the guys are the brains. Couldn't do without you." He said it with a straight face. For all they knew, he meant it. In a way Benson was flattered. But he didn't dare admit it to Vinnie, who was fuming. "All those fuckin' politicians at Headquarters put their heads together, Billy. They never caught us so now they're gonna get even by makin' us stay on this detail until we put in our papers."

Vinnie had to be wrong about that. Homicide was an elite unit whether you made any scores or not. If the brass had a hard-on for them they could have been buried in some jerkwater squad out in Queens. Or even worse, put into a busy house in the West Bronx where they'd be up to their eyeballs in ghetto squeals with the Internal Affairs Division watching their every move. They could be entrapped in a million ways, if that's what the brass wanted. It seemed to Benson, at least, that somebody was trying to get the maximum use out of them. But he didn't dare suggest it to Vinnie.

Then the papers started running stories about crime in the garment center. There were a hundred investigations going on—the FBI, the IRS, Immigration, the Treasury Department. Everybody was generating information on thefts, shylocking, tax evasion, use of illegal aliens in sweatshops, union corruption, you name it. Everybody but the NYPD. There were stories about how easy it was to outfox the cops, how you could steal right under their noses. How reputable manufacturers were arranging thefts of their own goods and then selling them to certain retailers for cash, in addition to pocketing the insurance claims that the police verified for them. The Department was looking real bad on this. A shake-up was inevitable.

When it came it hit the whole Midtown South area. Precinct captains were transferred, inspectors took early retirement, every detective had to take a lie-detector test. The Major Cases Unit moved in to concentrate on the garment center.

And when the smoke cleared, Benson and Crow found themselves on the Safe, Loft and Truck Squad with instructions from Inspector Duffy—"the king of the altar boys," Vinnie called him—to make frequent and public arrests in the area. "I don't care if it's a kid shoplifting a package of jockey shorts," Duffy had said to the new members of the squad. "I want the public to see that we're on the job out there."

The first few months they worked back up. The squad put undercovers in the garment center, Spanish kids pushing Cadillacs, contacting other Spanish kids who were walking a few racks the wrong way. Nothing big, but the collars were on the street. Benson and Crow with three or four of these mutts pushing the wall. It didn't mean anything, but it looked good, and that was what Duffy wanted.

Then their break came. There had been a burglary in a Pierre Cardin showroom. Five hundred designer suits, all sizes. The place had been covered by a private security outfit which operated a silent alarm and radio-dispatched car. By the time the guards showed, the perps were gone. Another nowhere squeal, but just for drill Benson checked the personnel sheets on the two security guys and *bingo!* there was a photo of a guy he recognized from Sunnyside. Bobby Flynn, a weasel they used to call Bunky. It had been at least twenty years, but Benson recognized that squinty little bastard right away. The name on his sheet was Dennis Parker. A phony name.

"I think I'm gettin' a hard-on." Benson said. "What do those Cardin suits retail for?"

"Five, six hundred," Vinnie said.

"I definitely have a hard-on."

Benson pulled Bobby Flynn's yellow sheet. He had a record going back fifteen years. Burglaries mostly, one grand-theft auto, one assault with a deadly weapon on his wife. All told he had done six years in Rikers and Greenhaven.

Benson called the security company and asked for

Mr. Parker. "This is Brady, Safe, Loft and Truck Squad, Mr. Parker. We'd like to get a statement from you on the robbery."

"Sure, sure, anything I can do to help."

Benson made a date at a Blarney Stone near the Post Office. He got there fifteen minutes late. Vinnie sat in the car while he went in. Bunky Flynn was drinking shots and beers in the corner; his ashtray was overflowing. Benson clapped him on the back. "Bunky Flynn, they didn't kill you yet?"

Bunky almost swallowed his Marlboro. "Jesus, Billy Benson."

"Look what happened to Bunky Flynn." Benson fingered the blue jacket with Arrow Security written in gold letters on the breast pocket. "You're the last guy I'd expect to see protectin' other people's property."

"I've cooled out a lot since the old days," Bunky said with a nervous smile. "What about you?"

"I'm a cop, Bunky."

Bunky was a good criminal. He stayed calm even though he had just shit a brick. "Jesus, no kiddin', Billy," he said. "Last time I heard of you it was when you made All-City."

Benson smiled. This was fun. "I'm on the Safe, Loft and Truck Squad now, Bunky."

Bunky looked around for the bartender. "No kiddin', Billy," he said casually. "Lemme buy you a drink."

"I'm Brady, Bunky. I'm the guy who called you."

Vinnie came in right on cue, walking up behind Bunky. "This the stool?" he asked, glaring.

Sure it was an old trick, and sure Bunky had seen it

before. But with Vinnie Crow you could never be sure that he wouldn't devastate you just for the fun of it. Bunky was pro enough to know what they wanted. He sighed and shook his head.

"The pinch stops here, fellas."

Vinnie took him by the arm. "Let's talk about it in the car."

They walked him out and frisked him for a wire— you never knew who was double-banging who anymore. Vinnie got in the backseat with Bunky. "Names and numbers, Bunky."

Bunky shook his head. "I'm no stool pigeon."

Vinnie backhanded Bunky with his ring hand, the hexagonal high school ring with the sharp edges. Blood poured from Bunky's lip. Benson handed him a handkerchief.

"What's this with the code of silence, Bunky? You know better than that."

"This is wiseguys, Billy," Bunky pleaded.

Vinnie put his huge hand over Bunky's face. "I'll put your head right through the window, Bunky. I'll kill you, Bunky. Nobody would miss a fuckin' squirrel like you."

"Be careful, I got asthma," Bunky said in a muffled voice.

"Let him alone, Vinnie," Benson said.

Vinnie sat back. He took Bunky's Marlboros out of his pocket and gave him one. Bunky knew the game, but he looked to Benson for sympathy anyway, which just showed how well the game worked.

"I never gave anybody up before, Billy," he said.

Vinnie grabbed Bunky by the hair and slammed his

head against the front seat. "You'd give up your mother for Rangers tickets, you lyin' bastard."

"The man's struggling with his conscience, Vinnie," Benson said. "He's got to think it over."

"What's to think? Either he tells us what we want or I mutilate his fuckin' face."

Bunky came up, shaking his head groggily. "I can take care of you guys."

Vinnie sneered. "What are you gonna do, sign your check over to us every week?"

And Benson just shook his head sadly. "We got you by the balls, Bunky."

"Okay, okay," Bunky said. "There's a guy throws us a few bucks, me and my partner, and we respond late to the alarm. Fifteen, twenty minutes, to give him time to clean the joint out."

"Who is this guy?"

"Richie the Greek."

"Don't know him."

"Richie Mavropides, Olympia Trucking. He calls us when he's gonna hit a spot on our route."

"How does he come to know your route?" Vinnie asked, grabbing Bunky by the back of the neck. "You spottin' the scores for him, too, Bunky?"

Benson removed Vinnie's hand. "So what if he is," he said gently. "He's makin' a dollar, right, Bunky?"

"I ain't gettin' rich," Bunky said, wiping his split lip.

Vinnie reached around him and opened the door. "Tell your story walkin'," he said and shoved Bunky out into the street.

Olympia Trucking was in a garage on Thirty-eighth Street, off Tenth Avenue. The driveway was closed, entrance door locked, no way to get into the building. No one answered their knock.

There was a blue Seville with Jersey plates parked on the sidewalk in front of the driveway. Vinnie went up to the car and pulled off the windshield wipers. Then Benson got out his keys and started cutting his initials into the passenger door. A big guy in a dark blue suit came out of the garage. He had black hair, bushy black eyebrows. He was tieless, his white-on-white shirt stuck out of his pants; a gold birth sign and a Greek cross glittered in the matted black hair on his chest. The garage door opened and two guys in mechanics' overalls, carrying wrenches, came out.

"What the fuck do you guys think you're doing?" the big guy said.

Benson wiggled the tin. "You Richie?"

"Yeah."

"This your car?"

"Yeah."

Vinnie came around from the other side of the car. Richie's eyes widened, his eyebrows raised, and he backed up an inch.

"We want those suits, Richie," Benson said.

"What suits?"

"Let's go inside, Richie."

Richie chased the mechanics with a jerk of his head. He led Benson and Crow through the entrance door and down a narrow corridor. They could see the garage area through a glass window. Two ten-ton trucks and a van, that was Olympia Trucking.

"Nice little business, Richie," Benson said.

Richie grunted. He took them into a tiny, cluttered office. There were nude calendars on the wall from different suppliers, a desk piled with invoices, old filing cabinets. Richie sat on top of the desk and reached for the phone.

"What are you doin', Richie?" Vinnie asked.

"Callin' my lawyer."

"This ain't a pinch."

Richie kept dialing. "The day I believe a fuckin' cop . . ."

Benson was the closest so Benson hit him. He caught him with a short right just under the heart. Richie went "Woof," doubled over and fell off the desk, landing on his knees. He crawled around for a while, trying to catch his breath. Vinnie stood over him.

"I know a hundred-twenty-five-pound Puerto Rican can take a punch better than you, Richie."

"This oughta prove we're not pinchin' you," Benson said. "We'd never leave ourselves open to a charge of police brutality."

"I don't have the fuckin' suits," Richie gasped. He crawled behind the corner and stuck his head in the wastebasket.

Benson waited until he finished puking. "Who'd you fence them to?"

"Don't fence 'em. I steal 'em on contract."

"Don't get technical, Richie," Vinnie said, yanking Richie up by his hair.

"Lemme sit down for a second," Richie whined. "I'll give you the whole thing."

They helped him over to his desk. Vinnie went out and got him a cup of water. Benson wiped the vomit off his shirt. Richie was white. It looked like he was going to have a heart attack. "It's over for me," he said.

"Nothin's over," Benson said. "You give us the fence, you stay in business. We'll go away, it'll be like nothin' ever happened."

Richie shook his head. "You don't understand. It's the wiseguys."

"They won't know nothin' about it."

Richie shook his head vehemently. "You don't understand. It's Sally Fish, he knows everything. He's got fuckin' radar, you can't put nothin' over on him."

"Who's Sally Fish?"

"Sal Pescatore. He's the man. He's movin' in on the garment center. Hijackin', burglary, even diamond heists gotta be organized through him."

"Where's Sally Fish from?"

"Bensonhurst. The Marino family."

"Frankie Carbonaro's runnin' that," Vinnie said.

"Yeah, yeah, this kid Sally's his nephew. He's the main gee in the garment center. You sell a fuckin' tie on the street and he comes around for his end."

"What'd he give you for the suits, Richie?" Vinnie asked.

"Fifteen grand."

"For five hundred suits! Thirty bucks a suit. You got ripped off."

"You're tellin' me? I had to make two trips out to the asshole of Brooklyn."

Richie didn't have an address or a phone number on this guy Sally Fish. Nothing but a social club on Elizabeth Street where Richie had gone to meet him. They were sure he had a yellow sheet with his last known address, probably a prison record. But to pull the sheet would leave a trace, however faint. So they sat in the car thinking. Then Vinnie said, "What was the name of that guy who had the jukeboxes in Brownsville?"

"JoJo . . . JoJo somethin'."

"Don't matter." Vinnie started the car. "He was hooked in to the Marinos."

JoJo hung out in the back of a video-game parlor on Eighteenth Avenue in Brooklyn, making deals while the kids played in the front room. He had a neighborhood kid watching at the window for him. Another kid, in a dark suit, white shirt open at the collar, fancy haircut, stood in the back. The guy at the window didn't budge as Benson and Crow came in. As they walked to the back they could hear the kids whispering, "Cops."

The kid at the door in the dark suit stepped out in front of them. "Can I help you?"

"Yeah, I need a blow job," Vinnie said. "Whaddya say?"

"You look like John Travolta, you know that?" Benson said.

The kid slid back.

JoJo was a moonfaced, beardless guy, pear-shaped like one of those rubber clowns that bounced up when you punched it. He was drinking coffee and eating pastry at a little Formica table with a couple of old guys from the neighborhood. They got up muttering "Excuse me" as they backed out.

JoJo watched them carefully. Vinnie sat down and fingered the box of pastry. "Cannoli, my favorite. May I?"

JoJo pushed a dank lock of black hair out of his

eyes. He had stubby gray fingers, nails bitten down to a black rind.

"I'm not shleppin' quarters in Brownsville anymore, gentlemen," JoJo said.

Vinnie licked custard off his fingers, doing his slob routine. "Hey, you're a big shot now."

"We're from the Youth Squad." Benson said. "We hear you been fixin' those video games."

"I can't be stakin' every cop who floats in here."

Vinnie looked at his watch. "Two-minute warning, JoJo. Two more minutes of wise remarks before I shove these guinea cupcakes in your face."

"We're lookin' for Sally Fish, JoJo," Benson said.

"I don't give information," JoJo said.

"We know, you're a big shot, JoJo," Vinnie said. "Give us that line about you make a phone call and we're walkin' a beat in the South Bronx," Vinnie said. "Now that you're a big shot, you gotta learn all those lines."

Benson threw his memo book onto the table. "Put his address down there, JoJo, and we'll go away. What's the big deal? You're gonna tell us anyway."

JoJo looked out of the corner of his eye at Vinnie. He wrote the address. Vinnie picked up the box of cannoli. "A big shot like you can always get more."

Vinnie stopped off for a can of Coke to wash down the pastry. Back in the car he said, "With all this detective work we're doin' I feel like Sherlock Holmes today."

"You looked like you had rabies with that cream on your mouth," Benson said, laughing.

Sally Fish lived in a luxury apartment building on Ocean Parkway. White stone and glass, a circular driveway, and a doorman in livery. The doorman was sitting on a white sofa reading the *Enquirer*.

"Mr. Pescatore at home?" Vinnie asked.

"Who's calling?" the doorman asked, without looking up from his reading.

"Good friends."

The doorman looked up and read cop, not that it took a lot of perception with Benson and Crow. "Eleven D."

"Don't buzz him. We want it to be a surprise," Benson said. But as they got into the elevator they saw the doorman running to the house phone. So they got off at the third floor and began walking up the stairs. Halfway up they heard hurried footsteps heading down toward them, and at the seventh-floor landing a guy in a cashmere overcoat almost ran into them. He was anxious, but he wasn't sweating; he even half-smiled when he realized he'd been outmaneuvered.

"What's the hurry, Sally, you don't owe us any money," Vinnie said.

"Who are you?" Sally asked. He wasn't big, but he was thick like a laborer, and there was no fear in his eyes.

Benson fingered the coat. "Nice." He checked the label. "Pierre Cardin," he said, rhyming it with "tin."

"Card*an,*" Sally corrected, rhyming it with "tan."

"Got any suits like this, Sally?"

"Couple."

"Let's go see 'em."

They went upstairs to the eleventh floor. As soon as they were inside they knew they had their man.

"The buck starts here," Vinnie said.

The living room was done in black and white. White

sofas, black-lacquered coffee tables and a curio cabinet with silver plates and service dishes behind the glass doors. A white bar with a black-lacquered counter, white carpet with black slashes.

"Somebody spilled paint on your rug," Benson said.

"That's a reproduction of a Franz Kline painting," Sally said. "Ever hear of him?"

"I heard of Pierre Cardin," Benson said.

Sally went to the phone. "I don't know nothin' about no suits, but I know you guys ain't gonna believe that, so I'll just call my lawyer."

Crow took the phone out of his hand. "You've been givin' out burglary contracts in the garment center, Sally. We got a thousand fingers pointin' right at you."

Sally shrugged regretfully. "I'd like to help you guys. . . ."

"Let's see your bedroom, Sally," Crow said.

The bedroom was black and white. There were black silk sheets on the bed. Benson fingered them as Crow went into the bathroom. "Sexy."

"Yeah, I like throwin' blondes on there," Sally said. "Nice young blondes with white skin. Matches the decor."

Vinnie came out of the bathroom, wrapping a towel around his clenched fist. "You wanna tell us about those suits, Sally?"

"Wish I could."

They cuffed him spread-eagled to the bedposts and went to work. Vinnie hit him a few shots in the chest with his towel hand, then Benson slapped him in the ribs with the blackjack. Sally's body twitched with every shot, but he didn't make a sound.

Benson wrapped the jack in a towel and smacked him across the mouth. "You're not gonna be goin' down on any young blondes for a while, Sally."

Blood dripped from Sally's split lip. "I heal fast," he said.

Vinnie unwrapped the towel, slowly. "You're gonna be pissin' blood for a week, Sally."

"I don't have nothin' special planned anyway."

Vinnie snarled and hit him in the kidney just under the ribs. Sally bounced twice, then lay there for a minute, clenching his teeth to keep from moaning. Benson and Crow stood over him, watching.

"You guys are from the old school," he said in a choked voice. "I give up."

Vinnie took the cuffs off. There were deep red welts on Sally's wrists. "You get A for guts and F for brains, Sally."

Sally turned over on his side. "All of a sudden I got partners?"

"Either that or ask your Uncle Frank to find something else for you because we'll put you out of the garment business."

"Okay, okay." Sally rolled over onto his stomach and muttered into the pillow: "Get me a handkerchief out of that dresser against the wall, willya? Top drawer."

Benson opened the drawer and found a roll of fifties as big as his fist wrapped up in two thick rubber bands. "Shouldn't leave so much money laying around, Sally."

"What money? There ain't no money there."

Benson slipped the roll into his jacket pocket.

"There's a bottle of Chivas on the bar in the living

room," Sally said. He tried to sit up, but could only make it halfway and fell back on the bed, clutching his side.

Benson patted him on the shoulder. "You stood up good, Sally."

"How'd you guys catch up to me anyway?" Sally asked, wincing with every word.

"Good detective work."

Vinnie came in with the bottle and three glasses. Grunting with pain, Sally rolled over and sat on the side of the bed.

"Y'see, you're getting better already," Vinnie said, handing him a glass.

"Here's to you, Sally," Benson said. "You got balls."

They clicked glasses and drank. Sally tried to stand but couldn't make it. He motioned to Benson. "Gimme a hand."

Benson held out his arm. Sally grabbed it and lifted himself painfully.

"Why don't you take it easy for a minute?" Vinnie said.

"Nah." Holding Benson's arm, Sally limped into the living room. He reached under the counter and sprung a lock. A hidden panel flipped down, revealing stacks of hundreds held in place by metal clips. Sally pulled a stack out from under one clip and threw it on the bar. "Fifteen grand. You tell me the guy who gave me up."

Vinnie shook his head.

"Not even I'm that greedy, Sally," Vinnie said.

Benson slid the stack across the counter. "Can't blow a stool. Not even for an old friend like you."

"Okay, okay." Sally flipped the stack to Vinnie, who caught it in his big mitt and just stared down at it. "Chump change, gentlemen. You keep it."

Vinnie raised his eyes reluctantly and looked over at Benson.

And Sally gave out with that harsh, braying laugh that would become so familiar to them. "You fuckin' cops are a pisser, you know that? You had yourselves all programmed for a little score, right? Maybe a G-note. A day's pay. Instead, you stepped in shit right up to your eyeballs and you don't know what to do about it." He poured himself another drink and limped out from behind the bar on his own power. Benson and Crow exchanged looks. This guy *was* a fast healer.

"There's eight grand in that roll. Plus the fifteen makes twenty-three big ones and you deserve it for runnin' me down because I'm smart. You know the word 'wiseguy.' It was invented with me in mind." Sally laughed and sat down on the couch. "Yeah, you got a big fish, alright. So big that it's gonna turn around and put the hook in your mouth." He opened an onyx cigarette case on the glass coffee table. It was full of cocaine. "Gotta take my medicine," he said, digging the powder out with a silver spoon. "You guys want a taste?"

"No, thanks," Vinnie said.

"Pharmaceutical, fellas. No benzene, no nothin'. Right from the Merck's factory to your table." Sally took a snort. "I use it to think, like Sherlock Holmes did, you know. That's why I don't understand why more cops don't do coke when the greatest detective ever mainlined it, for Chrissake. Oh, well, what do I know? Sit down and put that money away and stop lookin' at it like it's poison ivy.''

They sat down. They knew the kind of workout they had given this guy, but his movements were normal and he seemed completely recovered.

''I'm not through playin' Santa Claus with you guys,'' Sally said. ''Now I know you took a while locating me and you've got to account for your time with the squad commander, right? So I'm gonna give you a pinch. Now whaddya say to that? Am I a stand-up guy or what?''

''What pinch?'' Vinnie asked suspiciously.

''So glad to see the power of speech has returned to you,'' Sally said. He took another snort and leaned back with his eyes closed. ''Talk about blowin' away the cobwebs.'' Then he lunged forward. ''Calico Maiden, remember?''

Vinnie looked over at Benson.

''Dresses,'' Benson said. ''The truck was hijacked and they shot the driver.''

''Freelancers from New Jersey,'' Sally said. ''They were asked to stay out of the garment center. In a nice way, you know. So now they made threats. Said they wanted a sit-down. Next thing you know they'd be bringin' alotta *gavones* from Atlantic City into the act. Alotta aggravation. My Uncle Frank don't like that. He had a solution to the problem, but I think I got a better one. You guys are gonna arrest 'em. You look good. They look bad. Everybody's happy. I'll give you their names, the names of the retail stores they deal with. All you gotta do is write it down in your little memo book. Whaddya say?''

''What do we have to do in return?'' Benson asked.

Sally smiled. "Only everything."

The proposition was simple. They'd get an envelope every month, 10 percent of whatever Sally had netted. Every once in a while he'd throw them a collar. "This way we kill two birds with one stone. I get rid of a nuisance, you guys become Dick of the Month." All they had to do was keep him informed as to everything that was going on in the Squad, which meant what cases were getting hot, what stools were coming forward. "Like I said, only everything," Sally said.

Benson remembered Sally's quick looks back and forth between Vinnie and him. And then that laugh again in which he threw his head back and showed his teeth like a horse. That laugh that made you want to shove your fist down his throat.

"Gentlemen, this is a happy day for me," Sally said, as he walked them to the door. "You see, criminals really have just about everything in their lives—adventure, color, variety, wealth, the company of interesting people. But the one thing they lack is a sense of security. Well, now I have that, too, thanks to you."

"The guy's mockin' us," Benson said to Vinnie in the elevator.

Vinnie patted his pocket. "He paid for the privilege."

"There's just enough cop left in me to be offended that this prick commits a felony right under my nose. I'd like to go back there and pinch him for possession and attempted bribery. There's just enough cop left in me to do that."

"Too bad," Vinnie said, "'cause there's no cop left in me. No cop at all."

They'd had two years and change with Sally. Sally

was as good as his word. He threw them enough good collars to make them stars in the squad. Once a week they'd meet at a restaurant for a big meal. Sally would order a ton of food and leave it untouched while he did his nonstop monologue about how smart he was and what *he* did and what *he* said. And about how his Uncle Frank was coming out of nowhere to take over the five families. At the end he'd slip Vinnie an envelope with a tiny "v" penciled in the corner. There'd be two, three, sometimes four grand in it. Vinnie would get a humble look on his face and duck his head, almost like he was bowing.

"You look like a dog comin' for his Alpo," Benson told him one night.

"I am," Vinnie said.

And then later, after they had whacked up the money and were drinking in Quigley's, Vinnie confessed to him.

"I gave him Flynn and Richie the Greek."

Benson's hand shook so badly he had to put his drink down. He was filled with fear. "Now he's gonna kill 'em."

Vinnie looked away in anguish. "Hey, we've been givin' him stools for a year and a half."

"Yeah, but we never gave him names."

"We didn't have to. We gave him the job. He knew the crews. The guy's no shmuck, he could figure out who was givin' him up."

"Yeah, but it's not like giving up names, Vinnie."

"Bullshit it's not. You wanna jerk yourself off, go ahead."

"You didn't have to do it."

"Look, we're in. We're part of his operation

whether we like it or not. And we gotta go all the way because now we're protecting ourselves. Those two guys could link us with Sally, and they would in a second."

"That's bullshit, Vinnie."

Vinnie slammed down his glass so hard it splintered. He turned and screamed in Benson's face loud enough for everyone in the joint to hear. "*You're* bullshit. Ten pounds of shit in a five-pound bag, that's you. We're in, you understand, so we gotta act like we're in."

"So we get out," Benson yelled back.

"We can't, asshole. We're in until we die, you understand?"

Benson heard voices outside the squad room. Suddenly the TV was off and everybody got real busy. A second later Duffy came walking through the door. He walked right by Benson like he didn't see him and down the hall through a door that McKinnon was holding for him. McKinnon went in after him. He came out a second later and waved at Benson. Benson made believe he didn't see him. He knew how to play that game, too.

"Benson," McKinnon called.

Benson still didn't look at him. Either he came down or he said what he wanted. Benson wanted the whole office to hear him being summoned. They weren't going to treat him like a collar until he was one.

McKinnon walked toward him. "Inspector Duffy wants to see you."

"Oh, okay." Benson rose slowly, stamping out his cigarette, and followed McKinnon down the hall. It was like Vinnie had been giving him a message from the grave. He was out, but Benson was still in. There was a satchelful of money at the Port Authority. There was Sally Fish.

It made sense now. From that very first day Sally had been looking to get even for that beating they had given him. But first he wanted the names of the stool pigeons who had given him up. A guy like Sally could wait. He played with them for two years, working on Vinnie, working patiently until he got what he wanted. Vinnie would be alive today if he hadn't given up those names.

And now Sally would go after that money. Sally would go after him. That was what Vinnie had been trying to tell him. "First things first" meant get Sally before he gets you.

Benson walked into the bare office and looked calmly into Inspector Duffy's angry face.

"I want to know everything you know about Vincent Crow," Duffy said.

Benson sat down with a smile. "Vinnie was hung like a police horse, Inspector. Everything else you already know."

THEY'RE NOT GOING TO LET ME GO

The sergeant's name was Momigliano. He smiled as he watched Karen staring at his nameplate. "It's a mouthful," he said, and pronounced it for her. Then he got her coffee and took her out in the living room so she wouldn't have to stare at Arnie's crumpled body under the covers. He held her gently under the arm with lightest pressure, steering her toward the couch by the window. He had tired brown eyes and enormous shaggy brows and exuded a comfortable smell of leather; Karen had never been close enough to a policeman to get his odor. He sat next to her, his knee brushing hers, and took down her statement in a spiral notebook with the tiniest blue lines. He printed laboriously, making Karen stop in her recitation while he caught up. He didn't ask any questions, just took down everything she said. Karen looked over his shoulder. His lettering was surprisingly neat and graceful.

When it was over he patted her on the knee, letting his hand rest for a moment as he said, "I'm afraid you'll have to wait here until the detectives come. Won't be long."

After an hour and two more containers of coffee, the detectives still hadn't arrived, so Karen sought out the sergeant in Arnie's bedroom. Cops were poking around in the drawers and closets. Two cops had raised the mattress, causing Arnie's body to roll to one side where another cop braced it while they searched. Everyone stopped and stared at Karen when she entered.

"Sergeant, I'm very tired," she said. "Could I possibly talk to the detectives later in the morning?"

The sergeant took her by the arm again, the pressure a little firmer. "They should be here any minute now, Miss Winterman," he said. "Would you like another cup of coffee?"

So she sat for another hour. The apartment filled up with policemen, but none of them spoke to her. They'd walk into the bedroom, confer in low voices, turning to look at her. Then they'd walk out, each of them giving her a quick look as they passed.

Karen tried to pull her skirt over her knees. She had come out barelegged. Those stupid spike heels Arnie had bought her were the first shoes she had seen in the closet. Should have worn slacks. Should always wear slacks.

The technicians arrived with their cameras and little black bags. Then a policewoman, a slim, pretty redhead, sat down across the room and smiled at her. Karen got up and smoothed her skirt, aware of the curious stares, and walked back into the bedroom to find Sergeant Momigliano. By now they had turned the place inside out. Arnie's clothes were piled in the middle of the room and a technician was going through them. They had taken the covers off his body and were photographing it from every angle. Momigliano walked quickly over to stand between her and the body. "Anything I can do for you, Miss Winterman?"

"I'm not an expert in these things, but aren't there an awful lot of policemen here?"

"Several units respond on a homicide like this."

Homicide? For a moment Karen couldn't breathe. Her feet went numb. "I have to see Arnie," she said. She tried to walk quickly around the sergeant, but the spiked heels wobbled. The policewoman came out of nowhere and grabbed her around the waist. "I want to see his face," Karen explained. "Poor Arnie, let me see his face one more time before he goes away forever."

And then she was lying on the couch in the living room with a cold towel over her forehead.

Somebody shook her gently. "Miss Winterman . . ."

She sat up and a violent pain erupted behind her eyes. She pinched the bridge of her nose to relieve the pressure, but the pain was so intense she reeled with nausea.

"You'd better not steal anything," she said. "Arnie's grandmother has an inventory of everything in the house."

WHY DON'T THEY CALL ME DOCTOR?

They put her in the backseat of a gray sedan. The policewoman held her arm throughout. "I wonder if I could just stop off at my apartment and change into something more, uh . . . suitable," she requested. The policewoman just repeated what Sergeant Momigliano had said before in exactly the same tone. "This won't take long. You'll be home in an hour."

A loose spring in the seat pressed against Karen's spine. *Why am I accepting all of this? Why don't I explode in a tirade of indignation and demand to be taken home immediately?* She was acting guilty. It made her wonder if many other innocent people were made to confess to crimes they didn't commit by this nonspecific sense of guilt that was just waiting for an accusation to take form. "The Miranda Ruling and the Oedipus Complex." Wasn't a bad idea for a paper.

Karen kept her eyes closed against the pain in her

head. At one point someone in the front seat asked, "Were you making a house call, Doctor Winterman?"

There was a suppressed chuckle and a whispered rebuff. Karen could feel the policewoman shaking with quiet hilarity. *They're putting on an act for my benefit. It's like Arnie said about them.* "Cops are practical jokers. They get off playing dirty tricks on people."

They took her to the 19th Precinct, upstairs to a door marked 19th Squad where a group of detectives were drinking coffee and watching *Good Morning America*. One of the cops gestured toward an office. "This way, Miss Winterman," the policewoman said. She ushered Karen into an office where a man paced impatiently.

The office smelled of fresh paint. There was a splintered desk in the middle of the room, two folding chairs against the wall. The man had swart, pouchy Hispanic features. His thick-heeled leather boots clunked like a flamenco dancer's. He was squeezed into a pair of Sergios with a large golden belt buckle in the shape of a ram. His soft silk shirt was unbuttoned, exposing a brown hairless chest. A diamond ring twinkled on his pinky. His long, thick fingers were yellow with nicotine. The nails were large and muddy. Karen hated him on sight.

"I'm Lieutenant Saldana of the Narcotics Squad. Sit down, please, Miss Winterman. Want some coffee?" He didn't even wait for an answer, but opened the door and shouted, "Can we get some coffee in here? How do you take it?"

"Black," Karen said.

"Two blacks," Saldana shouted. He slammed the door and sat on the desk, staring down at her. The bulge of his crotch seemed to be aimed at her like a concealed weapon. Another primitive police trick, Karen thought. They want to intimidate you with fatigue, confusion and the size of their genitalia.

"How long did you know Arnold Feinstein?" he asked.

"A little over a year."

"See him regularly during that period?"

"Yes. He was a patient. I saw him twice a week, sometimes more when he was working on a project for me."

Saldana looked down at her bare legs. "Told you everything about himself, did he?"

"Everything appropriate to our relationship, yes."

Saldana slid off the chair and began pacing again. "Appropriate, huh? Did he tell you he was running a million-dollar-a-month cocaine operation?"

The door opened before Karen could answer. An angry red-haired man in a baggy brown suit entered the room. "What are you doing here, Lieutenant?"

Saldana stepped between Karen and the red-haired man. "I lost an important operative last night, Inspector Duffy."

"Major Case Unit has been assigned this case," the red-haired man said.

The muscles in Saldana's buttocks tensed up as if he were digging into the ground. "If you think I'm gonna stand in line . . ."

The red-haired man walked around him, grabbed a chair and put it behind the desk. "Good morning, Doctor Winterman, I'm Inspector Duffy," he said, emphasizing the Inspector. "Oh, Lieutenant, ask Sergeant McKinnon to come in, will you please?" he said to Saldana, then turned back to Karen. "Sorry to keep you waiting like this, Doctor." Unlike the others, he didn't give her the once-over but stared directly into her eyes until she wanted to turn away, but she felt that if she did it would, in some obscure way, be an admission of guilt. So she stared back and heard the door close quietly behind her. "We feel that your uh . . . patient's death is linked to another case we're very anxious to clear up."

The door opened behind Karen. Duffy looked up, his cheeks twitching. His voice cracked like a whip through the bare office. "Why'd you let him in here?"

A man in a gray suit brushed Karen's shoulder. Karen couldn't see his face, only got a whiff of sweat and nicotine and a look at his hand trembling behind his back.

"The girl was from his unit . . ." the man began haltingly.

The inspector shut him up with a look of such implacable scorn that Karen felt the man's career was ruined for life. "I want him out of this building," the Inspector said. "I don't want to see his face around here. I don't want him talking to anybody associated with this investigation."

The detective in the gray suit did a quick about-face, anxious to get out of the room and away from his boss's contempt.

"And I want everything on Evelyn Aponte," the Inspector continued.

"We've got her jacket. We've got all the reports she filed. Statements from other cops she worked with."

"Get her fives, too," the Inspector said. "I want to

know every case and every dealer she's been assigned to since she joined the unit.''

The door opened behind Karen.

''And get Saldana out of the building. Now!''

The door closed softly.

The inspector slid a pack of Luckies toward the edge of the desk. Karen shook her head. ''Now that you've softened me up, you're going to use the fatherly approach, is that it?''

The inspector looked steadily at her.

''This isn't a game, Doctor Winterman. We're not using some technique on you here.''

Fight back, but don't be defensive. ''When you keep a person waiting for three hours . . .''

''You were kept waiting because I gave orders that anyone connected with the death of your uh . . . patient be held until I could speak to them personally.''

Why did he stumble over the word "patient"?

''And I was detained on another matter.'' The inspector turned away to avoid blowing smoke in Karen's face. ''This little incident with Lieutenant Saldana was not staged for your benefit, if that's what you were thinking. These things happen.''

The inspector took a notebook out of his inside pocket. ''The deceased was participating in a pilot program you were running for the Parole Board.''

''I am still running it,'' Karen said.

''Did you know *he* was running a cocaine-smuggling ring that was distributing between fifteen and twenty kilos a month in the New York area?''

''That's not possible. . . .''

The inspector closed his notebook and stared at

Karen again. "Mr. Feinstein was under investigation by undercover agents of the Narcotics Squad. His operation had been infiltrated by an undercover police-woman, Detective Evelyn Aponte. Detective Aponte was killed last night in a shootout at the River Royale Hotel. Three other police officers were also killed in that shootout. The perpetrator escaped. Now I know that a confidential relationship exists between a doctor and a patient, but you can see why we're anxious to get as much information as we can about Arnold Feinstein."

"Inspector, I can categorically state that Arnold Feinstein was not running a drug ring."

The Inspector looked intently at her. "You knew him that well."

Don't flinch, don't fidget. "I knew him well enough to know he was incapable morally and emotionally of such criminal activity."

The Inspector opened his notebook again. "We have reports from Detective Aponte implicating Mr. Feinstein and identifying his apartment as the place where contacts were made, deliveries arranged—" the Inspector's voice dropped—"murders planned."

"That's just not possible," Karen said.

"We have surveillance reports from other operatives identifying this apartment as a meeting place for drug distributors." He raised his hand to emphasize. "High-level distributors. We have a list of phone calls made from this apartment to drug distributors throughout the tri-state area. . . ."

"He would have told me."

"Mr. Feinstein's name first shows up in a recorded conversation between Detective Aponte and a drug smuggler named Sammy Pena," the Inspector said. "Sammy Pena was later murdered in an after-hours club in the Bronx on Mr. Feinstein's orders."

"Arnold Feinstein was definitely not a murderer."

"This man you saw outside Feinstein's apartment. Can you describe him in more detail than you gave the officer at the scene?"

"Not really," Karen said. "You see I wasn't really thinking . . ."

"There's a witness who says he saw the two of you together."

"No. Well, yes, I mean . . . just for a moment. We spoke. . . ."

"You don't know the man."

"No, of course not. If I did I would tell you."

The Inspector took an envelope out of the desk drawer and slid it across the desk at her. "Could you identify these photos for me, Doctor Winterman?"

Karen got dizzy at the sight of the smooth white borders sticking out of the envelope. *My God, the snaps!* She had forgotten all about them.

Arnie had gotten this weird idea. How much would *Playboy* pay for a centerfold shot of a shrink? The Sexiest Shrink in the World, they would call it. At first she demurred, but Arnie started snapping away with his Nikon and before long she got into the spirit, posing in those petulant provocative poses she knew so well, having worked on a Feminist Collective Committee Against Pornography in her senior year of college, where she had put together an exhibit of photos from mail-order "stroke" books to high-fashion monthlies, intending to show the institutionalized degradation of women. Then Arnie made up a fantasy:

She's a beauty-contest winner trying to get into the big time. He's a *Playboy* editor. Psychodrama. He made her get dressed and ring the bell. They played the whole scene, right down to the ultimate humiliation where she goes down on her knees for the centerfold. Arnie took pictures of it all, saying, "Hold that pose," while he stopped to reload. It went on until dark, this little game. In the shivery chill of the damp afternoon, they had spun a little fantasy cocoon around themselves. Arnie had an insatiable capacity for this kind of play. He pushed her further and further into it until she became that pathetic girl from a small town outside of Rochester—God knows she knew enough of them. When it was over and she lay semidressed and despoiled at his feet, she said, "Now I know why so many women permit themselves to be abused in this way. Now I understand." And he had laughed. "You have a way of turning everything into an experiment. Everything relates back to your dissertation." And they had laughed together, the spell broken.

Now the harmless childishness of that day had evaporated into a sinister collection of snapshots that the inspector intended to use against her. Okay. "Never waste time explaining things to a cop," Arnie always said. "Just try to make the best deal you can."

"What do you want from me?" Karen asked.

"Arnold Feinstein was your lover, wasn't he?"

"Yes." No use lying now.

"That's a violation of professional ethics, isn't it?"

"Yes."

"It could damage your career."

"Are you trying to blackmail me, Inspector?"

"Trying to get you to cooperate, Doctor Winterman. For your own good."

"I've told you the truth, Inspector."

The inspector shook his head calmly; he didn't seem at all upset. "I don't think so. I think Arnold Feinstein became your patient first, then your lover. That you were fascinated with his life style, the glamor, the money, the element of risk, the shady but colorful characters in a drug dealer's life. That you also developed a psychological dependency on cocaine, which Feinstein encouraged because that was an element of his power over you and others."

He's trying to implicate me. "This is the purest fantasy, Inspector."

"I think you knew a lot about his dealings. Probably met a lot of people he had business with. He would keep you in the dark about the dirty side of it, the murders, the unsavory connections. You would think of him as kind of a modern day bootlegger."

"That is completely and utterly . . ."

"You took a walk on the wild side, Doctor Winterman. A lot of people do it. A lot of people find the Arnold Feinsteins of this world irresistible."

Karen's mouth went dry with panic. *They're going to arrest me. They're not going to let me go home.* "Inspector, please, you're making a big mistake. . . ."

"Now I'm going to release these photographs to the press and to whatever professional association regulates you people, Doctor Winterman. I'm going to close your program down. I'm going to insist on testing your urine for the presence of narcotics and repeating the test at random intervals. I'm going to try to indict you for obstruction of justice. . . ."

Tears rose in a boiling vapor behind her eyes. She turned away.

Inspector Duffy stubbed out his cigarette and rose slowly, like an analyst at the end of the hour.

"I've got no particular interest in ruining your life, Doctor Winterman. I'll hold these photos for two days. You come back with some information, I'll tear them up. If not . . ." Inspector Duffy shrugged and smiled. "Have a good day, Doctor Winterman."

SIDETRACKED

Edmund iced his ankle all night long. It didn't stop the throbbing or take down the swelling, but at least it numbed the ankle so Edmund could focus on something other than the pain.

For hours he lay in bed staring at that photo. Karen Winterman, Ph.D. She was a pretty woman, and soft, too. Not like one of those flashy white bitches who thought they were slick, doing drugs and talking real uptown just to be hip. Ph.D. meant she was educated. Not the kind of chick to get involved with Sally Fish.

At 7 A.M., Edmund swung off the bed and came down hard on his ankle. It was swollen stiff, but he could walk on it. He put on the Sergios, the hooded sweatshirt and the Yankee cap, the street look. He poked around the bed for the Nike high-tops, and saw the valise. Damn, but this chick was the first person he'd come across who might be able to deal with the valise. And he was going to put her to sleep? Damn!

Thomas had given Edmund the valise when he went off to California to work on the space program. The thing was plastered with steamship stickers that Edmund's father had accumulated during the thirties when he traveled to Europe and South America with the Lunceford band. Inside was every record that Thomas Senior had been featured on. There were the sides with Lunceford where Daddy sang with a trio and took most of the tenor solos. And the septet sides he had cut in New York during the war, when he traveled up and down the East Coast working small clubs, but was barred from the USOs and the larger clubs because he was a black leader with white guys in his band.

"This is our tradition," Thomas had said. "Now you're in charge of it."

The idea was to put Daddy in his rightful place in the history of jazz. Thomas had gotten most of the material together, records, sheet music, press clippings, even something he called "oral history," which was a collection of interviews he had taped with musicians who knew and had played with their father. Now he wanted to interest some record company in a memorial album. One thing Thomas has neglected to do, he said, was to take the original pressings and acetates to a sound lab and get tapes made, so the stuff could be played without fear of permanent destruction. That would be Edmund's first task. Thomas had an inventory list of the contents of the valise. He had a list of dealers and collectors who might have access to the missing sides, another list of critics and musicians who might have press clippings. Thomas had everything in order, like a shopping list. First get the tapes made. Then go to the jazz magazine, then the record companies. . . .

"You understand how important this is," Thomas had said.

Edmund didn't understand. He never understood anything Thomas said. Sometimes he doubted he and Thomas were even brothers. Thomas was eight years older, big, black and broad like Daddy. Edmund was light and slim like Mama. "Pared down," Daddy would say, patting him on the head. Thomas had this gift—he could add a column of figures in his head. He could memorize a page out of the phone book. Edmund had no interest in numbers. He sat in the back row in school, and if he had a teacher who called on him too much he just stopped going. He never knew the answers, anyway.

Thomas went to Bronx High School of Science. He would bring these chumpy white boys home and Mama would make them Sloppy Joes on hot-dog rolls while they sat around talking about how first the state does this, then the people do that. . . . Edmund would tip out of the house, ashamed for the kids on the block that his brother was hanging out with these little gray faggots.

Then Thomas went on full scholarship to MIT and moved out of the house. By then it was just Edmund and Mama. Daddy had moved out to St. Albans with the nurse he'd met in the alcoholic ward at Jacoby Hospital. Mama didn't seem to mind. "I won't put up with his drinking, he can do whatever he wants about it."

But Daddy still came around on weekends. Edmund would awake to the sound of old-fashioned jazz records and would know Daddy was there, sitting in the kitchen with his horn case under the chair. When Edmund came in, Daddy would clench his fists and dance around, flicking jabs. "Hey, champ. . . ." And Mama would shake her head disapprovingly. "He gets enough of that on the street."

Then Daddy would reach out to Edmund, a dollar bill between his fingers. "Go out and get yourself some ice cream."

"Don't send the boy away," Mama would say.

Edmund would move in front of Mama, glaring up at this black giant of a man, who swayed and smiled in front of him.

"You don't have to protect your Mama from me, champ. Tell him."

And Edmund's mother would put her hands on his shoulders. "Go out for a while, honey, I'll be alright."

That was all before Edmund started hanging out at the old man's apartment. All before he realized that the dollar bill had been about Daddy getting over. All before Daddy had gotten sick and shrunk down to nothing. Edmund remembered that moaning creature in the hospital room, all that hard bulk just melted away, reaching out an emaciated arm to him. "Hey, champ. . . ." And outside the Jenkins Bros. funeral home a few days later when Thomas took him aside and said, "You know Daddy was a lot older than he looked. Sixty-five at least." Thinking back, Edmund realized he must have been crying, to have Thomas say that odd, consoling thing to him. But he didn't remember feeling anything except the cold and the impatience to get the thing over with so he could get back on the street.

Skinny as he was, Edmund could fight. He could waste dudes three or four years older, fifty pounds heavier, it didn't matter. From the outside people said he was fast. From the inside it was like from the time he was a little kid he always knew what a dude was going to do before he did it, so he always got the jump. From the outside people said he was stronger than he looked. From the inside it was like there was always a split second when a dude went slack, and if you could get there with something when that happened you could make people go flying. But the biggest thing about him, people said, was that he was cold. Cold meant taking a bat to a dude's head, or smashing him with a garbage-can cover when you've got him down. It meant going for the throat or the eyes, things that most of the other kids—bad as they thought they were—wouldn't do. From the inside it was nothing but fear. You had to put people out so when you walked away they wouldn't come back at you. You had to hurt them so bad they wouldn't even think of getting even.

While he was still a kid Edmund had really wasted some dudes. He'd gotten a rep on the block. Everybody was afraid of him. Everybody but the old man.

The old man lived in a smelly little basement apartment on Manhattan Avenue and 106th. Day and night there was always someone in his pad. Either some old dude with a conk and alotta jewelry or a bunch of strung-out white boys looking like they were ready for anything. Or a cop sitting in front of the TV drinking a beer. The old man was so fat he could hardly get up the three steps from his apartment to the street. He had a wide ass that went from his knees to his shoulder blades, and his breasts jiggled like a fat lady's behind.

But day or night you could always find a nice young bitch laying up on his couch. They came for the dope—the old man had it all—and they did whatever they had to for a taste.

It was the old man who had picked Edmund off the street. One day he had waddled across to the park side with a paper bag. "You wanna make twenty dollars, boy? Take this up to Shorty's Bar on a Hundred-and-thirty-second and Lenox. Ask for Cherokee, he'll give you the bread." Edmund started hanging out at the old man's pad after that. The old man fed him pork chops, red beans and macaroni and cheese. They would watch the ball games and the boxing matches and the old man would tell him stories about how everything was fixed so the "big boys" could make money. The old man drank VO by the quart, but never touched dope. "You don't wanna be sellin' this shit to support your own habit," he told Edmund. And one hot summer night the old man called Edmund into his bedroom where he was sitting gasping for breath on a bridge chair, a sheet of fat hanging off his belly right between his legs so you couldn't see what he had. There was a brown girl on the bed, sweat shining off her like she'd just been running around the block.

"I'm too hot to move, Edmund," the old man said. "You go ahead."

So Edmund crawled on the bed with this desperate bitch, and did it for the first time, the old man huffing and giggling behind him.

By the time he was fifteen, Edmund was out of school and working full time for the old man making pickups and deliveries. Thomas was on some kind of deal at Bell Labs and living out in New Jersey. He

came in on weekends, and once Edmund heard him
and Mama in the kitchen and Mama saying with a sob,
"I've lost my baby to the streets." And Thomas came
out to the park side afterward. He was wearing khaki
pants and black loafers with a ratty old tweed jacket.
"Joe College," Edmund said.

Thomas wore glasses with thick gold rims. He took
them off and folded them carefully into a case. For
one heartstopping moment, Edmund thought he was
going to start something, but it was nothing like that.
Thomas took a pint of Gallo sherry out of his jacket
pocket and took a slug. Then he wiped off the rim and
passed it to Edmund.

"I miss the block, Edmund. I miss hangin' out in
the park, just rappin' with no rhyme or reason to it.
You don't make friends out in the world like you do
on the block, you know. Maybe it's because I'm older,
maybe because I'm around mostly white people now,
I don't know. You're lucky to be around here."

Lucky? Edmund didn't have any friends, Thomas
had to know that. Thomas was the popular one, not
he. Those old winos who couldn't remember their own
names were always asking about him. *Your brother put
a man on the moon yet? Tell him to come back to the
park, we on the moon every night.* Thomas was loose
with people. He had the knack, like Daddy. Edmund
was a loner. He spent all his time out on the street
with the same dudes, but he felt nothing for any of
them. Or they for him. They respected him because
he was bad and because he worked for the old man.
That was it. Nobody ever called up or came by the
house to see what he was into. When two or three

dudes would split downtown to go to a show they never asked him.

After they finished the bottle, Thomas had taken him back into the apartment and given him the valise.

"I'm going to California, Edmund. I hope to be married by the end of the year. My old lady's white and I gotta deal with her family."

Edmund reeled from the sugary wine and Thomas put a heavy hand on his wrist.

"You know, Daddy was a great musician. It's up to us to see that he gets his recognition."

Edmund nodded.

Thomas gave him a rusty key. "This is the key, man. Don't lose it."

Edmund nodded. Later that evening he slid the valise under his bed and placed the key on top of it. The next night, after Thomas had left, he was walking down a deserted street near the Brooklyn Navy Yard with a shopping bag full of grass when he spotted two white dudes in a car across the street from the house where he always made the drop. He turned and walked casually back toward the subway. When he heard the twin slams of the car doors he began to run. He turned a corner and dumped the grass in a trash can. They got him just as he was vaulting the turnstile as the subway was pulling away.

"Never give the man a hard time," the old man always said. So Edmund stood calmly while they frisked and cuffed him. Gave his real name. In return they bought him coffee at the precinct and let him use a phone in the squad room to make his call to the number on the slip the old man gave him, which turned out to be an old lawyer named Irving Kaminer, who told Edmund, "Keep your mouth shut. I'll work something out."

As soon as they heard Kaminer's name the detectives got even nicer. They didn't put him in the crowded little detention cell where a junkie was retching and moaning while two other dudes tried to beat him into silence. They let him sit, one hand cuffed to a pipe, in a corner of the room. A white-haired detective typed his name and address laboriously on an old typewriter, cursing every time it skipped. He held Edmund's hand gently over the ink pad while they took his prints. The atmosphere was casual, almost congenial.

Kaminer, the lawyer, was a bald old Jew in a baggy gray suit. He didn't look like much, but all the cops gave him a big greeting. He had a worn-out briefcase full of cigarettes and candy and he went around the room passing the stuff out to everybody, even the dudes in the cell. "You smoke Winstons, right? Who wants a Big Payoff?" And everybody laughed because it was a candy bar. Edmund watched it all go down, wondering what kind of clown the old man had hooked him up with.

Then Kaminer disappeared into the lieutenant's office. He was gone for about an hour, during which time the cops watched the Johnny Carson show and those dumb dudes started beating on the junkie again.

When Kaminer emerged, the white-haired cop jumped up without a word and unlocked Edmund's cuffs. Kaminer walked Edmund into an empty office, pausing to call over his shoulder, "Somebody order some hamburgers up here, willya? I'm starving." And slipping a fifty to the white-haired detective. "Hamburgers all around, Jimmy."

In the office Kaminer sat Edmund down and put a hand on his shoulder. "You've got to go to jail, son," he said. "That can't be avoided this time. You understand that."

Edmund nodded.

"But the fellas here like the way you handle yourself. They could get you on possession with intent to sell. And Sullivan Law. You had about fifteen pounds. The weight would become fifty in court, you know how these things go. We could say you never had the package in your possession. They'd just lie and say they found it on you. You'll get heavy time in a state prison. You understand all this?"

Edmund nodded.

"The fellas here think you're a stand-up guy, so they want to make an offer." Kaminer took out a smeared white envelope overflowing with white betting slips. Edmund could see the numbers and initials scribbled on them. Kaminer handed Edmund the envelope.

"They'll forget the grass, the gun. You just plead guilty to possession of policy slips. You see, the fellas here have a business relationship with the bookies, but they have to make a gambling arrest every once in a while just to satisfy Headquarters. So they have an ingenious solution to this problem. They take a deserving young man like yourself, let him plead to the lesser charge, and everybody's happy. Meanwhile, you get thirty days in Rikers. You'll only do fifteen, as opposed to the three or four years you'd do on the marijuana charge." Kaminer looked him in the eye.

"Christmas only comes once a year, son. Take the offer."

"Okay," Edmund said.

Kaminer patted him lightly. "Good boy."

The cops jammed the other dudes into a prisoner van but drove Edmund to night court in a detective car. Kaminer was outside the courtroom when they arrived. "It's a zoo tonight," he told the white-haired detective.

"We'll get him on right away," the detective said.

The courtroom was jammed with witnesses, relatives, cops, lawyers. The cops shoved through the crush right up to the bench. The judge, a gray-faced man with sagging jowls and pouches under his eyes, watched their progress without interest. The white-haired detective said something to the clerk, who went behind the bench and whispered in the judge's ear. The judge looked down at Edmund and nodded.

"He got a lawyer here?" the judge asked.

Kaminer, standing right next to Edmund, didn't say a word as the clerk continued whispering.

"Got the papers?" the judge asked.

The clerk whispered.

"Thirty days," the judge said.

They took Edmund to Rikers in a van filled with prisoners. The first night he slept in a dormitory with all the other new arrivals. The guards kept the lights on all night long. You could tell the repeaters from the first-timers because they slept like babies under the sputtering fluorescents, while the new kids sat up smoking and looking around, their acts worn down and their fear showing through.

The next morning the guards marched them into the cafeteria. "Lookit the new bitches," someone said.

After breakfast Edmund stood on line waiting to use the phone. Kaminer had assured him that they would call his mother and tell her he was alright, but he knew they hadn't done it. When he got two or three guys away, a big black dude came out of nowhere and shoved in front of him. "Get the fuck outta my way."

Edmund didn't even take a breath. He jammed a thumb in the dude's eye and got a hand in his bushy Afro, but someone grabbed him from behind and threw him down hard on the stone floor. A foot came down on his face as he turned. He took a numbing kick in the back. Footsteps were clattering down the hall. "Hey, break that shit up." He took another kick to the back of his head before he was jerked up by his armpits.

"Motherfucker tried to push in ahead of me," the big dude said quickly.

The guards shoved him against the wall face first and frisked him.

"Motherfucker's crazy," the other one said.

Out of the corner of his eye he saw the two dudes who had attacked him. Ugly motherfuckers, looked like brothers, with the same bushy mustaches, standing there laughing. He could feel the blood trickling into his eye and down his cheek. In a second he'd be blind.

There was a ballpoint pen sticking out of the guard's shirt pocket. The hand gripping his neck eased up, it was something only Edmund could feel. The two dudes went slack, that was something only Edmund could see. It was that moment, that space between the ticks of a clock. Only Edmund lived there. He reached up—so easily it seemed—and grabbed the pen. He moved within that space, punching a hole in one dude's neck with the ballpoint, then feinting high and ducking under the other dude's awkward swing to bury the pen right up to the clasp in the soft flesh of his side.

It cost him a beating. They hung him by his wrists from an air vent and jacked him in the back and ribs until he blanked out. He knew why. He had made the guards look bad. They would have to file a report, explain why they weren't at their posts by the phone. He had to pay for causing them embarrassment.

They brought him to trial for assault. His mother sat sobbing in the front row. His brother took the week off. Both of the dudes got blood poisoning and the trial was delayed while they waited to see what would happen. They both recovered.

Kaminer and Thomas got into an argument. Kaminer wanted Edmund to cop a plea. He'd get simple assault, they would give him a year, he'd be out in five months. Thomas wanted to fight it. These two men were convicted murderers who were in prison on another charge of homicide. Why should Edmund be punished for protecting his life when the state obviously wouldn't do it?

"You make a political issue out of this, you make the system look bad," Kaminer said. "That's the one thing the system will not tolerate. Your brother has to play ball and do it my way."

"You're nothing but a parasite," Thomas shouted back. He stood threateningly over Kaminer. "You're fired."

Kaminer looked up, mild and unafraid. "It's not as easy as that." And he looked at Edmund.

"I'll take the deal, Thomas," Edmund said.

Thomas backed off. He sat down next to Mama and looked at Edmund as if he were seeing him for the first time.

So Edmund went to Attica. The guards gave him a nickname—Mr. Bic—for the pen he had used on those two dudes. He had a rep now. Wherever he went people pointed him out and whispered his story. In a place where guys his size were in constant danger, nobody came near him.

And then one day, in the yard by the basketball courts, Hutchens, a drug dealer from Harlem, approached him. "Somebody wants to meet you, bro."

He took Edmund around behind the equipment shed where a white man was laying out packages of coke on a grating. He was one of the mafia guys who sat together in a corner in the cafeteria. Curly-haired dude, hair sticking out of his shirt collar, wild-eyed like he was wired all the time. Broad shoulders, thick in the chest, long arms, knuckles pounded smooth from all the punches he had thrown. He looked up with a crazy smile.

"Mr. Bic. I got a nickname, too—Sally Fish."

Three days after Edmund got out, they had found his brother Thomas in his office at Edwards Air Force Base, a bullet in his brain. Mama was convinced he had been murdered by his girlfriend's parents. "They'd never let a colored boy in the family," she said. She stopped eating and taking care of herself, just sat in the living room all day muttering, "That's what I told him about race mixing, that's what I told him." It was only when she had died and Edmund was moving out that he found the valise under the bed, the key still on top of it. Only then that he remembered his promise.

"Do something for Pops," Thomas had said. But what could he do? Getting records made, visiting critics and students and DJs—organizing shit like that was a white man's scam. It was done in a white man's world. Except for a few cops, no white man had ever looked him in the eye. When he went into stores or restaurants he could feel them all freeze like he was about to pull down on them. In the subway sometimes he'd hear these white boys talking about something and it was like a foreign language. "There's plenty of home boys dealing with jazz," Thomas had said. "You can talk to them." But the homes froze quicker than Whitey. They knew the difference between black and bad. How in hell was he gonna show up anywhere with a valise full of yellow newspapers and scratchy old 78s and get anybody to listen to him?

And still, the thought of that valise under his bed made Edmund crazy. The thought that one day he wouldn't be coming home to that apartment. He'd be in jail or worse—laying in a gutter with a bunch of bullets in him. They'd come and take this valise away. Burn it without even checking to see what was inside. The old man's memory would go up in smoke. Sometimes he'd be thinking about it and his chest would tighten with fear. It would get so bad and last so long that he would forget what it was that made him scared in the first place and would go back through the thoughts until he realized the fear wasn't about being pinched or wasted, but about his father's records burning in an unopened valise.

The thing was to find somebody to do it for him. One of them white jazz fans Thomas had hung out with. Just give him everything and "Go, man, you deal with it." But who?

And now finally someone had come into his life. This chick, Karen Winterman, Ph.D. She was white and educated and fine. She could talk to people. She could put this over.

Only thing was, Karen Winterman was going to sleep. By tomorrow there would be no Karen Winterman.

The fear tightened in Edmund's chest. But this time he knew where it came from.

WE BOTH LOVED HIM

By 4 A.M. Karen's anxiety level was so high she associated every ambient sound—voices on the street, car doors slamming, the elevator rattling up and down—with the imminent arrival of Inspector Duffy.

She had the classic fantasy of imprisonment. Guards walk her down a long, dark corridor, women jeering from the cells. Rats scurry under her feet as she is shoved into a dark cell. The door clangs shut behind her. A woman rises out of the gloom offering her cigarettes from a rumpled pack: a blowsy blonde, her black roots showing, with rotted teeth and pitted cheeks, fat sagging off her arms.

She tried to do a diary entry, but her hands were too clammy to hold a pen. She tried to think of someone she could call, someone to see her through these terrible hours until daybreak. There was no one. No friend or colleague she could risk her secret with.

Arnie was the only one who would have been there for her.

Arnie. She had to see him one more time. She had to say good-bye. He had no relatives aside from his grandmother. Bubby would be alone in her grief. Arnie had always wanted her to meet Bubby. "The two women who love me should get it on," he would say. But she had refused, saying it was against the rules of psychoanalysis for the analyst to get to know the patient's family, and she had broken enough rules already. When he persisted, she balked, reluctant to be presented as a fiancee (how else would an old-fashioned Jewish woman view her?), to endure the revelation of her gentileness. Now it was too late. Now the two women who had loved Arnie could at least come together at his graveside.

Karen grabbed the phone book. Feinstein . . . Feinstein . . . no good. The book was only for Manhattan and Bubby lived in Brooklyn. Besides, her name wasn't Feinstein.

She rummaged around among her files. She had two hundred and forty pages of notes on Arnie, two audiocassettes, his probation report, a three-page autobiography he had written for her. Nowhere did he mention his grandparents' names. There was a video he had made after a three-day binge. He had given it to her a few days before he went off to Florida. "Arnie and company," he said, "the lower depths." She had never gotten around to watching it. Now there was no time.

Only one possibility remained—Inspector Duffy. Karen called the 19th Precinct. The phone rang for minutes. Thinking she had misdialed, Karen tried again. And again the phone rang on and on until finally a sleepy voice at the other end murmured "Nineteenth Precinct."

"Maybe you can help me," Karen said and asked where Arnold Feinstein was reposing, explaining she was a close friend who wanted to pay her respects.

"Who is this, please?"

"I'm Doctor Karen Winterman. Mr. Feinstein was a patient of mine."

She had a sense from the silence that the voice knew who she was. "Hold on, please."

Minutes went by. Karen thought of all the patients she had put on hold: depressives, borderline schizophrenics, hysterics in a breakdown mode. Then the voice was back. "Arnold Feinstein is reposing at the Seagate Funeral Home, 1826 Neptune Avenue, Doctor Winterman. The funeral is scheduled for this morning at eleven o'clock."

Karen waited out the dawn on her unmade bed, nuzzling the sheets where she and Arnie had lain so often. His scent lingered, unobscured by the deodorant smell of the detergent, the traces of perfume. She sank into this cloud of smells, found Arnie's odor and let it enfold her, imagining Arnie with his drowsy, post-coital smile drawing her to him.

She lay awake and aching as the darkness grayed around the edges. "The between times," Arnie had called those gray hours between twilight and night, night and morning. They were the most excruciating for the drug user, the one because it signaled another day wasted, the other because it signaled another sleepless night about to lead into another wasted day. "The long, slow parade to the grave. Muffled drums, dress blacks. The pallbearers are gaunt and hollow-eyed. They shuffle like *kazetniks*'' (the Yiddish word for concentration-camp survivor that Arnie always used). ''It's amazing how much druggies and *kazetniks* resemble one another. Among other things, they are both inconsolable.''

At eight o'clock she rose. Her arms and legs were like lead. A cold shower didn't help. It was more than physical. She had a feeling of dread.

She had a black evening dress, but it was low-cut; low in the back as well, so she couldn't even wear a bra. She had a little russet half-jacket; she would just wear that over the dress. She looked at herself in the mirror for a long time before deciding it was respectable.

Walking through the lobby she got a glimpse of herself in the mirror—last mirror before you hit the street. The sleepless night showed in the deep shadows under her eyes. Prison pallor, hunted eyes. You can always tell an ex-con, Arnie had said. They stay pale, cell-block gray, no matter how many hours in the sun or under a tanning lamp. They stay jumpy, no matter how many years they've been out. They can never look you in the eye because they learn that eye contact means you either want to fight or fuck. Karen ducked under the friendly look of a neighbor. She had no taste for small talk. The simplest question might make her burst into tears. She peered into a car window as she put on her lipstick. It was like dabbing color on a corpse.

She hailed a cab. The driver, twitchy and sharp-featured, looked her up and down as he pulled up. ''Only Manhattan, no Brooklyn,'' he said in a heavy

Spanish accent. "Only airport, no Brooklyn." She could see him laughing as he drove away and realized he had been faking the accent.

The next driver just shook his head. "You'll get there faster with the subway, lady."

Finally, a gypsy cab screeched up. The driver, a young light-skinned black man wearing a Yankee cap, rolled down the window. "Anywhere you want to go, miss."

They crawled through rush-hour traffic down the West Side Highway to the Battery Tunnel leading to Brooklyn. The driver's eyes flicked in and out of the mirror. *The way I look, he probably thinks I'm a tart after a hard night,* Karen thought. *He'll probably want to take the ride out in trade.* She avoided his eyes and stared out the window. *What a city. Your lover is murdered. The police threaten you. An old woman holds the key to your inner peace. A cabdriver lusts for you. These things all happen in the space of twenty-four hours.*

Karen had lived in New York for six years, but had never been out of Manhattan. She was amazed at how different Brooklyn looked. Even the people seemed old-fashioned, provincial, as if from an earlier time. When the driver pulled on to Neptune Avenue, she saw the crumbling buildings, the vacant lots. He turned onto a street on which only one building was left standing, a dilapidated two-story affair of crumbling brick, a tattered awning flapping, graffiti scrawled on its outer walls. The Seagate Funeral Home. Karen paid the driver, her eyes averted carefully.

A gaunt old man with a patchy gray beard and lips

that pursed spasmodically stood at the door, watching as she climbed the steps. A black skullcap was perched on top of his head. Like a circus tent, Karen thought, and then was struck by the strangeness of that association.

She asked for Feinstein, and the old man led her through the darkened foyer to a room under the staircase. In a corner, a plain pine box was standing on a dolly draped with black curtains. A handful of old men and women sat silently on bridge chairs. The men all wore skullcaps, the women veils. They sat and nodded to their own private thoughts.

Karen asked for the grandmother. They pointed to an old woman on the far side of the room, leaning on the handle of a heavy wooden cane. What is her name, please? Karen asked.

Mrs. Krakauer, she was told.

The woman's isolation from the other mourners, the bitter introspection of her expression, made it clear that she wanted to be left alone. But Karen had come too far to turn back.

As she crossed the room, Karen passed the pine box and realized that Arnie was in there. In this threadbare room, in that flimsy wooden box. Arnie was under those wooden slats in a shroud, his face the color of cement.

Karen paused a moment before taking the last few steps. The old woman looked up.

"Mrs. Krakauer, I'm Karen Winterman. I was a friend . . . I was Arnie's analyst."

The old woman rose slowly, arms trembling, lips moving. Karen stepped over to help her. The old woman pursed her lips and spat loudly on Karen's dress.

Karen retreated. "Mrs. Krakauer . . ."

The old woman lunged at her, swinging the cane. Karen raised her hand. Pain shot up and down her arm through her elbow. The pain drove her to one knee. "Mrs. Krakauer, please . . ."

The old woman raised the cane. Karen tried to get up, but her heel caught on the torn carpet. The cane came down on her shoulder. Pain shrieked through her. She heard the whoosh of the cane and then felt a blow to the cheekbone that made the room go dark and the air howl around her. She felt the floor with her hands and knees. The old woman grunted with every blow. Karen felt the blood streaming into her eye. She cried out, "Help me!"

Edmund had done everything right so far. Pick up the gypsy cab from the Dominican on Amsterdam Avenue. Pay the guy fifty bucks, he didn't care what you did with the car. Camp out in front of the building early enough to make sure he was there when Karen Winterman, Ph.D., came out. She's gonna stand out in the middle of the street looking for a cab. You just happen to be there. Give her the big Sambo grin. I'm clean-cut, I'm cool. Working my way through college. She'll get in the car. Anywhere she wants to go there's a way. East Side, you drive through Central Park. Turn into the Ramble parking lot. Jump in the backseat and choke the chick. Won't take more than a minute. West Side, you drive down Eleventh Avenue, tell her you're avoiding the traffic. Early morning, there's nobody around. People mind their business down

there anyway. Down any side street, same deal. Get
the rug out of the trunk, wrap up the body and tie it
with twine, looks like you're carrying a carpet. Back
in the car and drive upstate around Warwick. There's
a lot of black people up there so you won't look out of
place. Into the woods, dump the body. Case closed.

It had all worked fine until she got in the car. She
was going to Brooklyn, which meant he could pick any
spot. Coney Island, she said. Even better. There were
blocks and blocks of deserted buildings around that
neighborhood. Just take her into one of them, they
wouldn't find the body for days.

Instead, he had taken her where she wanted to go.
A hundred spots had presented themselves, a hundred
places to pull in and do the thing without nobody
seeing. He had passed them all by. And when she got
out, he realized the gig was going to be complicated.
Because now he had to wait until she came out, pull
up, give her the smile and convince her that he had
just been driving by when he saw her come out and
figured she'd be wanting to go back to Manhattan
again. She'd get paranoid when she saw the same guy.
Start thinking this nigger wants to rape me. He'd have
to overcome all of that. Or else just get out and drag
her in the car and do it right there. . . .

Then he saw her backing out of the building, her
hands in the air like somebody had a gun on her. She
stumbled on a loose piece of cement and went down
the steps.

An old lady, limping on a cane, came out after her.
From across the street Edmund could see the way the
rubber-tipped bottom of the cane bulged out a little.
He'd seen that before; the cane tip was hollowed out

and filled with lead. Old folks in Harlem used it. This old lady stared down at the chick, her face all twisted with hatred. Then she limped down the steps. Edmund knew what she was going to do. She was going to step back and smack that chick with the cane. His heart fluttered in panic. *Watch it!* Too late. The old lady spread her legs for balance and flicked the tip of the cane across the chick's face. She switched her feet like a baseball player and backhanded the chick. Fast for an old lady, Edmund thought. Fast for anybody.

Other people appeared at the door and Edmund thought, *They'll grab the old bitch. They'll stop her.*

But nobody moved. They stood there watching. The chick was crawling around picking up all the stuff that had fallen out of her bag. She had lost her shoe. It was out in the gutter. The old lady came at her, dragging that one bad foot behind her. The chick looked up and said something. She thinks it's over, Edmund thought.

The old lady grabbed the cane like an ax and brought it down. The chick clutched her head and retreated. The old woman limped to the curb. She picked up the shoe on the tip of the cane and flipped it into the street toward Edmund's car. Sobbing, the chick came out to get it. Mascara was streaming down her cheeks. Her forehead was bleeding and there were bruises on the side of her face. Edmund ducked under the seat— couldn't let her see him—and lay there as she retrieved the shoe, and leaned against the hood to put it on. She kept repeating something. It was hard to make out through all the crying, but it sounded like "I loved him too."

Edmund waited until the footsteps had faded before raising his head. The people on the steps of the funeral parlor were watching the old lady limp back toward them. An old man jumped down to help her, but she shook him off.

Halfway down the street the chick was stumbling blindly away all hunched over. Edmund started the car. She was going in the wrong direction on the demolished street, heading right into the leveled area that stretched for blocks, a desert of ditches, broken pavement and junk left by the bulldozers. In the background was the El train and beyond that rose the skyline of Manhattan. She would have to walk a mile across this trash to get anywhere. People would see her blood and bruises, her torn clothes. She might have a problem.

Edmund stopped the car and watched the lonely figure struggle across the bleak landscape. There were a few buildings still standing. You never knew who was hanging out in them. Edmund watched just to make sure she didn't buy herself some more trouble.

I gotta kill this woman, he thought. I gotta kill her soon.

I'M THE EXECUTOR

I want to be cremated," Vinnie Crow liked to say when he was half in the bag. It was a familiar routine played for the benefit of younger cops in saloons all over the city. Always the straight man, Benson would ask, "What do you want us to do with your ashes?"

"Drop 'em in the Silex at Headquarters. If I give the Commissioner the galloping shits, I'll know my life wasn't in vain."

For Vinnie death was just as bad a double bang as life had been. Not only was he not going to be cremated, but they were laying him out at the Francis X. Crowley Funeral Home on Tenth Avenue in Brooklyn, the same place, even the same reposing room, where they had laid out the man Vinnie hated most in the world—his father. Heading into Brooklyn on the Expressway that morning, Benson had to smile at the thought. Those two had trouble staying in the same borough together, and now they were stuck side by side until Doomsday.

He had lain awake for the second night in a row, while Doreen fussed and mumbled next to him. She sensed his wakefulness and this disturbed her slumber. But she wouldn't come out of it enough to talk to him or even to whine "Go to sleep, Billy" like she always did.

She had always hated Vinnie and was glad he was dead. But at breakfast that morning she hadn't dared say anything, just stared at him with that "I told you so" look that made Benson want to throw hot coffee right in her face. She had told him so a thousand times. "Vinnie Crow thinks he's so smart. He's gonna get himself in trouble one of these days. And you too for tagging along behind him." Big fucking insight. Everybody knew that, especially Vinnie. He'd seen it coming, which was why he'd stashed the money.

He sat in rush-hour traffic all the way into the Port Authority. Two hours of stewing about Doreen. Had she ever stopped to wonder how he managed to get the $150,000 house, the two cars, two color TVs, compact disc player and a closetful of clothes for Betty, not to mention all the fancy sacks she bought with bows and belts and all kinds of camouflage for her fat ass?

When he finally got to the Port Authority Building, Benson circled it twice looking for familiar cars or faces. When he saw none, he still wasn't satisfied, and he drove up to Fifty-fourth Street where he stuck the Pinto by a pump in front of the 14th Precinct. Then he walked down Ninth Avenue up to the back entrance of the building and let the rush hour surge take him right past the bank of lockers.

Benson walked by the lockers with his head down. Right away he pinned the stakeout. There was a Spanish kid nodding on the bench, and two rows behind him was a white kid, long-haired, with a hoop earring like a pirate. The only thing missing was a sandwich board with ANTI-CRIME printed on it. In the archway leading to the bus station, two guys in baggy suits were leaning against the wall trying to make believe they had a reason for being there. That would be FBI or DEA or some hicks from the Organized Crime Strike Force. A crooked cop shaking down a junk dealer meant big headlines. Big headlines meant more money for their budgets, so they all wanted a piece of this one. And they'd all converge on him at once if he went near that locker.

Benson kept walking, his head down. I'm so far ahead of these hooples I can smell their farts before they have lunch, he thought. Let 'em sit on that locker three shifts a day. I won't be back. Sorry, Vinnie, you died intestate.

Benson sat in a coffee shop in the arcade watching the people watching the locker. The city cops were good. They kept to their act. But the suits, standing there with the newspapers over their faces—anybody who watched cop shows on TV could pin them.

Benson turned back to the Greek behind the counter. "You sell a lot of coffee in this joint."

"This is nothing," the guy bragged. "You should have seen when there was a PATH strike. No trains, so they were running buses night and day. I sold forty thousand containers one week. So what I did, I bought half interest in the company of guy who makes the cups." He showed Benson a blue-and-white Styrofoam cup with some old Greek building on it. "You see these before?"

"Yeah," Benson said. "Yours, huh? Smart idea."

The guy beamed. Little weasel greaseball. Looked like he hadn't had a shave or a shower in a week, you could smell him across the counter. But he owned this joint, and you could bet half the people working here were his cousins, all illegals he was paying two dollars an hour. And he owned half a fucking paper company to boot. And meanwhile, Vinnie Crow, who pulled babies out of burning buildings, bled to death in some fleabag last night for a satchelful of money that was going to get lost in the property clerk's office until some bright guy slipped out with it.

Benson stepped out of the Port Authority Building into a White Rose. He sat by the window for a while watching the back entrance. Nobody came out after him. Either they hadn't spotted him or they had orders to sit on that locker. Or they had a guy so good that Benson couldn't pin him. Either way it didn't matter. It wasn't a crime to take a walk through the Port Authority Building.

Benson took the Battery Tunnel into Brooklyn. It was 11:30. They were probably just setting up the chairs in the funeral home. The M.E. had released Vinnie's body early in the morning after a full autopsy, head and body ripped open, all the vital organs and the brains—which Vinnie would say weren't so vital—removed. It was rough to embalm a guy with a hole in his face, especially since Vinnie alive wasn't a beauty even after a good night's sleep. They'd pack the face with cotton and clay, stick a lot of powder and rouge over it and lay him out there for the world to see. Jesus. Couldn't take that without a drink.

Benson pulled off the Brooklyn-Queens Expressway and drove over to a gin mill right across the street from the docks. He remembered the joint as packed from morning to night with longshoremen who just had time for a shot and a beer before going back to the ship. Now it was empty. The same old Irishman with a face like a cobblestoned street puttered around behind the bar.

"I remember you had to fight for a stool in here," Benson said.

"That was before they put the containers in the ships," the old guy said. "Now they pay the guys to stay home."

Benson thought of the Greek guy at the Port Authority. Somebody goes up, somebody comes down. From one minute to the next you didn't know where you were gonna be. How many times had he and Vinnie sat and watched a guy in a club spending money, buying drinks, wall-to-wall broads, laughing because he had just made a score and thought he was in the clear. And in the next second his world collapsed. No more drinks, the broads disappeared. The money was heading for the lawyer's pocket.

He finished his drink. Twelve-fifteen, still too early. He took the local streets stopping at another saloon every couple of blocks, throwing down shots of vodka with beer chasers. It was a little after one when he pulled up in front of Francis X. Crowley's. It was a runty three-story building, the kind where the family lived on top of the store, only in this case the store was a funeral parlor. The facade had been redone with bright red shingles. A little white awning extended out over the picture window on the second floor. Benson could see people moving around the room, putting up wreath stands, laying bridge chairs against the wall. In another minute he'd be looking down at Vinnie's ruined face.

There was a saloon across the street. He sat by the window for an hour drinking steadily, warm vodka, beer that seemed to go flat as soon as it came out of the tap. How many times had they squatted on a house and Vinnie said, "Keep your fingers crossed there's a saloon across the street"? And when there was, they would stand by the window tanking up and joking around until the mutt showed, and then Vinnie would say, "Showtime." And they would go out, just like that, without thinking twice. Into dark hallways, through doors where you didn't know what was waiting on the other side, anywhere they had to go. They'd traded shots with guys, fought them, taking knives, guns, Uzis, grenades away from them. They'd collared a lot of dangerous guys. Goddammit, you couldn't take that away from them!

Benson sat there for an hour watching the people come and go. Finally, when he'd reached his limit and knew that one more drink would tip him into bingeland, he walked the long mile across the street.

It was one of those neighborhood undertakers that could do one funeral a week and still net a hundred Gs a year. A bunch of cops from the old Seven-Three were standing outside the room smoking. They all muttered hellos. A few of the guys got a glint in their eyes like they were remembering some wisecrack from the old days. Tommy Preston, who had been another one of Finnerty's boys, pointed into the reposing room at Vinnie's son, Anthony.

"Little prick asked us not to smoke in the reposing room as a sign of respect," he whispered indignantly.

Benson dropped his cigarette in a sand bucket by the door. "Maybe somebody's allergic."

"Bullshit." Tommy blew smoke into the reposing room. "I come here to do the right thing and he treats me like a mutt. The kid hates cops, Vinnie told me a hundred times."

Benson caught Anthony's angry eye and looked away. The kid was built like a toll booth, just like Vinnie, but he had the dark complexion, the black hair and long eyelashes of his mother. Benson remembered the night the kid had pitched a no-hitter in the American Legion playoffs. They'd been at dinner with Sally Fish, all of them drinking pretty good and getting sloppy. Vinnie had raised his glass and said, "Here's to my boy. He's the only thing that keeps me from sticking a gun in my mouth."

Always coming in second-best, Benson had slobbered something about Dennis, his boy, becoming all the things he couldn't be.

And Sally had looked at them with that shit-eating grin, saying, "I wish I had kids. I really do."

And when he went to the can to load up, Benson had turned to Vinnie. "That prick's laughin' at us."

And Vinnie had patted his pocket in the patented gesture he used whenever Benson complained about Sally.

Benson shouldered by Tommy Preston. "Let me get in there."

The reposing room was small and square, with a maroon carpet worn in places, linoleum peeking through. Vinnie's coffin took up one whole wall. A crucifix loomed over it, the head of the Savior pointed toward Vinnie's head so that it would look as if the two were looking each other in the eye.

The place was packed. The air conditioner was rattling away but didn't seem to be doing much good. People nodded to Benson and stepped aside to let him through. Carmela was sitting at the foot of the coffin, fidgeting on a rickety bridge chair. He floated on a wave of warm vodka toward her, his arms outstretched. She rose to meet him, smoothing her dress over her thighs.

"Billy," she said, reaching for him. Her black dress was low in the front and he could see the outline of her breasts. "Enormous jugs," Vinnie used to say. "The first time I saw them I started shaking like a Ford with afterspark. They're still worth half a hard-on. The other half I make up out of the events of the day. Most of the time I just don't bother." She was waylaid for a moment by a priest with a soggy handkerchief. With a regretful look at Benson she endured the priest's condolences. In that moment he sobered up. Clawing through the stagnant air, he almost gagged on the powdery stink of the deodorizer they put on bodies to camouflage the smell. *I'm drunk as a skunk,* he thought. *My best friend in the world got blown away and I'm looking down his wife's dress. Jesus, God, forgive me my thoughts!*

He stumbled and steadied himself on the coffin as Carmela pushed through the crowd, waving her hands like a blind woman.

"Billy . . ."

Her tears were cold against his cheek. Old tears shed hours ago. But he felt the warmth of her breasts right through the dress and remembered that dark women always had a little halo of baby hair around their nipples.

Carmela took him by the hand. "I gotta talk to you alone, Billy."

She led him into a small adjoining room where the three girls and two boyfriends and Anthony were sitting in silence.

"Kids, Mr. Benson and I have to discuss something," she said.

Benson mumbled condolences to the girls as they passed. Only Anthony hung back, glaring at Benson like he was ready to fight, until Carmela gave him a shove. "Anthony, please, don't start . . ."

As soon as the kid closed the door she turned wild-eyed to Benson. "Billy . . ." She took his hand and clasped it to her breast. "Is it true what they're saying about Vinnie? Tell me, Billy, I gotta know."

Jesus, I should have known this was going to happen, Benson thought.

"The IAD came to the house this morning," Carmela said. "You should have seen them. They treated me like a suspect, Billy. Made me stay downstairs in the kitchen with a policewoman. My husband's not even in his grave and they're going through his things. That little twerp told me the wife is usually in on it. It's usually the wife who drives them to it, she said, by nagging them about money. I never nagged Vinnie about money, Billy, you know that."

Benson slid his hand away and patted Carmela on

the shoulder. "Don't pay any attention to those dirt-bags."

"They said he'd been working for some drug dealer, Billy. They said he had probably stashed two hundred thousand dollars or more. I told them they were crazy, we never had enough money to finish out the month. They asked me about you, Billy."

"Don't worry, Carmela."

"I said you were the most honest, most considerate man ever born, Billy. I swear I said that. But they said you were a thief, too. That Vinnie had told this Puerto Rican woman about you . . . said they were going to get you, too, Billy."

"They ain't gonna get nobody 'cause there's nobody to get." Benson walked Carmela over to a window seat. "Vinnie was the straightest cop in the world, Carmela. And the best. He never took a nickel from anybody and I oughta know because I was right there with him."

Carmela covered her face. "If he did he was even a crueler man than I thought, Billy."

"Don't say that, Carmela."

"It's true," she sobbed. "If he was dishonest he could have at least let a little of that money come into the house instead of spending all of it on whores or somewhere else."

"Carmela, I swear . . ."

Carmela reached blindly for Benson's hand. "We lived on air all these years. I don't know how we did it. The only thing we've got is the house and that's because my father paid the principal for me. I never told Vinnie. The way he felt about my father he would have killed me. I just put the mortgage money away every month in a special trust fund for Anthony's college.''

Benson felt he had to say something. ''Vinnie loved you. . . .''

''Don't, Billy.'' Carmela put her fingers over Benson's lips. ''Vinnie wasn't happy with me, I know that. We were both miserable.''

Benson felt the tears boiling up behind his eyes. ''Carmela, please. . . .''

Carmela pressed harder against his lips. ''No, no, I want you to hear this, Billy. A hundred times I wanted to leave him. Once, after a night of hell, Billy, pure hell, I had my bags packed. But where was I going to go with no money? You know how Vinnie was, Billy. He would have cut me off without a penny, not that he had anything to give anyway. So I stayed because I couldn't go, you understand? I was trapped in this misery, Billy. And now, God forgive me . . .'' Carmela sobbed and squeezed Benson's hand. ''God forgive me for saying this, but I feel like some terrible load has been taken off me.''

Benson's head seemed to explode with grief. ''You don't mean that, Carmela.''

''He's better off, too, Billy,'' Carmela whispered. ''Believe me, he is. These last few months he's been like a man possessed with a devil, I swear to God. At least now he's been delivered from his torment. Maybe he can find peace.''

''Carmela . . .'' Benson couldn't stop the tears. He dropped down on his knees.

''You were his only friend in the world, Billy.'' Carmela said. ''From the very beginning, when you guys were in Brownsville, he used to say, 'In case anything happens, Billy will take care of you.' He always said that about you."

"I will, Carmela," Benson said.

"Only last week he repeated it. He must have had a premonition. They say you get them just before you die. He sat at the kitchen table and wrote his will in his memo book. 'I'm making Billy Benson my executor. Anything happens he'll take care of you. He'll make sure you get everything you've coming to you.' "

"I will, Carmela," Benson said, struggling to stem the tears.

Carmela knelt next to him and pressed his head against her bosom. "You gotta take care of us," she whispered. "Please, Billy, please be there for us."

Benson had never been this close to Carmela. Her odor fell gently over him like a warm coverlet; warm wisps of her breath curled around his ear, around and around maddeningly until he felt he could rise up and tear the building down brick by brick for her.

This is love, Benson thought. And to Carmela he said, "I'll take care of you. I swear on my mother's grave."

A SUCCESSFUL NEGOTIATION

By six o'clock Benson knew exactly what he had to do. It was as if Vinnie had sent the plan to him from beyond the grave. It was the kind of move that Vinnie would make.

He slipped out without saying good-bye to Carmela, even though he felt her eyes on him. He drove down Coney Island Avenue and stopped at a cop hangout on Caton Avenue across from Prospect Park for a little morale booster. He sat alone at the far end of the bar where he could see the door. The place was full of guys he knew, some of whom he'd just seen at the wake. A few drinks were sent his way, but no one came over to commiserate. You knew the IAD had someone in a joint like this, watching who drank with who, who the cliques were. Benson could tell he was a marked man. Nobody came near him.

After five vodkas with beer chasers, Benson was ready. He drove over to Ocean Avenue and up toward

Sheepshead Bay. He was looking for a restaurant called the Tiebreaker. He finally found it down the block from the municipal tennis courts. He drove past it, looking for a van, a truck, any sign of a surveillance unit. Diagonally across the wide avenue was a Con Ed excavation. A construction trailer had been thrown up behind it. That was it. They were clocking everybody going in and out. The excavation might even mean they were tunneling under to install eavesdropping equipment. If the Feds were doing it, the sky was the limit as far as money was concerned.

Benson parked the Pinto in a dark area by the tennis courts. It didn't matter whether they saw him or not. It took them months to develop a case; he'd be in and out with everything done in two days. Thirty seconds, if he didn't get what he wanted. He opened the trunk and removed the 9-millimeter-Browning from the hollow spare tire. Strapping on an ankle holster, he walked the long block back down to the restaurant. Overhead, the leaves rustled in the old trees that lined the street, trees that had been planted a hundred years ago, before anybody living today was born. Were they maples, oak, elms? Benson had never been curious about trees before. Funny time to turn into a nature lover.

The Tiebreaker had a vivid neon sign that looked out of place on the old brown brick facade of the ancient low-slung building. Its logo was two tennis racquets crossed at the handles like swords, with a shimmering ball that bounced up and down between them. As you entered through the oak-and-plate-glass door, you could feel the heft of another era. And if you looked up you would see the old sign painted in *fin de siècle* script: Murchison's, est. 1897.

In its day, Murchison's had been the finest steak house in Brooklyn. Old-timers spoke about it with the same reverence as Lundy's in Sheepshead Bay, Michel's on Flatbush Avenue. Built to cater to the wealthy Protestant families that lived in elegant mansions on Ditmas Avenue, it had outlasted its clientele, hanging on long after they and their life style disappeared. Now that there weren't enough Protestants in that neighborhood to form a basketball team, it existed as a kind of pleasing anachronism. Eating at Murchison's was the kind of ritual gesture you made without understanding its origin. The Jews and Italians who had moved into those brownstones and mansions used it in the same way as its original customers for Sunday dinners, special occasions like Mother's Day, birthdays, anniversaries, maid's night out. Frankie Carbonaro used it as a place to hold court.

Five nights a week he would arrive around eight and sit alone at a big round table in the back near the stairway that led to the bathrooms. The place was a singles hangout at night. It drew a big crowd from the tennis courts.

But Frankie made no concession to the sporty style of the clientele. He wore Laurens and Armanis, tieless over a plain white shirt. He was short and dark, with the huge hands and simian gait of a bricklayer, which his father and his grandfather had been. He had thick black hair which crept over his collar. His black eyes seemed bottomless to those who could endure their stare long enough to form an opinion. His features were thick, brows bushy, jowls hard as iron. He never smiled, and you had to be very sensitive to him to know when he was amused because he was never amused by the predictable things. Every weekday night he sat there until closing at 1:30 A.M., smoking Pall Malls and drinking Rob Roys straight up. People came to see him. They sat for a while, sometimes for less than a minute, and left quickly when the audience was up. The bar always did very well. Although none of the customers ever looked in Frankie's direction, they knew he was there. And although none of them would ever dare speak to him, they liked to be in his presence. Rubbing elbows with racketeers is a favorite preoccupation of Brooklynites. They have an unshakable conviction that racketeers frequent the best restaurants. They are fascinated by these bigger-than-life characters they've read and seen so much about. And the racketeers know this. They know how swashbuckling their lives seem to the nine-to-fivers, the guys who sweat the rent and get palpitations when their taxes are audited. Although their lives are lonely, secretive and full of fear, they play up this daredevil, freebooting image. They advertise themselves with their clothes, their rings, their cars, their loud, patronizing behavior in public.

Frankie Carbonaro did none of this. He was all business. He was a boss who had the power to put seventy-five guns out on the street. Who was trying to pick up the pieces of a family that had lost its power bases as the neighborhoods in Brownsville, East New York, Bushwick and Williamsburg had changed populations. Who had to face defection from his own ranks and depredation from the other families. He was a man who held a lot of lives in his hand. It took balls to confront him on his own ground. A man who did it would have to be very secure in his position, or so insecure that it didn't matter anymore. Either a sure winner or a sure loser. It didn't matter which, both types were equally dangerous.

As Benson entered the joint, he could see the wise-guys standing two deep at the bar. They had come to beg for favors—he hadn't. He pushed his way through to the front of the line, breathing vodka and "cop" on everyone who turned to protest. He got to the point where he could see Frankie lighting a Pall Mall when a runt in a windbreaker, chewing the soggy end of a cigar, popped up in front of him. This was Al Lucito, Uncle Al, everyone called him. He was Frankie's driver and bodyguard. It was supposed to be a sign of Frankie's power that he traveled with this ineffectual little man as his only protection, but Uncle Al was a banger. According to Sally, he had clipped at least fifty guys since being made in the early fifties, and was still in action for Frankie C.

"Gotta take a ticket tonight, pal," Uncle Al said, planting himself in front of Benson.

Benson flipped open his wallet and flashed the tin. "Free pass."

Uncle Al didn't budge. "Not even for you, pal."

Benson stared down at the little man. "I'm not your pal, you greasy guinea bastard." And he walked around him to Frankie's table.

"I got a beef to straighten out with you, Mr. Carbonaro," he said loudly.

Frankie pointed to a chair. "You're not helping yourself by letting everyone in the joint know you're here."

"Everybody knows I'm here," Benson said. "The Federal Government is taking home movies of everybody who walks in and out of this joint."

Frankie winced. "There's nothing like cops for gettin' nervous. Why don't you tell your story sittin'?"

Frankie knew all about the surveillance. He also knew about the bugs that were continually being planted in the restaurant. He had a Russian electrician working for him, a guy named Ilya, who'd emigrated in the early eighties. The guy was a genius when it came to bugs, wiretaps, transmitters. Every week he came in dressed as a porter and cleaned the joint from top to bottom, deactivating every bug the cops had installed. The Strike Force had to be completely nuts by now, thinking that they had all this defective equipment. So maybe they were trying a new approach with this guy.

Benson sat down and lowered his voice. "Your nephew killed my partner."

"I got four nephews," Frankie said.

"Sally Fish, your button in the garment center."

Frankie also had a little gadget that Ilya had given him. It looked like a light meter and could detect a transmitter at ten feet, could even pick up the frequencies from one of those tiny Panasonic recorders they were marketing these days. He slipped it into the palm of his hand and got no reading. The guy wasn't wired.

"My nephew Sal owns a store on Utica Avenue, Feinstein's Audio."

"Your nephew was running hijacking and burglary out of the garment center," Benson said. "My partner and I were in business with him up until last night when he had my partner killed."

"Hey, if the kid has a secret life . . ."

"He was also dealing coke. I don't know how big because he closed me out, but big enough to get an undercover policewoman on his case and big enough to use my partner."

"This is news to me," Frankie said.

"Yeah?" Benson leaned in close. "Here's some more news. I want the mutt who shot my partner."

"I thought you said my nephew Sal did it," Frankie said.

"His shooter, that's the guy I'm talking about right now. I'll get to your nephew later. I want him. I want the money my partner had stashed in a locker at the Port Authority. And I want Sally Fish himself with his head on a fuckin' platter."

"Seems to me you should be talking to Sal about this."

"I'm talking to you," Benson said. "You're the boss. You made alotta money with us plus we made life real easy for you. And you paid us back by banging my partner out in a sleazy hotel room, disgracing him and his family forever."

"These things happen."

Benson lit a Marlboro and blew smoke in Frankie's face. "You're supposed to be such a good judge of character. At least that's what Sally used to say. 'My Uncle Frank's a fucking genius. He can look in your eyes and see right through to the fuckin' circuits in your brain.' "

"That's a very good imitation of my nephew."

"Look into my eyes, genius," Benson said. "See my circuits? The wires are crossed. Everything's sparking, fuses are blowing like fuckin' crazy."

Frankie held up his empty glass. Uncle Al came by with a new cocktail.

"Everything okay, Frankie?"

"And what are you gonna do if it's not, you guinea pimple," Benson said, turning to look up at him.

Frankie waved Uncle Al away. "So you scared an old man."

"You think I'm showboatin' you?"

"There's not much else you can do."

Benson's eyes bulged. He winced. His voice broke into angry fragments. "Your brain's not workin' so good today, genius," he said. "I'm a walkin' corpse right now. Inspector Duffy's not gonna stop until he hangs me. That's why I'm here with the eyes of the world upon me. I don't give a fuck, you understand. I can do whatever pops into my head. Stick a Thirty-eight in your ear maybe, Boss. Or go out to Locust Valley and blow your wife and four daughters away. That's five shells, which means there'll be one for me and I won't even have to reload."

Frankie turned slightly to look directly into Benson's eyes. "You should know better than to threaten a man's family."

Benson stared back without flinching. "I can sit down for fifteen minutes with Duffy and walk out with total immunity after I tell what I know about you. They'll give me a new identity, even, and a job in a McDonald's in fuckin' Iowa."

"You don't know anything about me," Frankie said.

Benson smiled. It was time to make the prick sweat. "You should know better than to trust a cokehead with dangerous secrets. Little Sally boy gets a noseful and he loves to talk about his Uncle Frank."

Frankie stared at Benson. "Only nice things, I hope?"

"You be the judge," Benson said. "They call you Frankie the Cowboy, but never to your face, because you don't like nicknames. You got the name because you started out cowboying, sticking up three or four bars a night with your cousin Bruno Cannozeri, who you later killed when he started bragging about his association with you and telling stories of the early days."

Frankie shook his head. "You could get that reading the *New York Post*."

"They say the CIA hired you to crack safes in foreign embassies and fixed a bank rap for you as payback. A guy like Duffy would love to follow that up."

Frankie shrugged and wiggled his glass again. His nephew Sally was in the office listening to this. Frankie wanted to make sure he stayed put.

"Here's a little something else Duffy would cream over," Benson said. He stopped as Uncle Al came by to snatch Frankie's glass. "Hey, tough guy, bring me a shot of vodka with a beer chaser." Uncle Al looked at Frankie. Frankie nodded.

"Make sure the office is locked before you do anything else," Frankie said.

"You were the guy who hit the stools in the Brunelli case. They were under police protection, but you guys bought a cop named Reynolds and he told you they were going to the fights at the Garden the next night. So you went the night before and hid in the bathroom all night and the following day. The two stools came in to take a piss like you hoped they would. Reynolds steered them to the right bathroom and waited outside. You popped out of a stall, shot 'em with a silencer, dumped the gun in a urinal and walked out like nothing was happening.''

"You're tellin' war stories," Frankie said. "A thousand people were fingered for that thing. And a thousand more took credit for it."

"Yeah, but only Reynolds knows who did it."

Frankie yawned and looked at his watch. "Reynolds is dead. Wrong time wrong place-type deal. He was sittin' in a saloon that got knocked over, went for his gun, and they shot him."

Benson shook his head slowly, enjoying the moment. No matter how smart they were they could always be sandbagged because they were always covering up.

"According to Sally one of those guys was Uncle Al," he said. "If they show a photograph, one of the witnesses might make him." He leaned forward and poked Frankie in the chest. "You get it now? I'm talkin' about taking apart your operation piece by piece. This Duffy's a bulldog. He's one of these guys who couldn't pass the priest test so he became a cop."

Frankie nodded. "I suppose you made a tape of all you know which will go to the DA in case of your untimely death."

"Maybe I did, maybe I didn't. You can't take any chances."

Frankie nodded. "Okay, I'll give you the shooter—dead. You can't have him alive because I can't take the chance that you'll turn cop at the last minute and arrest him."

Benson nodded. "Okay."

"I'll give you the money no questions asked. But you can't come back to me and say you got short-counted."

"If I come back with a beef I won't be talking," Benson said. "Now, how about the main course?"

Frankie wagged his finger at Benson. "Sally you don't get. He's my big sister's only son. I don't double bang my own blood."

"Sally killed my partner. He's gotta pay."

Now it was Frankie's turn to lean in and lower his voice.

"You guys signed up with us. Nobody made you. You got dirty with us. You made alotta money for a little work. You had fun with my nephew the raconteur. You don't turn around and say, 'Hey, we were only kidding, we wanna go back to the old rules.' Sal was the crew boss here. He made a decision, according to you, to do this thing. And I'm backin' him a hundred percent."

"There's no deal without Sally," Benson said.

Frankie moved in an inch closer. "Then everybody does what they have to do. You talk about killin' families, I can kill a few families, too. Now you came in here with three points, you got two. I would consider that a very successful negotiation if I were you."

Benson sat back, shamed by Frankie's steady gaze. Suddenly it seemed he was acting like a stool pigeon. He felt he had to justify himself to this man.

"We did good for Sally. He made out real good with us."

Frankie shrugged. "Yesterday's news."

"Just the same, he didn't have no business killing Vinnie."

"I wasn't there," Frankie said. "You accept my terms?"

Benson wavered. Somehow he'd been outmaneuvered. What would Vinnie do in this situation?

Vinnie would drop the prick where he was sitting.

"There's alotta people waitin' to see me," Frankie said, looking toward the bar. "Their business is just as important to them as yours is to you."

"What are my guarantees?" Benson asked.

"It's safer for me to deal with you than to take you out. That's your guarantee."

Drop him, just drop him. Go out like a man. But then the state would get the money and Sally Fish would get a walk.

"This isn't a quiz show," Frankie said, baring his teeth and showing his impatience. "You don't get a chance at the jackpot next week."

"I accept," Benson said quickly.

"Write down a safe phone number and give it to Uncle Al on your way out," Frankie said. "Oh, and look," he said as Benson rose slowly, "it's none of my business, but instead of hitting every saloon in Brooklyn like you're planning to do, why don't you go home and get some rest? Sleep deprivation is a very dangerous syndrome for a man in your position."

THIS GUY'S A TIME BOMB

Frankie watched the big cop barrel through the crowd at the bar, then he waved to Uncle Al. "Get that little bastard out here right away."

Uncle Al went into the kitchen. He came out followed by Sally Fish, who was smiling and clapping and mouthing "Bravo, bravo!" Sally was wearing black leather pants and a cowboy shirt with pearl buttons and buckskin fringe. He had a turquoise bracelet on one wrist, a turquoise clip on the other, a turquoise chain made with beaten-silver links around his neck.

"Brilliant, Uncle Frank. Talk about in like a lion out like a lamb. Talk about the matador and the bull . . ."

Frankie waved his nephew into silence. "How come you dress like a fuckin' hairdresser?"

"Tex-Mex, Uncle Frank." Sally sat down and whipped out his cigarettes. "It's the newest. I like to stay on top. I don't see spending seven hundred dollars for a suit, then jumping up and down on it for a week before I put it on. With all respect, that's the Meyer Lansky look, Uncle Frank."

Sally sneaked a sideways look at his uncle. The man was definitely not amused.

"Shitcan the rebel act, Salvatore," Sally said in a mock lecture to himself. "Be humble, Salvatore. Grovel, Salvatore."

Frankie sat motionless, waiting.

"Okay, so I shot my mouth off a little bit, I'm proud of you. I got a ton of respect for you and it comes out like that. I didn't say anything that's not common knowledge, right?"

Frankie didn't answer. Sally could hear Uncle Al wheezing with repressed laughter behind him.

"I was talkin' to two corpses, you know what I mean? In my mind they were over from the day they gave me a workout in my apartment. It was just a matter of time. Now one of them's asleep and the other guy's got his pajamas on. So who's hurt?"

Frankie wiggled his cocktail glass. Uncle Al swooped in and took it out of his hand.

"You're not gonna bullshit your way outta this, Sal," Frankie said.

"I'm sorry, Uncle Frank."

"Sorry don't cover it, either. Not this time. This time you gotta make it good. The problem with you is that nobody ever punished you. From the time you were a little kid your mother wouldn't let anybody harm a hair on her pretty little boy's head. Your father, he should rest in peace, didn't have the balls to go up against her. So you skated. I've been letting you skate, too, for my own reasons."

"Maybe they got something to do with the money I earn for you," Sally said.

"I think I could get along without your contributions, Sal. Especially if your big mouth and degenerate life style made you a liability."

Sally raised his hands protectively. "Purgatory talk, Uncle Frank. That proves you're mad. Look, I'll clip this cop tonight, if you want me to."

"You're not gonna clip him, Sal. You're gonna do business with him."

Sally jumped up so suddenly that Uncle Al, returning with Frankie's cocktail, had to sidestep to avoid a collision.

"The guy wants to kill me."

"Give him the shooter," Frankie said. "Get him the money."

"That's absolutely fuckin' impossible, Uncle Frank," Sally said.

"Sit down, Sal." Frankie shook his head at Uncle Al. "Everybody's jumping around tonight. Everybody's taking positions."

"That money is in a locker at the Port Authority," Sally said. "You gotta figure they got every cop in the city watching it."

"You're a smart boy, you'll find a way to snake it out."

"This colored kid is the best. It would be like ripping up a fuckin' Rembrandt."

The bottom dropped out of Frankie's black eyes. "I told you when I gave you the garment center that you had to resolve your problems personally."

"I did."

"Four times you came to me. Four names, four

175

problems you wanted to solve. I gave you the okay. But you never said anything about using a banger."

"I thought I was understood. I don't have the time to handle those things myself."

Uncle Al giggled. "Busy man."

Sally realized from Uncle Al's impudence that he had said the wrong thing. "This guy is better than anybody. I've been using him on this other thing." Sally tapped his nose. "He did eight things for me last year."

"Eight?" Frankie pushed his untasted Rob Roy aside. "You never told me."

"You said you didn't wanna know nothin' about that thing, remember? You said I should run it with a separate organization."

"Eight is an unacceptable risk."

Sally sat back with a regretful smile. He was on sure ground here. "It's the business, Uncle Frank." Then he moved forward, speaking earnestly. "You're dealing with two kinds of lowlifes, junkies and psychos. When they get outta line it's sleepy time. You can't talk 'em back, you can't threaten 'em. They're like fuckin' animals. They take one bite out of you, they're gonna take another one."

"Bad management," Frankie said.

"Didn't I prove I knew how to run that thing?" Sally said. "We cleared five million three in the past two years and that's with no exposure. We're invisible in that business."

"You miss the point, Sal," Frankie said. "It's not about being invisible, we're too big for that. Sooner or later something happens and they put us on the map. They say, Frankie Carbonaro is consolidating the rackets in the garment center, let's get him. So now they gotta make a case. That's where the real war starts. They'll spend ten million bucks to put you and me in jail. With the electronics they got now they can look up your asshole from across the street. But as long as they can't make a case against us, as long as we're careful . . ."

"I was careful," Sally said.

"They got eight shots at this kid. Twelve, really, with the four cops he clipped the other night. Is he gonna stand up if they get him solid on one? Why should he be loyal when he can give you up and get a free ride? You're not thinking, Sal. You're putting too much of that shit up your nose."

"I'm thinking that the way out of all of this is to clip one drunken cop. As we speak, the prick might be wrapping his car around a pole. That's how easy it would be. Why get complicated?"

"Because I say so, Sal. You don't want to take orders from me, that's your privilege."

Sally shivered and drew up his collar. "Whoa, did somebody turn up the air conditioner in here? You know I'd go through a wall for you, Uncle Frank."

"I know what I see. I told you to do something, you didn't do it. I tell you to do something else, you give me an argument."

"You're not worrying about this tape he said he made?" Sally said. "I can't believe that. I mean, you *know* none of that is admissible . . ."

"Except if it comes from a guy who's been hit, you understand? A dead man with no plea to cop, no ax to grind."

Sally considered this in bitter silence. Uncle Frank

always had an answer. Always. "Okay, I'll concede that, Uncle Frank."

Frankie showed his teeth in his version of a smile. "This isn't a presidential debate here, Sal. As far as I'm concerned you put a time bomb in my little girl's bedroom and you don't wanna take it out."

Sally got up in a hurry. Uncle Frank mentioned his family as a way of showing how serious the situation was. The discussion was now officially over.

"I'll take care of everything, Uncle Frank. Just the way you said."

"Don't bother coming around until you do," Frankie said.

Sally took a few steps backward and Uncle Al was next to him, slipping a piece of paper into his pocket. "Here's the cop's number." And then, calling after him as he picked his way through the bar crowd, "You goin' out tonight? Goin' down to the Village? You can get broads wearin' those kinda clothes? I don't believe it." Uncle Al turned to Frankie with a sloppy, toothless grin. "It's the new breed, whaddya expect? He's better than most."

Frankie lit a cigarette. He didn't like to discuss things with Uncle Al. But that didn't deter the old man. "It was worse than a slap in the face the way you talked to him. Because he really respects you. He wants to sit up there with you one day."

"He wants to sit here alone," Frankie said. "Get the little prick back here."

Uncle Al caught up with Sally as he was getting into his Porsche Targa. "He needs you back for a second."

Sally slammed the door. "What is this second-rate mind-fucking? The money I've made for him I don't deserve this kind of treatment."

"Yeah, yeah, you tell him that," Uncle Al said. "Tell him right now."

"Something I forgot to tell you," Frankie said as Sally stood in front of him. "This stupid nickname, Sally Fish, get rid of it. I don't like havin' some cop spit it in my face."

Sally clenched his fists behind his back. He had inherited that nickname from his father, who got it because he ran a betting operation out of a fish store in Sheepshead Bay. His uncle knew that. His uncle knew how much that tradition meant to him.

"Anything you say, Uncle Frank."

Frankie ground his cigarette out and looked around Sally at the impatient supplicants at the bar.

Sally turned and followed his eyes. "Standing Room Only tonight, huh, Uncle Frank?"

Frankie fished for another Pall Mall. "You still here, Sal?"

"I left fifteen minutes ago," Sally said. He turned and brushed angrily by Uncle Al, who jumped aside with a gleeful grin and called after him, "Don't go away mad, Sal."

Outside, Sally floored the pedal on the Targa until it was revved to screaming. Then he jammed the car into first and made a screeching U-turn across Ocean Avenue, the back end of the car flying out.

Back at the Tiebreaker Uncle Al had moved a guy in a cowboy hat and spangled jeans jacket to the head of the line. He hurried back to Frankie.

"This guy is from that trucking company in Arizona," he said, bending to Frankie's level so his voice wouldn't carry. "He's the guy Nathan Hirsch asked you to straighten out."

"Alright," Frankie said. He looked at his watch and checked his electronic gadget. "I'll give him five minutes."

THREE

LOVE IN THE BIG CITY

Karen Winterman's cheekbone was bruised, her jaw swollen to almost double its size from the blows of Bubby's cane. Her knees and arms were skinned raw from falling down the steps and she felt a deep pain in her side whenever she breathed too deeply. She would have to go to a doctor. Have to lie about a fall or an automobile accident. Couldn't say *"I went to my lover's funeral and his grandmother tried to kill me, Doctor. Can I have a refill on my Valiums?"* She wouldn't get them.

Inspector Duffy was on her answering machine. His voice, terse and quiet, sent a chill through her. "Doctor Winterman, this is Inspector Duffy. Please call back as soon as possible." And then, because there had been no other messages, it came right back. "It's been three hours and I haven't heard from you, Doctor Winterman."

Karen's hand shook so badly she had to grab her

wrist to turn off the machine. Her body bucked uncontrollably. Strange moans came out of her. Then she was on her knees, her face pressed into a throw pillow, sobbing, "What am I going to do? What am I going to do?"

Downstairs, Edmund was parked across the street from Karen's building trying to decide the best way to kill her. For the third or fourth time in an hour, he took out the long-barreled .22 and fitted the silencer to it. He sat for a while staring down at it without comprehension. It was like if you say a word over and over it loses its meaning. He didn't know what this cold, twisted piece of metal was for. He couldn't put it together with that shadow moving behind the drawn blinds on the third floor.

Edmund removed the silencer. His ankle had stiffened from so much time in the car. It would mend in a few weeks but would never be completely healed, not after all this time without treatment. He would never be able to count on foot speed again. Or luck either. He'd used up his lifetime supply of both getting away from the River Royale.

That woman upstairs was lucky. She didn't know Edmund and she wasn't acting like she knew anybody was after her. And she sure didn't know that she could be a minute away from being dead. It was a small six-story building. No doorman, only a buzzer and a speaker to let people in through a front door you could open with a credit card anyway. One of those buildings where the super was never around and probably didn't even live on the premises. Edmund could go in through the basement entrance carrying a laundry bag so in case anybody saw him he was just going to do his wash. Take the elevator to her floor. It's always gloomy in those hallways. Anybody passes a young black dude in a gloomy hallway doesn't stop for a second look, anyway. They just book on by, thanking God he ain't there for them. The move was to ring the bell and press the .22 against the peephole. Listen hard for the sound of footsteps because sometimes there was carpet and the chick could be barefoot. First the footsteps, then the click of the peephole being opened from the inside. Count one and squeeze the trigger. She'd just be putting her eye to the hole and the dumdum would blow her brains out. It was fast and quiet. A pop and a tinkle. You're back on the street in two minutes.

But what if she didn't take a peek? What if she just opened the door? Then you just backed her into the pad and shot her in the living room.

What if she asked who it was? Edmund was ready for that, too. "Doctor Winterman, I saw you out in Brooklyn today. Could I talk to you for a moment." Then she either clicked the peephole or opened the door.

Killing was easy. Getting in and out of the building could be a problem. But it wasn't. So the chick was dead any time Edmund wanted her to be.

Edmund fitted the silencer back on to the gun barrel. It was early yet. In a couple of hours the street would be quiet. In the dead of night there would be no traffic in and out of the building.

I'll do it after midnight, Edmund decided.

He closed his eyes, but the girl's tearstained face rose up in his mind. Couldn't deal with that. He opened his eyes, but it lingered. Edmund had learned to go by the eyes. Bad people had empty eyes. No feeling, they looked at you like you were a piece of furniture. But this girl had a lot in her eyes, didn't take but a second to see that. She looked like a little girl who'd had her feelings hurt and didn't have anybody to make her feel better.

Edmund felt a twinge of sympathy for her. What could a chick like this have done to make a stone murderer like Sally Fish want her dead? Maybe he had gotten the whole thing wrong. He was really after somebody else and somehow this chick had gotten mixed up by accident. Maybe Edmund would bang her out and Sally would come around the next day and say, "Oh, well, these things happen, you hit the wrong broad. Gotta do it all over again." Maybe if he went upstairs and talked to her . . .

"Shut up!" Edmund slapped the butt of the gun against his ankle because he knew that would be the thing that would hurt the most. There was nothing he could do to save her. Go up and talk to her, you blow everything. That was out. Walk out of the gig, Sally makes a phone call and somebody else does it. That was out. Try to talk Sally out of it and he'd get wasted along with the chick. That was out.

No, the chick was dead. Somebody was going to make ten Gs out of it.

Edmund rubbed his throbbing ankle.

Might as well be me. Might as well.

Without thinking, Benson had scribbled the number of the Francis X. Crowley Funeral Home on the piece of paper he gave to Uncle Al.

"We'll contact you in a coupla hours," Uncle Al had said.

It was the only safe number he could think of, but as soon as he arrived there he was sorry. He could tell by the abundance of parking spaces in front of the building that most of the visitors had left. It would just be family and close friends. He'd have to put up with hostile stares from Anthony. There would be no way to get Carmela alone, to at least give her a hint of what he was trying to do for her.

And then he almost dropped dead as he walked into the family room. Doreen was sitting there with Carmela. Doreen for Chrissake, he should have thought of that. She was wearing the same black dress she had bought for her niece's wedding, but it was at least a size too small and you could see her thighs all squeezed together on the little bridge chair.

"Where've you been?" Doreen asked, with the look that answered her own question. *Out getting bombed, that's where he's been.*

Carmela patted the chair next to her. "Come sit with me, Billy."

The coffin was still open. Christ and Vinnie in a staring match. Benson sat down uncomfortably. What if it were true that the dead stayed conscious for days before they were buried? There were stories of people who'd been brought back from the dead and spoke about floating in a blue haze around their relatives. Some of these people had reproduced conversations that had taken place around the operating table or the coffin.

Carmela took Benson's hand. "It's like all of us are together again, isn't it, Billy?"

Yeah, only one of us has got a bullet in his windpipe and might be listening to everything we say. Even reading our thoughts, because they say the dead have the power of telepathy as well. Something to do with lack of friction because they have no corporeal substance. Benson had read about it once in a magazine in the police surgeon's office, and it had stayed with him ever since.

"Remember how we all used to go out in the old days?" Carmela said.

"Don't torture yourself," Doreen said.

"I'm trying to remember the good things, Doreen, for God's sake."

Dumb cunt, Benson thought. Can't even pay a condolence call.

Carmela turned to Benson, taking his other hand now. "We had fun in those days, Billy, remember? We used to laugh a lot. We were all such good friends." She gave him an anguished look. "What happened, Billy? All of a sudden we just stopped going out together."

"Well, you know, the kids came. . . ."

"Vinnie spent more time with you than anybody, even me, Billy. I know he told you things. And you told him, too."

Doreen leaned over with interest.

"What happens to people, Billy?" Carmela sobbed. "Why do we all make each other unhappy? Everything started out so hopeful, you know. Young couples in love one day. And then it seems like the next minute you're not talking to each other, each in your own little world."

"Vinnie loved you and the kids, Carmela," Benson

said lamely. Doreen stared daggers. Well, what the fuck else was he supposed to say?

"He confessed to me, Billy. He told me about the hookers, the drinking, everything. . . ."

Oh, Jesus Christ.

"It was when he became involved with that Puerto Rican woman. . . ."

Oh, Jesus Jesus Jesus . . .

"That woman who was in the room with him, Billy. He had been seeing her for months."

"Did you tell the detectives about her?" Benson asked.

"No, of course not. I didn't tell them anything. You could just see they were looking to make a case against Vinnie. Crucify a dead man, that's what they want to do."

Benson looked around the room. He wouldn't put it past those mutts to have a wire in here. "I never knew."

"Oh, Billy, for God's sake," Doreen said angrily.

"It's true," Carmela said. "Vinnie told me. He said he was ashamed to tell Billy about her because of the cocaine. Also because he was her slave. He was ashamed for you to know that, Billy."

With all these standing floral pieces, it would be the easiest thing in the world to hide a mike. Hell, they'd even stick it in Vinnie's lapel. They had no respect.

"He was going to run away with her, Billy."

"Maybe you shouldn't talk about this right now. . . ."

"She made an addict out of him, Billy. She gave him so much of that junk. He showed me that night, a huge bagful of it. It made him crazy, he admitted it.

When he took it he thought of her. Even if it was three o'clock in the morning he would get so he had to see her and he would run out of the house.''

"You shouldn't think about this now," Benson said.

"For God's sake, let her talk," Doreen said. "Can't you see it's therapeutic?"

"What are you, a psychiatrist all of a sudden?" Benson snarled.

"You see how much anger we feel?" Carmela moaned. "My God, marriage is supposed to be a sacrament. Instead, it's a living hell. . . .''

"It's the job, Carmela," Benson said. "It makes you crazy after a while."

"It was the cocaine. You know we hadn't had uh . . . relations for months. Months, Billy. There was a lot of resentment on both sides. After he made me get the abortion last year . . .''

Doreen grabbed her arm. "Carmela . . .''

"Oh, Billy knows, don't you, Billy?"

"Well, I . . .''

"It was an accident, but I wanted the baby. With all the kids out of the house it would have been nice to have someone to keep me company. But Vinnie made me go to the clinic with all those little black girls from Bedford-Stuyvesant. It was the most humiliating thing that ever happened to me, Billy, I swear. And afterwards they fitted me for a diaphragm, you know, and I wore it, too. I used to say to him, 'You made me commit a mortal sin and now you won't even touch me.' ''

Carmela's skirt was hitched up to her thighs. Nice brown legs. Soft and smooth, he could get on his knees right there and run his tongue from her toes to the scratchy patch around her thighs where she shaved. All those brunettes had thick clumps of hair around their . . . Jesus! Benson closed his eyes and fought back the vivid pictures in his brain. She thinks I'm carried away with grief. Jesus Christ, if she only knew what was going on in my sick brain. He opened his eyes. Doreen was glaring at him. She knew. He didn't know how, but she knew. The cunt had one talent in life—reading his mind.

"The cocaine made him crazy, Billy," Carmela said. "One night he woke up covered with sweat. His side of the bed was drenched. He said he was going to see her. I pleaded with him, tried to reason with him. Finally, I stood in front of the door. I said I would call you, call his squad commander. Anything to keep him from seeing that woman. You know what he did, Billy?"

Oh Jesus . . .

"He took all my clothes and shoes out of the closet, everything, and threw them out the window into the backyard. Then, he took off my nightgown, ripped it to shreds. . . ." Carmela was blubbering so hard she could hardly get the words out. "He tied me up in a sheet and stuck a pillowcase in my mouth. My own husband, Billy. I lay for hours breathing through my nose. I prayed that he'd come home before the kids woke up, so they wouldn't find me like that."

Benson remembered the rapist they had collared who had tied his victims up in sheets and cut holes where their private parts were located. They'd flattered him into confessing, telling him how original his method was. Oh Jesus, Jesus . . . Vinnie had used this guy's technique.

He turned toward the coffin. *Vinnie, you sick bastard. Mistreating those hookers was bad enough, but your own wife . . .*

A fire erupted in the pit of his stomach. He doubled over. It felt like his guts were about to dribble through his fingers.

"You okay, Billy?" Carmela asked, touching his arm.

"Yeah, yeah, I gotta go to the john."

He staggered out into the hall. Behind him he heard Doreen say, "Drunk as usual."

An old white-haired woman stood at the top of the steps watching him labor up. She held out the phone.

"What's this?" he asked.

"You Detective Benson?"

"Yeah." The receiver almost slid off his sweaty palm. Sally Fish giggled on the other hand.

"Detective Benson, let me be the first to offer my condolences on the untimely death. I understand there's a little matter of some unrecovered funds you were anxious to resolve." Sally waited for an answer. "Is that correct?"

Benson gripped the phone tightly, but didn't say anything.

"We're going to expedite your recovery of that money, Detective Benson," Sally said. "All you have to do is park your car in the lot across from the Port Authority Building. Leave your key taped to the inside of the left rear tire. The funds will be deposited in your trunk early this morning. They'll be available when the banks open tomorrow."

Benson fell into Sally's rhythm. "What about the colored gentleman?"

"We have several options in that area. When we find the most feasible you'll be informed. Once again, let me offer my sincere condolences in your hour of grief. . . ." Sally's voice broke. He cackled wildly. "I share your sense of loss. I counted Detective Crow among my very good friends. . . ." He broke off again, wheezing with repressed laughter.

Slowly Benson hung up the phone. The fire smoldered deep in the pit of his stomach now. It was going to be there for a while. Nothing was going to change until he got Sally Fish.

After an hour, Karen was all cried out. She made herself a cup of tea and sat in the dark kitchen trying to make plans. She would have to leave New York, of course. The notoriety would die down after a while, but there would always be someone around who'd remember. Karen Winterman, the scarlet woman of psychoanalysis. She'd end up in a small college—somewhere in the Northwest probably, in a department with the rest of the has-beens and nonachievers.

"This is where our love took us, Arnie," she said. "You're dead. I'm ruined."

There was a bottle of Château D'Yquem left from the case Arnie had brought over one night. "The perfect wine for the rich junkie," he had said. "Sweet because that's what the junkie needs for his sugar jones, and vintage so he's not ashamed to buy it. I mean, imagine a guy stepping out of a limo and ordering a bottle of Night Train. . . ."

She opened the bottle and took out Arnie's file. There was that video cassette, "Arnie and Company," written in Arnie's spidery hand. She poured herself a glass of wine and dropped the cassette into the VCR. Arnie's voice came out of the darkness.

"Just sit down and do it already."

Then a gruff but oddly plaintive voice: "You know I can't talk about my family."

The tape sputtered as if from a clumsy splice and there was Arnie's living room. There was a mountain of cocaine in a package of tinfoil on the coffee table. Arnie sat in the armchair with that rubber-lipped grin he always got when he was very high, smoking a cigarette and watching someone move around.

"Okay, great, then you're not like me," he said, "because I'll tell you everything about my family. I'll tell you everything I know."

"That's 'cause you're a big-mouth Jew," the voice said.

"Okay, great" (Arnie always said that when he was high), "and you're a close-mouth mafioso, which means you're not like me, so stop saying you are."

"I am," the voice insisted. "We're like fuckin' brothers."

"Brothers are diametric opposites, in my experience," Arnie said.

"Twin brothers."

"Okay, great." Arnie leaned over to separate a mound of cocaine from the pile and divide it into neat little lines. "So talk about me."

"What do you mean?"

"Begin with how you met me. It's a funny story."

The voice was hoarse with disbelief. "You serious?"

Arnie snorted the coke through a kitchen straw.

"Sure, what do I care? Sit down on the couch, right on the piece of tape."

"What's this, for the FBI?"

"I told you what it was. A video I'm making for my shrink. I told you that. If you sit right on that mark your back will be to the camera, you'll be in shadow just like on those talk shows with the male prostitutes or the hit men who don't want to reveal their identities." Arnie giggled. "Of course if you're really afraid . . ."

"I ain't afraid of nothin'."

A broad hairy back slid onto the couch. There was a sheen of sweat along the shoulders. The head was obscured in the shadows. Only when the man leaned forward, a folded match cover in his hand, did Karen get a glimpse of tight black curls at the nape of the neck. Why wasn't he wearing a shirt? Maybe he was totally nude. Why was he sweating? Arnie kept the house glacial, industrial air conditioners in every room, even the bathroom.

It was because they had been up all night, maybe even for days, snorting coke. Arnie liked pushing himself, getting a huge amount and going on and on until his body gave out. "No food, nothing but coke and cigarettes and a little beer to keep the throat moist so you won't choke to death," he once told her. "You go and go until your skin is as clammy as a jailhouse wall. Your mind opens like an asylum on visiting day and all the loonies come scampering onto the lawn. It's not psychedelic at all. LSD makes you tell the truth, coke makes you hide it behind shadows of fantasy, veils of deception. It's what happens to your mind when your body breaks down. I guess it's like being in a concentration camp." And then he smiled slyly. "Or am I just symbolizing to keep you interested?"

There was no telling how long they'd been there. Arnie was cool enough in his crepe de chine ninja outfit. But then Arnie thrived on this kind of ordeal. The man with the broad back scooped coke off the pile and held the matchbox cover to his nostril, giving two explosive snorts, then bent over and did it to the other nostril.

"You know the first thing I ever saw of you was your ass?" the man with the broad back blurted.

Arnie smiled and crouched over his row of neat lines. "My dimpled Jewish ass, that's right. Tell it."

"Yeah. It was in D-block on Rikers. Over at the end where they'd closed the dormitories for painting or something. It was the place where they let the faggots go to get it on."

"So what were you doing there?" Arnie prompted.

"I had an envelope for the night captain of the block. He was getting food delivered for some of us from Primavera in the Bronx."

"Best Italian food I ever ate," Arnie said.

"That's because you're a Jew and don't know no better. Beppo's is better, La Casa del Mare on Mulberry Street, Jimmy's in Greenpoint. . . ."

"Okay, great, write a book about mafia eateries. Now let's get back to my ass."

"It was there up in the air," Broad Back said. "Right there in an old cell they were using as a tool room. A guy was sitting on your head, and they had your pants down and your ass up as I passed. And

Tommy Sconzo was there, a kid from Jerry Pinelli's family in Red Hook. . . ."

"Naughty, naughty, right?" Arnie said. "What happened then?"

Broad Back lit a cigarette. "Sconzo says to me, 'You want a piece of this?' "

"By way of background, it was my third day in," Arnie said. "I hadn't gone that long without getting high since I was fourteen. I asked this kid in the cafeteria and he said to come over to the old dorms in D-block. It was a setup. When I got there, this buddy of yours . . ."

"He's not my fuckin' buddy and you know it," Broad Back said angrily.

"This buddy of yours from Red Hook was standing there with a bag of grass and he said, 'Get on your knees, bitch, and I'll give you all the dope you want.' So I decked him."

Broad Back chuckled. "Yeah, you can throw a punch, I'll give you that."

"And then these other guys came out of nowhere and got me down," Arnie said. "And then you came along, my white knight," he simpered.

"Yeah and you're lucky I did. Guys who get gang-banged in the joint—it changes their life."

"The T.E. Lawrence syndrome," Arnie said. "So what did you do when you saw my buttocks waving in the breeze?"

"The only thing I could do."

"Explain, please," Arnie said, and he confided to the camera, "This is interesting."

"Let's just say I have a certain image to protect."

"You're a well-known man of the underworld," Arnie said. "You have hire- and firepower."

"Alotta firepower," Broad Back said, now warming to his narrative. "So I grabbed Tommy Sconzo and told him this shit don't happen on D-block as long as I'm here."

"And you became my protector," Arnie said.

Broad Back shifted uncomfortably. "You coulda done worse. You get hooked up with one of them big boots you'd be a jailhouse bride, white dress and all. You'd be doin' laundry all day long."

"Then you bribed the guards to let you into my cell at night."

"What do you wanna bring this up for?" Broad Back softly remonstrated.

Arnie wouldn't relent. "It happened, didn't it?"

"Alotta things happen in the joint that you don't ever talk about on the outside, Arnie," Broad Back pleaded. "In this life you don't talk unless you have a reason."

"I'm trying to get out of the habit of seducing middle-aged women and then stealing from them, that's my reason," Arnie said. "Now you came into my cell every night and sat on the cot. And we talked, right?"

"We never did nothin'."

"And after a week you touched my shoulder, remember? A few days later you slid down my arm and held my hand. If I'd stayed in the joint a week longer you would have tried to kiss me. . . ."

Broad Back shot up and disappeared from the frame.

"You see, you're not like me," Arnie said calmly,

bending over his lines. "I'll talk about anything. You, the big tough guy, you're scared. Truth is, you love me. It's not a love that'll do either of us any good. But it's love, I'd know it anywhere."

"I'll kill you for this," Broad Back snarled. A big hand came into the frame with the brief, green flash of a pinky ring. Then there was a crashing sound and then the camera was on the floor for a moment looking at a table against the wall as the hand punched the wall and Broad Back sobbed, "I'll kill you. . . ."

With that the screen went black. Karen snatched the cassette out of the machine. She lunged over the bed to the telephone and dialed the 19th Precinct. This time she asked for the squad right away and when the sleepy voice came on she identified herself first.

"This is Karen Winterman, I'd like to speak to Inspector Duffy."

And when Duffy came on seconds later she knew he had grabbed the phone because he thought he was going to get the confession he wanted. So she decided to tease him.

"Will you be there for a while, Inspector? I'd like to talk to you."

There was no urgency in his voice. He was too much of a pro for that. But Karen could feel his excitement because no one suffers the highs and lows more than a professional.

"Take your time, Doctor Winterman," he said.

Karen raced into the shower, bringing the cassette into the bathroom and laying it on the sink. She dressed down with slacks and a cardigan. There'd be no mistake about who she was this time. No gaping looks or stage sniggers as she walked by.

She paused for a look in the mirror. God, she'd forgotten about her bruised face. All the stiffness and pain had dissolved in the elation of her discovery. Duffy would want to know what had happened. And she would tell him. So what?

Too impatient to wait for the elevator, she ran down the back stairs. The street was empty, no cabs to be found. She ran right past the car where Edmund had been sitting, waiting for the right time to enter her building. As she passed he snapped the silencer off the .22 and slipped it into his pocket. Where was the chick going in such a hurry? She looked excited, too, like she was meeting her boyfriend. She oughta be happy. She don't know how lucky she just got.

Karen took a cab to the 19th Precinct. Her heart pounded as she rushed up the steps to the squad room. She knew exactly what she would do and say when they walked her into that bare office. He was sitting behind that splintering desk with a Lucky Strike dangling out of the side of his mouth. Karen rushed forward with all the excitement of a prize pupil and dropped Arnie's cassette in front of him.

"Here is the man who murdered Arnold Feinstein."

FOUR

A DESPERATE WOMAN

Sally's favorite thing was to get wired alone with the lights out. He loved the way the cocaine glowed on the mirror in the dark room. He would dip and toot, dip and toot, until he couldn't find his nose. Then he would lie back, eyes closed, while the drug sped through his bloodstream. In a while his motor reflexes would adapt to this sensory invasion. In this way he would add incrementally to his mental state. He thought of this as a training procedure, preparation for those times when he would be forced to do great quantities of drugs but still keep his head clear.

But this night Sally had overindulged, even for him. Sitting there in the darkness, he lost his focus and couldn't think. The cocaine burned white and harsh like a naked light bulb. It blinded him. Even when he turned away it glared in the corner of his eye. He was beset by visions. Not full-fledged hallucinations, just optical illusions where a shape in the darkness took on the contour of something or someone he knew, and it took an effort of will to convince himself that the thing wasn't really there.

Stay sober, stay cold, he told himself. *Think.* The thing broke down into four separate moves. *One:* Pluck the money. *Two:* Set Edmund up. *Three:* Take Benson out. *Four:* Kill that goddamn shrink before she puts the cops on me.

Sally wasn't afraid of death. He didn't expect to live out his natural term. But dying was losing; it meant you hadn't been smart, hadn't played the game well enough. And Sally didn't like to lose. He was a guy who lived on a tightrope. For him every birthday was a major victory. He was a desperate man. He would risk anything. But he needed a few more desperados for what he had in mind. He reached for the phone. A desperate woman was what he needed. A desperate woman was the greatest energy source in the universe, and little Ida was the most desperate woman he knew.

The phone hardly rang once before it was snapped up and a timid voice whispered on the other end.

"Ida," Sally said. "Ida, *mi vida,* it's Mr. Feinstein."

After the call, Ida turned off the lights. Mr. Feinstein said the people watching the apartment would think she had gone out. She sat there for hours, no cigarettes, no radio. She sat and concentrated on an image of Prudencio. It was only by concentrating on him that she could keep from hating Mr. Feinstein. Because Mr. Feinstein was the cause of their troubles. And now he was the only hope they had.

They had met Mr. Feinstein in Lima at the Café

Tres Hermanos, where they worked as tango dancers. By then they had been together for three years. Prudencio had taken her out of her house in Quito when she was fifteen to teach her how to dance. Her brother Manuel arranged it all. He was to be their manager.

Prudencio had the straight, shiny hair and high cheekbones of an Indian, but he danced *al español*. He taught her in a tiny studio to the sound of a phonograph. The records skipped, the mirror was so greasy she could hardly see herself, the air got so close she was offended at her own smell. But Prudencio never seemed to notice. He would work for hours on one step, playing the record over and over again. He never raised his voice, never criticized. He would take off his shirt and drape a towel over his shoulders where Ida had to hold him. He smoked while they danced, and with the heat and the odor and the stink of tobacco Ida would feel faint. Two weeks after they met he took her back to his room in the hotel. "We have to be married, *muñeca*," he said. And when she spoke about a priest he shook his head. "An artist cannot enter a church. He will lose his power." He stroked her hair and sponged her feet and was very gentle. She didn't mind it at all.

Prudencio taught her many tangos—Tango Mendocino, Tango de la Ciudad, Tango Largo, Tango de la Guerra—each with different steps and tempos within the same rhythm. Although the dances never varied and she came to know them in her sleep with the music that went with them, she was always surprised by something Prudencio did. It seemed that every night they were doing different dances. Prudencio's touch was so light that even though she knew when he was supposed to lift her, she would always be astonished to find herself swept off her feet. It felt as if she were flying under her own power. "Just look in my eyes," Prudencio told her. She did and saw only him. The audience didn't exist. The music seemed to be coming from inside instead of from an orchestra that was right behind them. She heard nothing but Prudencio's instructions. "Hold your head up. Proud . . . Proud . . . To the right, to the left . . . Wait for me. . . ." At the end, when the music stopped and she slid away, grasping the tips of Prudencio's fingers, into a deep curtsy, she would hear the applause and sense the people for the first time. It was like coming out of a dream.

Prudencio was sick with cocaine. *"La droga,"* he called it. His teeth were brown from smoking it. Every night he would argue with the manager for more money. Then he and Manuel would send Ida home alone and disappear into the streets to find the drug. After they smoked, Prudencio would come into bed with Ida and stroke her for hours, kissing her feet, murmuring things she didn't understand. When he slept, the sweat glistened on his chest. She would trace the blue veins pulsing in his neck, hold her hand over his face to catch the breath coming out of his open mouth. Sometimes he breathed so deeply, his chest would hollow and she could count every rib.

In the morning she would awaken to the sound of Prudencio coughing in the bathroom down the hall. It would go on and on, this racking sound, until Ida sobbed with fear—*"O Dios mío"*—convinced that this time his brain would burst from it. People in the other rooms pounded the walls and screamed insults. When the coughing stopped, Ida huddled under the covers praying for the sound of his footsteps, the whistle of his faltering breath. When he returned, pale and shaky, a cigarette burning between his fingers, he would be smiling shyly. "It is not the drug, Ida. The drug makes it better. Dries up my chest, the doctor told me." Then he would get into bed and she would hold him until he stopped shivering. *"Ida, mi vida,"* he would whisper, "you're so warm." And she would pray for forgiveness because in her soul she was grateful for the drug because it weakened him and made him need her.

The manager was a thick, bald man, not much taller than Prudencio, but broad as a barrel. He wore thick black-rimmed glasses and chewed long Cuban cigars. Wiry clumps of black hair sprouted on the backs of his hands and fingers. He gestured violently when he spoke, even about everyday things. When his hands stopped moving, the hairs would writhe and coil as if an electric current were running through them. He never had a pleasant word for her, always stared angrily as if she had committed the greatest offense against him and he was waiting for his chance to get even. He was the kind of man you couldn't live with, the kind of man who made everything hopeless.

One night Prudencio was sick and couldn't do the last show. He and the manager argued vehemently by the bar until finally Prudencio turned away with a gesture of contempt.

"Cabrón! I don't work here anymore."

The manager shouted, "Take your little whore and get out of my café!" He threw a wineglass, hitting Prudencio in the back. Prudencio turned and snarled.

He got his knife halfway out of his boot before the barman and the waiters were on him. They threw him to the floor and kicked him until he stopped moving.

The manager came and stood behind her. She felt his breath on her hair. *If he touches me I'll kill him,* she decided. Then he pushed her down. "Take your pimp home and stay out of my café."

They stayed a week in the room until Prudencio was able to walk. Prudencio sent Manuel into the streets to buy the drug. When he returned, Prudencio would weigh the powder on his jeweler's scale and accuse Manuel of cheating him. They would hiss angrily at each other, careful in the tiny room not to make too much noise. Then they would smoke. Ida never asked for it, and neither of them ever offered. She sat on the bed, her legs drawn up under her and watched the glowing tips of their cigarettes inscribing tiny circles in the darkness. There would be silence after they smoked. Prudencio crouched on his haunches like an Indian, his eyes gleaming. Manuel paced nervously, speaking with venom of people she didn't know. Of what they had said and he had replied. Of what they had done and he would do to them.

Prudencio would sit in silence, ignoring him. And then Manuel would begin to insult him. "Caveman, headhunter, what are you thinking? Where are your tattoos? Where is the bone in your nose?"

Prudencio never answered, and soon Manuel would leave, slamming the door so hard, dust fell from the ceiling. It was always the same between them. Once Ida asked Prudencio why.

"It is part of the smoking," he said. "It is our ceremony."

"But you are always so angry."

"Only Manuel," Prudencio said. "Because he doesn't understand the drug. No white man does. The drug was a gift to us, to the Indians. Why else would it only grow where we live? Why else would we be the only ones who can harvest it, the only ones who know its secret? The drug gives peace and beautiful colors only to us. To the white man only nerves and violence."

Then they had to leave Quito. Prudencio had taken Ida to the racetrack where he had worked as an apprentice, exercising horses. He dressed her up and took her to the jockey's clubhouse. They were mostly small brown men like him, and so they liked her as much as he had. Prudencio stayed until most of them left to race or watch the race. He picked the locks on their lockers and stole their money and jewelry. It was a big haul and he didn't share it with Manuel. Although no one had seen him, he was suspected because of his drug habit. They were in the café outside the station one night and a jockey got up from his table, screaming, "Thief, thief, watch out for the little thief!" Prudencio kept his head up, but his grip on Ida's arm tightened and he steered her through the door.

In Lima they danced for the owner of Tres Hermanos, a young blond American with a crazy laugh that had no happiness in it. Prudencio had smoked the night before and he was very stiff. His eyes watered and his breath hissed through clenched teeth. The American laughed and put his arm around Prudencio. *"Hermano,"* he said. *"Un otro hermano."*

Lima was a city of tourists. Nights would go by when Ida would never hear Spanish spoken in the club. People sat jammed into the little booths, whispering to each other. Sometimes it looked like an American film, the men with the boots and cowboy hats and beards. Ida would sit in the tiny dressing room off the kitchen and hear the waiters shouting for champagne. "*Dos* Dom Perignon . . . *Un* Cristal. . . ."

One night after the show, Prudencio was invited to a guest's table. Ida started to leave, but the owner took her by the arm. "He wants you, too," he said with that frightening laugh. Prudencio stood right there and let the American touch her.

It was Mr. Feinstein. In his white suit he also looked like an American film star—like Travolta or like Rambo. He wore a large emerald ring. He spoke a profane Spanish, using many impolite expressions. Prudencio looked uneasily at Ida, but didn't correct the man. Instead, he flattered him on his Spanish.

"We have many Latins in my city," Mr. Feinstein said. He smiled at Ida. "You will be very happy there."

They took a taxi across town to a passport photographer who remained open at two in the morning. Prudencio took her aside. Wetting a handkerchief with his tongue he rubbed off her makeup. Then they dressed her in a nun's habit. The men laughed a lot. Ida noticed a very young girl in tight jeans and high heels staring sullenly out of the darkness. Other men arrived. Mr. Feinstein poured drinks from a silver flask. They amused themselves making up a name to go with the passport. Each of them wanted it to be a nun who had taught them in school. Finally, Mr. Feinstein won and they typed Sister Josefa Bonventura. Mr. Feinstein took Ida's hand and said, "This woman used to beat me with a long stick, Ida. You wouldn't do that, would you?" The men laughed and sniffed cocaine from a cellophane bag the photographer had in his desk. They each had ornate golden spoons except for Prudencio, who sprinkled it onto his thumbnail, and Mr. Feinstein, who used a folded matchbook cover. Ida sat on a sofa in a corner. The girl with the tight jeans sat next to her but didn't say a word. It was dark and the blinds were drawn. They played a tango and Prudencio made her dance with him in her nun's habit. "We're going to America, *muñeca*," he whispered, giggling drunkenly. "We're going to be rich." It was daylight when they left. Ida kept her head down, ashamed to be seen in the nun's habit. Mr. Feinstein laughed. "She looks just like a bride of Christ."

The next day there was more intense instruction from Prudencio and Mr. Feinstein. Ida was to go to the airport by bus. She would be traveling with a group of nuns from a Carmelite convent in the country. She was to say nothing to any of them, but to keep her nose buried in her missal. If any of the nuns asked, she was to say she was traveling to America to raise money for Father Esteban Locatelli, who had a mission among the Indians in the slums of Lima. Father Locatelli had been ordered into "penitential silence" by the Vatican for his liberationist views and was called the "Red Priest" in the newspapers. The nuns would leave her alone after that.

They gave her a pocketbook, a small TWA bag, and a large leather shoulder bag with many compartments. She was to pack her clothing and cosmetics in the bags. When they got back on the plane after the customs check in Florida she was to bring the bags one by one into the bathroom and empty the contents into a laundry sack that would be behind the toilet. Then she was to leave the bags outside the bathroom door. When they arrived in New York Prudencio would return the luggage to her and she was to carry it off the plane. There would be a chauffeur waiting with a sign with her name on it. She was to go with him.

Prudencio would be on the plane with her, but she was not to speak to him or acknowledge his presence in any way. "This is very important," Mr. Feinstein said. "People will be watching you."

"What are we doing?" she asked Prudencio.

He smiled at Mr. Feinstein. "We're smuggling, *muñeca*. We are going to be very rich."

The next morning they drove her to a bus stop on the outskirts of the city. A group of nuns was waiting for the bus. "How did Mr. Feinstein know the nuns would be here?" Ida asked Prudencio.

"Mr. Feinstein knows everything," he answered. "He is a very powerful mafioso."

On the bus, one of the young nuns asked Ida where she was from and Ida told her the story. The young nun was quiet after that, but Ida saw the others looking at her and saw one of them speak to the Mother Superior.

She sat in the back of the plane. Prudencio sat across the aisle on the other side. She didn't look at him. The plane landed in Miami, Florida, and the passengers were instructed in Spanish and English to debark for Customs inspection. American Customs officers with flashlights rushed on the plane as they were getting off.

There were many different uniforms in the terminal. Policemen with huge dogs waited for the baggage to come off.

They opened everyone's baggage. Policemen stood by staring at the passengers. A blond woman with black roots and huge rings on all her fingers announced in Spanish that all the nuns were requested to form a separate line. When it was Ida's turn, two women took her into a small room with only a desk and told her in Spanish to disrobe. They wore a lot of makeup and jewelry and perfume. They talked all the while Ida took off her clothes about how they were Cuban and didn't believe in offending women of the church this way, but if you saw the tricks these smugglers used, then you would understand. They used the drug money to finance Communist revolution, did she know that?

When she was completely naked, one of them put on rubber gloves and went over her body while the other smoked a cigarette. They made her bend over and probed inside of her. They looked in her shoes, in the lining of her habit, in her underwear, talking all the time about how the Communists controlled the drug trade. They talked about giving her an enema, but decided she was too small. Ida didn't say anything, but she knew she had been denounced by the nuns on the bus.

When she got back on the plane she saw Prudencio in the back by the bathroom smoking a cigarette. After takeoff she went into the bathroom and emptied her baggage into the laundry bag she found there.

She left everything, even her pocketbook, outside the bathroom, and walked away just as she had been told to do. As the plane was landing, the stewardess asked her to take her baggage out of the aisle. She was surprised to find it there. Prudencio moved so quickly and quietly.

The shoulder bag was so heavy a man had to help her with it. The airline bag was heavy, even the pocketbook. By the time she got off the plane her back was aching from the weight. There was no inspection here. In the terminal she saw Prudencio carrying a leather suitcase he hadn't brought on with him. There was a man holding a sign. It was Mr. Feinstein, dressed in a black suit like a chauffeur. He rushed forward to grab the shoulder bag. "Here, let me help you, Sister." Outside, she saw Prudencio dragging the suitcase toward a taxicab.

Mr. Feinstein drove her to a building near a highway. In the streets she heard Spanish spoken. How strange to come from Lima, where she heard English, to New York, where she heard Spanish.

Prudencio was waiting in the apartment. He smiled and kissed her proudly. "You are my jewel."

"She is the best," Mr. Feinstein said. "There's not an American woman alive who could have done it." He gave Prudencio an envelope bulging with American money. "You have done beautiful work . . . beautiful."

When Mr. Feinstein had gone, Prudencio told her: "Sixty kilos we brought in. Mr. Feinstein says that is tripled here with the cut. There is an enormous profit."

Ida didn't understand what had happened.

"The smugglers can do anything, they have so much money," Prudencio explained. "They put the drug on the plane in the compartments for oxygen. The Customs people do not think to look there yet. It was my job to come back and get the drug out of the compartments and into the luggage."

The apartment had luxuries only the richest in Ecuador could afford. Wall-to-wall carpeting, tile bathroom, color TV, air conditioning in every room. On Saturday Prudencio would take Ida shopping along Queens Boulevard. There were so many stores. So many places to eat. Everything with an American name, but the customers were mostly Spanish or Chinese. On Sunday they went to church, and Ida prayed they would go back to that little club in Quito as soon as Prudencio had made enough money.

But she knew that would never happen. Prudencio was learning English. He had begun in Lima, a few words, smiling in embarrassment. But now she heard him speaking rapidly on the phone. In the stores he spoke only English, even to the Colombians. To Mr. Feinstein he spoke only English. Even to her, becoming impatient when she couldn't answer. But how could she learn English? Prudencio was out every day and night until early morning, and she had to stay in the house. Someone had to stay with the drugs and the cash, Mr. Feinstein said. Someone always had to be there. Sometimes late at night he would call, and Prudencio would go to the closet where they kept the drugs, take out some packages, and leave. Sometimes it would be days before he returned, but always with an envelope full of one-hundred-dollar bills, which he flattened out and hid in the false bottom of the suitcase he had brought in from Lima. He was nervous now, excited. He never slept, even when he was home. When they went out he would nod to strange men passing on the street. "I am becoming very important," Prudencio told her. But he looked old and stooped. His face was gray, his skin didn't shine anymore. "We will go dancing soon," he promised. "When I have time. . . ."

And then Mr. Feinstein called and Prudencio went out. But this time he wasn't gone for only a few days. A week went by, then two. Once Ida awoke to find somebody had slid an envelope full of money under the door. She stayed in the house, afraid to leave the drugs and money alone. But soon there was no food, and with all that money she was afraid to call the Chinese the way Prudencio sometimes did.

Then, when she thought she was going to starve, Mr. Feinstein called. "Turn off the lights and wait," he told her.

A few hours later she heard the key in the lock. Mr. Feinstein stood there in a black leather jacket. No jewelry, no flashy smile; he licked his lips before he spoke to her.

"Prudencio has been arrested, Ida," he said.

She began to shake. Mr. Feinstein held her shoulders tightly and made her sit down. "We have to get him out of prison, Ida. There are men in there, God knows what they would do to someone like Prudencio."

Ida had seen men on the streets of New York who looked like gorillas with red staring eyes and huge teeth. Prudencio was strong, especially in his hands and fingers, but he was small enough to have tried being a jockey in Quito. Ida knew he would fight to protect his dignity, but how could you hope to survive against such beasts?

"He sends you his love, Ida," Mr. Feinstein said. "He called me from prison to make sure I told you he was okay. He says you should be calm and do what I say, and I will get him out of prison and home. You do want to go home, don't you, Ida?"

Mr. Feinstein took all the money in the valise. "We will use this for a lawyer," he said. "And to bribe the police."

Next he gave her a little silver gun. "You must protect yourself. Use this on anyone who walks through this door, no matter what they say. I'm the only person you can trust. I'm the only one who can bring Prudencio back to you."

So she sat in the house as Mr. Feinstein had said. Soon she lost track of time. The days flowed into each other. She watched the television, slept, looked out of the window. Occasionally, Mr. Feinstein came with pizza or Chinese food, but he only stayed long enough to get the drugs. When she asked about Prudencio, he acted insulted. "I am working day and night to bring him back to you, Ida. I think of nothing else, believe me."

One Saturday he came and took her shopping. They went to a jewelry store on Queens Boulevard. "Prudencio wants me to buy his jewel a jewel," he said. He bought her emerald earrings set in gold. Then they drove in his car across a bridge into the city to a big restaurant, all metal and glass. The waiters wore tuxedos. They held Ida's chair and bowed to Mr. Feinstein. Champagne came in silver buckets. Mr. Feinstein stroked her hair and looked her in the eyes, forcing her to turn away in embarrassment. "A terrible thing has happened to you, Ida," Mr. Feinstein said. "But I am going to make you forget it." Then she knew that she would not see Prudencio for a long time.

And now she waited in the dark for Mr. Feinstein. She put on the emerald earrings for the first time since he had bought them for her. When he came in he noticed them right away and smiled. *"Muñeca,"* he said, and hugged her, pressing her to his chest and stroking her long black hair. "You are the bravest woman in the world. And the most beautiful." He kissed her gently on the forehead and looked in her eyes. This time she did not look away.

"You have trusted me, Ida," he said. "Now I will show how much I trust you. I have a very special job for you to do."

PLUCKED

At 5 A.M. that morning Benny Gutierrez was going into his sixth hour on the hard wooden bench across from Locker 416 in the Port Authority terminal. He had bummed up for the detail, ski cap, fatigue jacket, torn jeans and sneakers, the kind they gave away at the city shelters. Didn't need to "soot up." Six hours in the Port Authority would do it for you. Benny felt all slimy and greasy, and he hadn't moved off the bench.

He had an empty pint bottle next to him. He didn't look much different from the dozen or so other bums who were spread out around the area, some huddled up in their rags in the corners, others just laying out in the middle of the floor, making people step around them. At 6:30 the PA cops would make a sweep, rousting all of them so they wouldn't get trampled in the rush-hour crowd. At least one of those bums was his partner, Bobby Grayson. Bobby and Benny worked Anti-Crime in Times Square, and one night a week they had to bum up like derelicts outside of one hot spot or another. Bobby had a new baby at home and he would stuff a few dirty diapers into the pockets of his long overcoat just for a goof. Like clockwork, one of the hooples from the precinct would go over to roust him, get one whiff of those diapers and take off. Bobby had done it tonight. He laid himself down right in the middle of the passageway. When two of them useless fart sacks from the Port Authority had come over to prod him with their clubs, he had turned just enough so they got the full fragrance. Benny almost busted a gut laughing as they waddled off the set. He could see how Bobby's face was red from holding in the laughs. Bobby said he couldn't smell anything, his nose was so full of that beat-up coke they had taken off the hookers a few nights before. Bobby was a goof, there was no doubt about it.

But they couldn't clown around too much. The sergeant had said there would probably be guys from other agencies on their own stakeouts, so to be cool, and if anybody made a move on the locker, to be sure to get there first because there might be a jurisdiction hassle, you never knew. This was a big case, the sergeant had said. So Benny called his boy Edwin who worked in the Borough office and was sergeant-at-arms of the Hispanic Police Officers Society, and Edwin said that they were sitting on a couple of dirty cops, and rumor had it that one of them was Lieutenant Saldana, head of Narcotics. Benny giggled. "Bustelo gonna get his, bro?" The people in the Hispanic Society talked about Saldana all the time. How he was a loner, not getting active in the organization, when a guy with his rank could be real helpful to the younger guys. How he wasn't too cool, with his Jaguar and his big house on Pelham Parkway.

Still, Saldana had been around much too long to get tripped up in a stakeout. It was going to be a quiet night.

At about 3 A.M. Benny took a walk and smoked a jay. When he got back, nothing had changed except a few more bums were laying up and the phoniest maintenance guy he had ever seen was casing the lockers, pushing a garbage can on casters around and around like he expected something to drop from the ceiling. Benny mumbled and grumbled until he got Bobby's attention, and then he pointed to the dude. Bobby checked him out and then sat up suddenly with his neck stretched out like a psycho and shrieked, "FBI asshole, you don't tell me what to do!" The guy jerked around to see who was yelling. Benny had to hide his face, he was laughing so hard.

The guy was ridiculous. First of all he didn't look anything like a Port Authority janitor. He was tall and slim, with blond hair cut real short and gray around the temples and a smooth-shaven windburned face. Right there he was dead. No white man with seniority worked the graveyard shift in the terminal. Look around, all you saw was boots and *jíbaros* pushing the brooms. Second place, when did you ever see a fucking night-shift janitor with a clean shave and a sunburn? The guy was like a neon sign. FBI or Treasury, one of those white-bread operations.

The guy must have picked up the vibes because all of a sudden he rolled his little empty trash can behind the lockers, out of sight. Benny heard him poking around back there trying to make believe he was doing something. He turned his attention to the other loiterers in the area, trying to pin another ringer, but was interrupted by a low whistle from Bobby, and he turned toward the sound of high heels clacking on the terminal floor.

A nice tight little Latin chick was walking right toward him through the archway. She had black hair plaited in a thick braid right down to her ass. She was wearing a silk see-through blouse and a black leather skirt with a slit up the thigh. Three-inch heels . . . This chick was vibrating . . . Beep, beep, beep. . . . Benny sat up for a better look. This wasn't no piece of ghetto ass. Too much class, for one thing, and she wasn't tough enough, you could see that.

When she passed Bobby, he did his psycho act and rolled over so he could look right up her skirt. She looked down at him. He barked and clapped his hands like a seal in heat. She didn't say anything, just kept walking.

"Coño!"

The curse rang through the silence, bouncing off the walls of the deserted terminal. A chunky brother, square and low to the ground, tough to knock off his feet, was coming through the archway. Looked like a Cubano, a light-skinned black dude with a head like an oversized light bulb, wearing a short suede jacket, rings on all ten fingers, and about a hundred pounds of chain around his neck. Big hands, and he walked with the swagger of a guy who had never been hurt.

"Slow down, bitch," he yelled.

The girl kept walking.

"You know me, bitch," the dude shouted. "I don't

get that bread back, I'm gonna take it outta your skin."

The girl neither stopped nor speeded up. She kept walking at her pace, almost as if she didn't know he was talking to her.

As the dude passed Benny he shouted, "I said hold up, didn't I?" He took off after the little girl and grabbed her in front of a boarded-up newsstand at the end of the arcade. He spun her around and slammed her against the wooden facade. "You think I'm a hick? You think you can beat me . . . ?"

The girl started to say something in Spanish and he slapped her in the face with a crack that Benny felt. The girl staggered. He grabbed her chin and banged her head against the facade. "You gonna give me that money? You gonna give me that money?" Boom, boom, he banged her twice more. She started to sag. Blood poured out of her nose.

Benny rolled off the bench, Bobby jumped up, and they both ran toward the stand. Benny shouted, "Yo, bro, leave her alone," but the guy yanked her by the hair down to her knees and started smacking her again, yelling, "I'll teach you to fuck with me."

Bobby got to the dude first. He came around his back, grabbed a handful of his Afro and tried to pull him off the chick. The dude's head went back, but his arms kept pumping like pistons. Bobby jumped up on his back and they both went down hard, Bobby cracking his head on the floor. By the time Benny got there, the dude was up on his feet, kicking Bobby in the side. "Get your hands off me, bum." Benny tackled the guy. It was like hitting a wall. The guy took a swipe at Benny, smacking him on the ear with a heavy hand.

Benny rolled over and grabbed his blackjack. "Police officers, asshole."

The guy's jaw dropped. "Wha . . . ?" Benny jumped up and sapped him hard, right on the collarbone. Most normal people went to their knees after a shot like that. This guy staggered back like somebody merely had bumped him, and started rapping for his life.

"Hey, man, I want this bitch arrested, man. She tried to take me off. . . ."

Two other guys in windbreakers showed up out of nowhere. "Leave him alone," one of them said.

Bobby got up slow, but picked up speed and charged the dude. He threw a high karate kick and caught the guy on the cheekbone. The guy put his hands up wrestling style.

"You wanna fight somebody, motherfucker?" Bobby yelled.

"Leave him alone," one of the guys in the windbreakers said. They went over to the girl, who was sitting, dazed and bleeding against the wall. Now one of them came up to Bobby. "You're gonna screw up the detail."

"Fuck the detail," Bobby screamed. "I don't let no mutt kick me around."

Now the mutt decided to cop an attitude. "This bitch has a hundred dollars of my money. She said she was gonna get something for me."

"Oh, yeah, what was it?" Benny said.

"Don't matter what. She has my money."

The other guys flashed DEA ID cards. "Listen, *chamaco*, what do you wanna bet if we go through your pockets we find enough to send you to jail for five years.''

The mutt's eyes narrowed, but he backed up. "You can't search me without a warrant," he said.

"Probable cause. I saw a bulge in your pants. Don't tell me the law."

"Okay, okay, look, man, I'll tell you what it is." Suddenly the mutt looked real scared. "She's my old lady, man. We had a fight, man, and I got nuts on her. This shit hits you in a funny way sometimes, man, I'll admit that. You know like I know I got a problem. I been in detox, man, but it don't seem to last. If you just let me take her home . . ."

Benny walked over to the little girl. Her blouse was torn. She was holding a handkerchief to her bloody nose.

"You don't have to go anywhere with this man if you don't want to," he said in Spanish.

"No, he is my husband. . . ."

"Let 'em go for Chrissake," one of the DEA guys said.

Benny ignored him. "In this country your husband can't beat you."

"You guys wanna compromise this operation over a family dispute?"

Benny turned on the guy. "You wanna stay outta this."

"This is the Port Authority, pal," the other guy said. "We can spend the whole night getting involved in little beefs like this."

Bobby pointed toward the lockers. "Will you look at that chickenshit motherfucker? . . ."

The sandy-haired man they had pinned before was wheeling his trash can quickly away from the scene.

"Is he on this?" one of the DEA guys asked. "Where's he goin' in such a hurry?"

"Probably to call in for instructions. Don't you guys have to do that every ten minutes?"

The sandy-haired man pushed his trash barrel through the arcade into the darkened doorway of a candy shop. He reached into it and removed an old cloth satchel with frayed leather handles. The man walked through the terminal and out the Eighth Avenue exit. A white van was parked in a bus stop in front of the parking lot across the street. The man walked around and got in the passenger side. Sally Fish was eating a slice of pizza.

"Heavy," the sandy-haired man said, dropping the satchel on the back seat.

"I hope so," Sally said. He pointed to the pizza box, but the man shook his head.

"Nervous stomach."

"Nervous? About what? Makin' a move right under the cops' noses? You must be gettin' old, John."

The sandy-haired man held up his right hand. It was shaking slightly. Sally offered him a vial. He grimaced and shook his head. Sally flipped open the glove compartment and took out a pint of Fleischmann's. "I forget, John, you're a white man." He slipped an envelope out of his pocket. There was a tiny "j" penciled faintly in the right-hand corner. He waited until the sandy-haired man had taken a short pull at the bottle before handing him the envelope.

"How did it go?"

"Just like you said it would."

"Yeah, I dreamt this score."

The sandy-haired man slipped the envelope into his pocket without checking its contents. "It was like cuttin' the top off a box of cereal. Took about two minutes, maybe less."

"That's because you're a master, John," Sally said. "I needed the best and I got him and he proved it."

John grunted and took another hit of the Fleischmann's.

Sally drove up Eighth Avenue to a parking lot on Fifty-second Street. He let John out at the corner.

"This is one to tell your grandchildren about," he said.

"My grandchildren think I'm a plumber," John said. He slipped the pint into his pocket and walked quickly away.

A few minutes later, Santos de la Maria, known as "Rojo" for his light complexion and a reddish Afro, came out of the Ninth Avenue exit of the Port Authority Building, holding Ida under her arm. He looked across the street and saw a white van parked under the overpass. Then he hailed a cab and helped Ida into it.

The white van followed the cab to the rear entrance of the Post Office Building on Thirty-third Street. Santos and Ida got out and walked across the street. The van slid into the curb and they got in. Santos helped Ida into the back seat then turned to Sally, flushed with excitement.

"It went down just like you said it would," Santos said. "When we left, them cops was still arguing with each other. They forgot all about us."

"They're still arguing now, I guarantee it." Sally

slipped a small ravioli-shaped package out of his pocket and handed it to Santos. "How'd you like my girl?"

Santos turned solemnly to Ida and spoke to her in Spanish. "You've got more balls than any man I know."

He turned to Sally, switching back to English. "I never hit a woman unless she made me mad, you know, and I wasn't sure I could do it. You know what she said?"

Sally reached back and took Ida's hand. "What?"

"She said, 'Hit hard or the trick won't work.' That's what she said."

Sally squeezed Ida's hand and said, "The best." Once in Spanish and twice in English so she would know the words.

Sally drove uptown on the West Side Highway. By the time he got to 138th and Broadway, Santos had done the whole package and smoked three Salems. He got out in front of a bar called Domingo's and offered his arm to Ida to help her into the front seat.

Santos's eyes were shining. "Mr. Feinstein, it was an honor to work for you," he said. "A real honor. If you ever need anything . . ."

"I know the speech, bro, I've made it myself." Sally slipped an envelope out of his pocket. There was a small "s" penciled lightly in the corner. "Don't forget this."

Santos slipped the envelope into his pocket. "If you ever need a fire, man . . ."

"When it gets cold," Sally said.

He drove a few blocks down Broadway, then pulled over to the curb and switched the interior lights on.

Ida's jaw was swollen and her eye was closed. There was a thick patch of dried blood around her nostrils which made her breathe with difficulty. Sally touched the jaw and she winced. He touched the bruises on her shoulders where Santos had squeezed her. He kissed her fingers, one by one. "Tomorrow I'll buy you diamonds, the biggest you ever saw. You like diamonds?"

Ida lay back against the seat and let Sally stroke her knee as he drove across the Triboro into Queens. She closed her eyes and concentrated on Prudencio.

At 7 A.M. Benny and Bobby were due to be relieved. Benny peered through the rush-hour crowd that was already passing through the terminal at this early hour and saw Sergeant Lovinger standing by the lockers with a couple of guys who looked like they could be brass. Lovinger beckoned angrily.

Benny rolled off the bench and caught up with Bobby, who had gone over to the doughnut stand for coffee just before they showed up.

"You're gonna get reamed for that coffee," Benny said.

"Well, who the fuck ever heard of not getting a meal period just because we're on a surveillance?" Bobby said. But he dumped the container before they got to Lovinger.

They had to weave against the crowd. By the time they got close enough to see Lovinger's expression, they knew it wasn't about the coffee.

"This is Inspector Duffy, fellas," Lovinger said, indicating an angry-looking, red-faced guy in a rumpled gray suit, the kind these old-line detectives always wore.

"Did you men check the locker out during the course of your tour?" Duffy asked.

"Well, we've been looking right at it for eight hours, sir," Bobby said, hitting the "sir" defiantly. You had to give it to Bobby, he didn't take shit from the bosses.

"You have, huh?" Inspector Duffy said.

He walked them around behind the lockers. There was another bank facing out. One locker door was open. Duffy opened it all the way. A hole had been blow-torched in the back panel. Another hole had been torched in the back panel of the locker facing it. Locker 416 was empty. Benny and Bobby were staring into the two holes as a young guy in a London Fog and gold-rimmed glasses came over with the two DEA guys. They were white as sheets, the two of them, and looking nervously at Benny and Bobby.

"They say they didn't check the area during their shift," the guy in the London Fog said to Duffy.

Duffy nodded slowly, the muscles fluttering in his jaw. "Well did they check it before they started the tours, at least, so we can get a time fix?"

The two DEA guys shook their heads. Duffy scowled at Benny. He shook his head. "Well did anything unusual happen during the tour?" Duffy asked, exasperated.

Benny took a deep breath. "No, sir."

Duffy turned to the DEA guys. They shook their heads and shrugged. "Nothing out of the ordinary, sir."

Now Duffy turned to Lovinger. "I want to speak to the guys on the four-to-midnight right away. The terminal is more crowded during those hours. It probably happened then.''

Benny and Bobby looked innocently around the terminal. Benny shot a quick look at the DEA guys. They were looking innocently around in the other direction.

At eight o'clock the phone rang in Billy Benson's bedroom. He reached over his sleeping wife and grabbed it at the first ring.

"Benson? Billee Bensong?"

It was a girl with a heavy Spanish accent. Benson didn't say anything, just held the phone and waited. He had heard Sally Fish's spooky giggle in the background.

The girl spoke mechanically as if she were reading something she didn't understand. "Don' say I neber did nossin' for you, Billeee. . . ." And Sally's giggle turned into a shriek.

STRICTLY A HEMORRHOID JOB

It had been a long night for Duffy. He had been on the phone with the FBI and the DEA. They had all been caught with their pants down, and now it was ass-covering time. A guy named Locklear from the regional office of the DEA really had his balls in an uproar.

"I'm kickin' my two men right out of the Task Force," he said. He had one of those flat, twangy Southern accents that would make even "Happy birthday" sound like a threat. "I hope you're doin' the same, Inspector."

Duffy bridled. The guy had no right to make judgments on his men, but he deserved a little slack, considering the reaming he was going to get from his own bosses.

"I'm busting my Anti-Crime guys back down to uniform patrol," he said. "The sergeant's being transferred up to the West Bronx."

"Well, that's good," Locklear said. "I'm just concerned that there be some consistency in our reaction to this fuck-up."

This was too much for Duffy. "I'm not concerned with presenting a united front with the DEA, Mr. Locklear," he said. "These are punitive actions I have to take as a commander, even though I know that none of these men will be any good on the job anymore."

"You don't want 'em anyway, they fucked up."

"They're good men," Duffy said. "But they were put on a detail in which the politics were more important than the objective. You split the responsibilities, you split the attention. If this had been a one hundred percent police operation, they would have been sitting all over that locker instead of waiting for the other guy to do it."

"Well it's gone beyond that now, Inspector," Locklear said. "The thieves made us look bad, all of us, and I'm gonna get 'em for it. You certainly can't hold that against me."

"I don't."

"If you have any information to share I'd certainly appreciate it."

Duffy's neck tightened. He had the Winterman tape, the guy who had killed Arnie Feinstein and might have been behind the locker thing as well. DEA never pooled, none of those Federal operations did. They looked down on the cops and were always trying to beat them to the collar. But the rule was you had to share all information about drug traffickers with the DEA.

"I've got a videotape here that might be of interest," he said.

Locklear was at the precinct an hour later. He didn't look like his accent at all. He was a trim little guy with blow-dried blond hair. He had put on a three-piece suit, complete with gold watch chain, to come to a police precinct at 3 A.M. They offered him coffee, but he only wanted mineral water, so Duffy sent a car for a bottle of Perrier.

Locklear sat impassively through the tape. Duffy sat behind him and got the distinct impression from the way he leaned forward at one point, then pulled back, that he was trying to camouflage his reaction. When it was over he sat there shaking his head. "These people are all new faces to me."

"He's a new face to us, too," Duffy said. "We think the undercover policewoman who was killed was working on him."

Locklear took out a little black diary. "Well, I'm gonna give him a file number, Inspector. This will oblige you to notify us in case you develop any new information on the man. . . ."

"We'd appreciate if you'd reciprocate," Duffy said. "We have a quadruple homicide we'd like to clear up."

Locklear stood up. "I can sympathize with that." But he made no promises. And left without even shaking hands.

"McKinnon," Duffy said, "go downstairs and see if he's using the public phone."

McKinnon was up a few minutes later, shaking his head in astonishment. "Sometimes I feel like Doctor Watson on this job. He made a beeline for the phone outside the Community Service office."

"He's afraid we might have a wire on our phone,

and he didn't want us to hear what he had to say because he knows something. The lying little prick is trying to finesse me."

"What could he know?" McKinnon asked.

"Only one thing from that tape. He recognized the pinky ring. But he won't let us in on it because he wants to make the collar himself." Duffy crumpled an empty pack of cigarettes and threw it angrily across the room. "That's what law enforcement's all about in this country."

At 8:30 Duffy screened the tape for the guys from the Organized Crime Unit of the NYPD. By then some wag had put up a sign on the office door: "Sneak Preview." And someone had penciled under it, "Anyone caught with his coat over his lap will be prematurely ejaculated."

Duffy ripped the sign off the door. "Comedians. Four cops got killed and they're making jokes."

But he perked up at the sight of his friends filing wearily into the room. This was what cops were supposed to look like. Not some conniving twerp in a three-piece suit who was going to spend the next three years putting mutts in jail so he could go into private practice and make big bucks keeping them out. Not the FBI guys who measured each case by its publicity value, or the Government clowns who had a quota to fill and a budget to justify, so they inflated cases, bringing in guys who didn't belong, promoting small fry to supercriminals, passing themselves off as super-high-tech crime fighters, while all the time planes carrying tons of coke were roaring over their heads. Or the angry young blacks and Hispanics who looked on the bosses as worse villains than the mutts.

His friends were thirty-year men. Guys who had started on the beat the way every cop did and worked their way up, studying nights to pass their tests, working the extra hour or two to make a case, putting their asses on the line, earning everything they got. They were big, solid, thick in the waist, maybe a few scars on the knuckles from taking a shortcut now and then. Cynical? Sure, what do you expect? Twenty years a cop won't give you a very pleasant view of humanity. Still, these were guys who believed in the job, who loved the work. Incorruptible guys, never a black mark against them—not even an anonymous complaint. Bill Converi, head of the unit, Joe Feurey, who worked out of Brooklyn, and Dominick Paterno, out of Queens. Duffy had crossed paths with each of them over the years. In his favorite daydream, the one where he was appointed Commissioner, he always reached out for these guys and a dozen or so others. "Unbeknownst to these fine officers I have been watching them for years," he said in his fantasy press conference. "Now I will promote them to positions where their responsibilities will be commensurate with their abilities."

Duffy gave them a half hour to have their coffee and read the material.

"This guy Crow's name came up recently," Paterno said. "We developed an informant in the garment center, a guy named Robert Flynn, worked for a protection service. They caught him with a pound of smack in Sunnyside. He said he could give us a crooked cop and an OC burglary ring operating out of the garment center. He gave us a cop named Billy

Benson, and his partner, who he described. Crow fit the description.''

"Benson was Crow's partner," Duffy said.

"Yeah, well, we put him in protective custody, which he didn't want because he said the wiseguys would find out. And he gave us a guy named Richie the Greek, who he said was a contract burglar for some big wiseguy in Brooklyn. The next day Richie the Greek was hit outside his garage. A light-skinned black guy. Banged him out with a Twenty-two with a silencer.''

"We got a light-skinned black fleeing the scene of the murders," Duffy said.

"Yeah, I saw that," Paterno said. The four old cops cleared their throats and fished for cigarettes.

I love how we all try to hide our excitement, Duffy thought exultantly.

"Anyway, without Richie the Greek, we didn't have any corroboration on Flynn, so we had to let him out on bail. And they found him under the Queensborough Bridge with a Twenty-two in his throat the next day. No witnesses, but people in a bar said a light-skinned black guy had followed him out.''

"Same Twenty-two that killed Richie the Greek?" Duffy asked.

Paterno nodded.

Duffy turned off the light and rewound the tape.

"Don't we get popcorn?" Converi asked.

They watched the tape in silence. When it was over they shook their heads at Duffy's inquiring glance.

"Nobody knows him?"

"That means he's new," Converi said.

"There's something about the guy," Feurey said.

"Nothing that he says, really. Just an attitude. He's . . ."

"Overqualified?" Duffy said.

"Yeah, yeah. The way he talks to this kid Feinstein. Most wiseguys don't have relationships with civilians like that, even guys they boffed in the joint."

"Just the idea that he went along with this tape deal," Paterno said. "Most guys would never expose themselves like that."

"And this whole faggot thing," Converi said. "Most ex-cons don't talk about that. Wiseguys, never."

"So what does that make him?" Duffy asked.

"New breed," Paterno said. "They're all nuts, heavy into coke."

"If we don't know him, he's gotta be with Frankie Carbonaro," Converi said. "Frankie's been bringing a lot of new people in since he took over the Marino family. A lot of guys from Sicily, a lot of freelancers who had been kept out by the older guys because of their drug dealing."

"Frankie's cash poor," Feurey said. "The other families have the unions and the legit fronts. Frankie's power base was in downtown Brooklyn and the West Bronx, but the Cubans have ripped off most of his numbers banks. So he's been raising money with heavy crime, burglaries, hijackings, hotel jobs, bank jobs. It's all very tightly controlled."

"Frankie's smart," Paterno said. "The older guys hate him. The only way we'll get anything on him in the short term is if one of the other families gives him up."

"So we look for our guy in the Carbonaro family," Duffy said.

"Not easy," said Converi.

"We've been trying to get an undercover in for two years," Feurey said, shaking his head. "Can't even develop an informant. Frankie's too smart."

"He's got some Russian Jew out there in Coney Island who debugs his whole operation once a week," said Converi. "We had a transmitter in one of his park plugs and this guy found it."

"He doesn't sit down with the other four bosses," Feurey said. "We don't know how he communicates with them."

"So what do we do?" Duffy asked.

"We've got film on Frankie," said Feurey. "He's available to the public every night. Hangs out at the Tiebreaker on Ocean Avenue in Brooklyn across from the tennis courts. We have a van there. Infrared film, high-power mikes, the whole deal."

"It's a start," Duffy said. "We got some homework to do on this guy."

Feurey sighed, Paterno shook his head, Converi smiled. They had each picked up the same lead from the tape.

"I guess you were hoping I wouldn't notice," Duffy said.

"Rikers," said Converi.

"Right. The parameters are there. We begin the day Feinstein checked in and we take it to, let's say, three months after he checked out. If we don't get anything we'll go to four, five, etcetera."

"Does Rikers have a computer?" Paterno asked.

"If they do it's probably down," Duffy said. "Anyway, this is strictly a hemorrhoid job. We've got to go through all the prison records for some candidates."

"Maybe we can narrow it down to guys with Italian names," Paterno said.

"I'm glad *you* said that," said Feurey.

Duffy shook his head. "The guy could be Jewish."

"No way," said Paterno. "This is a mixed marriage with Feinstein."

"Hispanic?" Duffy said. "I know he doesn't have the Latin style, but he could be putting on that mafioso act, alotta these guys do."

"This guy ain't acting, but okay, you made your point," Paterno said. "Now how are we gonna work this?"

"We each throw a guy into the pot. We'll let my guy McKinnon run the deal. Send 'em out to Rikers and let 'em pull some candidates out of the file. Then, we'll show the photos to Doctor Winterman. She says she really only remembers the ring and the hair on his chest, but you never know."

Paterno got up and stretched. "The guys are gonna hate this detail."

"Fuck 'em," Duffy said.

And they all laughed.

BINGO!

At 11 A.M. the phone rang in Karen Winterman's bedroom. Although it was in easy reach on her night table, she let it ring three times before picking it up. It was a habit she had picked up in adolescence so that the occasional boy who called wouldn't think she had been sitting by the phone with nothing better to do. The question was, Why had she continued it into adulthood?

"Sorry if I woke you, Doctor Winterman."

It was Inspector Duffy. "I wasn't asleep, Inspector."

"I've got a batch of photos I'd like you to look at. Feel up to it?"

"Sure." She tried to keep the weary edge out of her voice, but he picked it up.

"I know the last few days have been a horror show for you. If you want to make it tomorrow."

"Actually, it'll take my mind off things."

"I'll send a car for you."

"I can find my way, Inspector. I'd like to get a little fresh air."

It was one of those sparkling Manhattan mornings where the sun glinted cheerfully, transforming the most depressing urban sight. The breeze was shivery, yet somehow contained a hint of the warmth to come. The kind of Manhattan morning where you walked along happily for miles before you stopped and realized you had nothing to be happy about.

Karen decided to walk through Central Park to the precinct. As she crossed the street a light-skinned black man popped up from behind a car and came right at her. He walked with a noticeable limp, wincing so painfully that she was almost tempted to ask if he needed help, but she didn't, of course, knowing her gesture would be misconstrued as a pickup. She speeded her pace and didn't look back.

By now she was a familiar figure at the precinct, and they let her walk unchallenged up the stairs to the squad room. Duffy awaited her in his little office. His desk was piled with manila folders. Cardboard envelopes overflowing with legal papers were stacked against the wall. Another phone had been brought in. It rested on the only other chair in the room. Duffy took out a crumpled cigarette, then shook his head and put it back in the pack.

"Please smoke if you want to," Karen said.

He smiled apologetically and lit up. "It's a bad habit I got into thirty years ago. At this point I can't think without a cigarette in my hand." He exhaled through his nose. Karen remembered her father exhaling that way—two jet streams of smoke widening as they came out of his nostrils. "I've been living on cigarettes and coffee for the last three days."

"Do you work with this much intensity on all your cases?" Karen asked. What a strange, stilted question, something you'd ask in a consultation, she thought.

"Depends on the case," Inspector Duffy said. "Some cases have a rhythm. . . ." He broke off with a shy smile. "Oh, well, you don't want to hear this." He handed her a black loose-leaf folder full of mug shots. "Why don't you just look these over?"

Karen scanned the impassive, unfamiliar faces. "They all look so bored."

"There's not a helluva lot to do in prison. Lucky, they're all subnormal. A normal person would go completely insane."

Karen flipped idly through the pages. "You really believe that all these people are crazy?"

"And stupid," Duffy said. "We'd never catch them if they weren't."

"So you're saying a smart person could get away with a crime."

"No. I'm saying a smart person never commits a crime because he weighs the risks against the benefits and decides against it."

"These people have a different definition of intelligence than you do."

"Yeah and they're in jail. I'm not."

She closed the book, shaking her head. Duffy handed her another one.

"So you believe in capital punishment," she said, making conversation.

"Sure."

"As a deterrent?"

"Of course not. You don't deter a mutt. He's too smart. He knows it all."

"So why kill him?"

"To get even, why else?" Duffy's tone was so bitter Karen had to look up. "Have people forgotten about that? I got a guy runnin' around town who killed four cops. When I catch him, and I will, he'll get twenty-five to life, if I'm lucky. Is that fair?"

Duffy ground his cigarette into an overflowing ashtray. "When I came on this job twenty-seven years ago, cop killers never came to trial. You killed a cop, you knew the cops were going to kill you. The public knew it, the press knew it. No problem. I remember there were two detectives in Brooklyn where I started out, Grady and Solloway, two guys in their fifties, who'd killed seven guys in twenty years, all cop killers. A cop killing was big news, it was so rare. Now we have fifteen or twenty a year. Guys trade shots with cops all the time now." He shook his head, "We're out there alone with no backup from the public. People seem to think that the more restraints they put on us the better off they'll be. And then they go around pissing and moaning about crime in the streets. . . ." He laughed and took out another cigarette. "Sounds like I'm running for Mayor?"

Karen smiled. Inspector Duffy turned away, then sat down. "Any luck?"

"I can safely say I've never seen any of these men before," Karen said.

"Keep looking."

Karen turned back to the folder. She could feel Duffy's anxious eyes. Then she turned a page and the man she had seen outside Arnie's apartment was staring up at her. The same dark curly-haired man. He had a smart-aleck smirk as if he had just made a crack and someone had told him to shut up.

"Just like in the movies, Inspector Duffy," she said. "This is the man I saw." And she read the man's name: "Salvatore Pescatore."

Duffy opened the door and shouted for McKinnon. McKinnon came in from the squad room in his shirt-sleeves. Karen was surprised to see his pistol in a holster attached to his belt; she had always thought cops kept their guns in shoulder holsters.

Duffy gave McKinnon the photograph and pointed to the pile of folders on the floor.

McKinnon squatted to go through the folders, putting his gun on the floor next to him. To think that they walk around with this appendage all their waking hours. She remembered how her fellow students had made such an issue of the weapon as phallic symbol, but McKinnon treated his gun more like an encumbrance.

"He's here," McKinnon said, pulling a file out of the pile.

Inspector Duffy barked into the phone: "Get me the DA's office."

"We'll have to verify his addresses," he said to McKinnon. "I want to get a writ for a wiretap and a search."

"Listen to this," McKinnon said. "Pescatore is the proprietor of a store called Feinstein Audio. . . ."

Duffy looked sharply at Karen. Her heart thumped violently. "Arnie had nothing to do with an audio store," she said. "He would have told me. . . ."

Duffy's eyes softened. "Get Doctor Winterman a ride home, McKinnon," Inspector Duffy said. "Right away."

Then he smiled at her. "I'm starting to think I'll make more progress on this case if I trust you, Doctor Winterman."

McKinnon walked her outside. "That's as close to an apology as he'll ever get," he said.

At 9 A.M. Benson went to retrieve his car at the parking lot across from the Port Authority Building. It had been there all night, and the attendant got ready to give him a hard time about a storage charge, but Benson gave him a twenty and he backed away, very humble.

The Pinto was where he had parked it. The key was where he had taped it. It didn't look like the car had been moved or tampered with in any way, but Benson wasn't about to check the trunk on Forty-second and Eighth. For all he knew, they had the cameras grinding and a hundred guys ready to jump him.

So Benson drove up Eighth Avenue to Broadway, and all the way up on Broadway to 156th Street. He picked up the Cross Bronx Expressway from Riverside Drive and crawled through the truck traffic to the Throgs Neck Bridge. It was tough spotting a tail in rush-hour traffic. You never knew who was behind you because he had to be, or wanted to be. But once he cleared the bridge and got on the Expressway heading for Long Island, he had clear sailing. With a handful of cars behind him, he could check which one, if any, was tailing him. He got off at a few exits, drove down service roads, and back onto the highway, checking

the mirror for a car he could pick up. When he was
satisfied he had no tail he drove up to Exit 70 and hit
the road leading to Montauk Point. Finally he reached
a wooded stretch of highway on which he was totally
alone. He pulled onto the shoulder and checked the
tires, pantomiming a man concerned about his car. He
opened the hood and looked inside. Then he went
around to open the trunk.

There was a beat-up old cloth satchel with a flowered pattern—the kind of bag your old Irish aunt
brought when she came to stay the weekend. It was
filled with hundred-dollar bills in stacks, rubber bands
doubled around each stack. Filled to the brim. Bulging
at the seams. There was no telling how much money
was there.

Benson got a wrench out of his toolbox and tinkered
around under the hood for a while. It was something
he had learned on stakeouts: go through all the motions. While he was playing around, he tried to calcu-
late how much money could be in that satchel. A
hundred grand? Two? Three?

After an acceptable period of tinkering, Benson got
back into the car and turned back onto the highway.
On the way back to the city he tried to remember how
many stacks had been on the top layer and decided on
ten as an arbitrary figure. The bag bulged in the
middle, which meant there would be more to each
layer, but ten was enough for purposes of approxima-
tion. Let's say ten across, forty deep. Let's say four
hundred thousand dollars.

Benson pulled in to a rest stop along the Expressway. Right up to a phone where he could reach out of

the window and make his call. He called the Crowley
Funeral Home and asked for Mrs. Crow.

"I don't know if she can come to the phone, sir." It
was that pimple-faced geek.

"Tell her it's Billy."

Seconds later, he heard Carmela's excited breathing. "Billy . . . ?"

"Carmela, I'm sorry to disturb you, but I've got to
see you about something."

"I'll be here all day."

"I gotta see you alone."

"Alone?"

"Can you get away for an hour or two?"

"I don't know, Billy. After all it's . . ."

"I'll buy you dinner, whaddya say? You gotta eat,
right? Nobody's gonna think you're bailin' out if you
go out to eat for an hour or two?"

"I don't know, Billy. The kids . . ."

"It's about the kids, Carmela. It's about their future."

"It's not that I don't want to. . . ."

"I'll meet you outside at seven o'clock, okay?"

"You're sure this is okay, Billy?"

"You won't be sorry, I promise you that. The one
thing you won't be is sorry."

"You okay, Billy?" she asked, full of concern.

"I'm more than okay," he said. His eyes brimmed
over and before he could cover the phone he sobbed.

"Billy, what's the matter?"

Benson let the tears flow. "This may sound weird,
Carmela, but today is the happiest day of my life."

WHAM BAM

At 4:15 that afternoon, Edmund swung off the bed, flexing his ankle gingerly, and tried to walk across the room to the window. This was after six Advils and seven hours of ice and elevation. Edmund held onto the bedpost and stood up. The ankle started to buckle, but managed to hold. He had to shift his weight onto the right side and drag his foot, but he could do it. The pain was intense, but he could stay on top of it. No time for a track meet, but he could move well enough to off a chick who wasn't expecting it.

Sally Fish had been by earlier with the down payment. For three solid hours he had snorted coke and rapped about how great he was and what genius moves he was making. And how he had gone beyond his Uncle Frank and every geep that ever lived because he was willing to innovate and experiment. New people and new ideas.

"You sound like a TV commercial," Edmund had

grumbled. He was waiting for Sally to go so he could ice his ankle.

But Sally was high. His silk shirt was soaked with sweat. He couldn't shut up, couldn't leave, couldn't do anything but rap rap rap.

"If you're so slick, tell me how to do this chick without making it look like a street bang," Edmund had said.

"Simple," Sally said with a smile. "It's wham bam / the lady's dead / where's my bread? It's a little New York tragedy, happens every day. Career woman living alone and liking it. Crack-freak burglar slips into her pad. She comes home too early. Death in the big city. Another promising career nipped in the bud. What are we going to do about these black men who roam the streets raping and killing? It's simply scandalous."

"You want me to make it look like a sex crime?" Edmund said.

"Make it look like the Dutch elm disease, bro, I don't care. Just make it. I'll accept delivery early this evening."

At 5:45 Karen Winterman entered her building. Her mailbox was overflowing with three days' worth of uncollected journals, solicitations—not one personal letter in the pile. She had to struggle around her armful of journals to get her key into the outside door. Had to push all her weight against the heavy glass door to open it wide enough so she could squeeze through.

Suddenly a brown hand appeared on the door frame. It was that man, the one with the limp that she had seen earlier that morning. He held the door with a courteous smile. She hesitated. You weren't supposed to let people into the building unless they had a key or were buzzed up. It had nothing to do with race; there were black people in the building who would jump down her throat if she violated the rule. Still, this man was a stranger. He would take it as a racial affront. After all, he was well-dressed and respectable-looking. Karen murmured "Thank you" and ducked under his arm.

The man limped after her into the elevator and pressed "2" hurriedly before she pressed "3." This was to let her know that he wasn't watching to see what floor she pressed—that he really had a destination. In the elevator the man looked down at his shoes so she wouldn't feel threatened by his glance. Karen could remember scores of encounters with black men in which rituals like these were repeated. Every encounter between the races is fraught with hidden communications, she thought. It was a good subject for a paper.

The man stepped out of the elevator at the second floor, keeping his head down. Karen wanted to smile or say "Have a good day," something to reassure him that she didn't consider him a rapist. But he moved too quickly. As the door slid shut she heard his foot dragging rapidly down the corridor.

Karen had three locks, three separate keys. With an armful of junk mail, it took her two minutes to get the door open.

The door of the back stairway creaked open. There was a dragging sound. Someone breathing. Karen turned and saw only a huge hand heading for her throat. She was lifted off the ground, twisted backward. An arm like an iron bar pressed against her Adam's apple. She couldn't catch her breath. A hand smelling of Ivory soap pinched her nostrils shut as she was pushed into the apartment. *Kick him in the shins. Bite the soft flesh between his thumb and forefinger.* Karen kicked out weakly. She twisted her head, fighting for an inch of air.

Reason with him. Put him at his ease. She tried to speak, but the arm pushed harder against her throat. Her chest heaved. The room whirled. She was falling . . . falling.

He's going to kill me.

In the darkness she heard a strangled sound.

"Please. . . ."

THE BOTTOM LINE

At 6:45 Benson pulled up in front of Crowley's. He sat in the car smoking a cigarette, watching the comings and goings. The second day, and Vinnie was still drawing a nice crowd.

At seven on the nose Carmela hurried down the steps, all hunched over and checking out the street like a burglar bailing out of a house. Benson reached over and opened the door. "Your carriage, madam."

Carmela had trouble getting in. "They certainly don't make these cars for women with tight dresses," she said. She gave her skirt a few futile tugs, then gave up and put her hands over her knees. "Don't look, Billy."

"I'll keep my eye on the road." He offered her a cigarette. "Meanwhile, you just relax, we're going to have a nice dinner."

Benson drove into Manhattan to Beppo's on Grand Street. The Chinese kid in the parking lot sneered at the Pinto with its body cancer and dented fenders. *Should I take the satchel out of the trunk?* Benson wondered. *Can't take it into the joint with me. Can't check it.* Benson heard the tires squealing as the kid parked the Pinto. There was nothing to worry about. With all the Caddies and Mercedeses in the parking lot, the Pinto was the very last car anybody would toss. They'd spend twenty minutes getting a Blaupunkt out of a BMW when all it would take to make five hundred grand was a screwdriver and a couple of good pushes.

Beppo didn't blink when they walked in. A quick "Good evening, Mr. Benson," and he walked them over to Sally's table next to the ferns where nobody could see them. Beppo gave Carmela a sly look on the fly before blending back into the woodwork. A few minutes later he jumped out from behind the bar as Benson headed for the bathroom.

"That your wife, Billy?" he asked.

"Vinnie's wife," Benson said.

Beppo shook his head and took another peek in the dining room at Carmela. Benson could see he was trying to put the two of them together in his mind. "Nice-lookin' woman, Billy. She Italian?"

"Stop starin' at her," Benson said. "The woman's in mourning."

Beppo shrugged. "Nice-lookin' widow, Billy."

Back at the table, Carmela fidgeted uncomfortably. "I feel strange in this black dress."

He took her hand. "I know. You think everybody can look right through you, everybody knows your business. But nobody knows nothin' and nobody cares. They got their own problems. If you ask 'em, they probably think you're goin' to the opera. C'mon, have a drink.''

"I'd better not."

He squeezed her hand. "C'mon."

With a shy smile she asked for an apricot sour. Then she had another. By the time the clams oreganata came, she was looking around the room with interest. "I always wondered what this place was like. I used to find the matchbooks in Vinnie's jacket pockets." She turned to him, her eyes shining. "It's a nice place, Billy."

They shared an order of *linguine frutti di mare*. Benson had *steak pizzaiola*, Carmela, plain broiled chicken. They had a bottle of Valpolicella and were about to order another when Beppo sent over a bottle of Asti Spumanti, "to go with dessert," the waiter said. Benson had cheese cake, Carmela, a *zuppa inglese* so rich in rum she got flushed and had to dab her face with ice water. "My God, this is the best meal I've ever eaten in my life, Billy," she said.

Benson moved his chair closer to her. "From now on you'll be able to eat like this all the time if you want to, Carmela."

"What am I gonna do, win the lottery? Vinnie didn't leave nothin' but debts."

"Vinnie took care of you, Carmela."

"On a detective's salary."

"Vinnie was a crook, Carmela. I'm sorry, there's no other way to put it. I was lyin' the other night."

Carmela lit a cigarette. She didn't look surprised.

"If he took money, he never spent it on his family," she said.

"I was in it with him, Carmela," Benson said. "We

shook down motorists, took payoffs from bookies, Christmas presents from storekeepers. We even tossed a few collars in our time. We did it every way we could, Carmela. If Vinnie bought it for being a crook, there should be a twin coffin and I should be laying next to him, I just want you to know that.''

"Billy, please. . . .'' Carmela slid over and put her arm around him.

"Vinnie hated the job, but he did it as well as any human being could, I swear to God he did. He saved lives. He made the streets safer. He put alotta mutts away, Carmela. Vinnie Crow never walked away from a beef in his life. He did what he was paid to do. Anybody says different I'll blow them away.''

"It's alright, Billy,'' she whispered soothingly.

"Nobody understands us,'' Benson said in a choked, child's voice. He looked up and saw the astonished faces of the other diners. Carmela dipped a napkin in a glass of water and patted the tears off his cheeks.

Benson stood up quickly. "Let's go back to your place, Carmela?'' he asked.

"Billy, my husband's lying in a coffin. . . .''

"I got something for you, Carmela. Something that'll change your life.''

She touched his hand, her eyes soft with concern. "Billy, are you alright?''

"Trust me, Carmela,'' he whispered earnestly. "I would never do anything disrespectful to you. I'd kill myself first.''

They drove back to Brooklyn in silence. As they crossed the Brooklyn Bridge, she turned to him. "Penny for your thoughts?''

"You don't wanna know, Carmela."

"I do, Billy. Tell me, please."

"I was thinkin' how nice it was to finally be alone with you after all these years. Okay? I said you didn't wanna know."

Carmela leaned over and kissed him, leaving his cheek wet with her tears.

The house was seventy, eighty years old and showing its age—"The haunted mansion," Vinnie used to call it. It was three stories of dark wood frame, listing a little to the right like an old man who couldn't stand erect. There was a light burning on the third floor.

"That's Anthony," Carmela said. "He studies up there day and night."

"We'll have to be quiet," Benson said.

Carmela took his arm and walked him around to the back door. "Vinnie and I moved downstairs a few years ago into the dining room," she whispered as they walked through the kitchen. "What with him comin' home late and all the arguing, we didn't want the kids to hear." She turned on the light. "We converted the dining room into a bedroom. Didn't need the space. This family never ate together, even on holidays. We were very unhappy, Billy. Vinnie and I hadn't . . . you know . . . for years."

"Wait here," Benson said. He went outside and got the satchel out of the trunk. When he returned, Carmela was sitting on the bed in a blue silk bathrobe.

Benson averted his eyes, but everywhere he looked there was a mirror, or a window even, where he could see her reflection.

"Here's Vinnie's last will and testament, Carmela," he said. He held the satchel high over his head and spilled its contents in Carmela's lap. She sat there gaping as the stacks of hundreds cascaded around her. Benson shook the last few stacks off the bottom and stood back, breathing hard. There was money everywhere, on the bed, the floor. A few stacks had even slid under the night table. There had to be sixty or seventy of the neatly banded packages, more than he had estimated.

Carmela picked up a stack. "Where does this come from, Billy?"

"It's an IRA, what do you care, it's yours. You're the next of kin."

Carmela's lower lip trembled. "This is dirty money, Billy. I can't take it."

Benson took Carmela's hand.

"You want me to give it to Inspector Duffy and say, 'Here's proof that Vinnie Crow was a crooked cop'?"

She sniffled and shook her head.

"You want me to take it out in the backyard and burn it?"

She looked at him in astonishment. "No."

"You have to take it for Vinnie's honor and your reputation. You have no choice."

Carmela picked a stack up off the floor. "But how much is there?"

"Maybe a half a million. Maybe more."

Carmela mouthed the words "half a million."

"There's fortunes being made in dope, Carmela. These dirtbags are makin' millions, billions, no kiddin'. They're gettin' away with murder, you got no idea. Vinnie figured he'd take a little dip along with everybody else. And you know what I say, Carmela? God forgive me, I say, God bless him. Because now his family is provided for much better than if he stayed straight for thirty years and died in a charity ward somewhere. That's the bottom line. That's what counts."

"My God, Billy, it's all hundreds."

Benson moved a few stacks out of the way and sat down next to her. "You're set for life. If you're smart."

"But I don't know what to do."

"Listen to me. You use the money to live, not for luxury. You put it in the bank a few hundred at a time just to cover bills. This way no large deposits will show up. You take loans out for everything, your boy's tuition, the girls' weddings. No problem now because you know you can pay everything back, and that's how you wash the money. You put the house up as collateral. No problem, right?"

Carmela reached under the bed to retrieve a stack. "But how long can the money last that way, Billy?"

"You're gonna make more with it. Money makes money. But you gotta be very careful because the IAD will be watching you. They'll use up a million man-hours to put a widow in jail. But you're gonna fool 'em, Carmela. You buy income property. You start out with a coupla buildings in this neighborhood. Go to the local bank. Use the death benefits and the Social Security as down payment. Pay the mortgage with the pad money, they'll never know."

Carmela made a helpless gesture. "I'll never be able to do this, Billy."

"Sure you will," he whispered urgently.

"Half this money is yours, Billy," she said. "You were Vinnie's partner."

"He kept me out of this one."

"Because he knew you wouldn't touch drug money," Carmela said.

"Okay, so I drew a line," Benson said, trying to keep his voice down. "That just makes me a coward, not a hero. Trying to have it both ways, so I can make the money and feel clean."

"I think you're a fine man, Billy," Carmela said, her eyes shining.

Benson turned away. "A fine man? If you knew what was in my mind . . ."

He got up and started throwing the money back in the satchel. "Find a good hiding place for it. You got a safe-deposit box?"

"Vinnie had one."

"Not Vinnie's. You get your own. They have to get a court order to open yours. You put a chunk of the money in it. Not all of it. Just a chunk. Then you get coffee cans or Baggies or anything, and you bury it somewhere safe. And don't tell nobody. Not your kids. Don't tell Doreen. I know how close you two are."

"We're not close at all, Billy."

"I just thought because you were always in the house . . ."

"I came to see you, Billy," Carmela said. "Since we're all telling the truth tonight—I always liked you better than Vinnie."

Oh, Jesus Jesus Jesus . . .

She looked up at him imploringly. "I know I shouldn't talk this way with my husband lying in his coffin."

Benson backed up, stopping at the door. "You've had a rough coupla days. . . ."

"The truth is that you were Vinnie's partner and best friend. I met you on my wedding day. I walked down the aisle and saw you standing there and fell in love. Love at first sight, Billy. That's the kind of a cruel trick that life plays on nice Catholic girls like me. I was only one man away from the one I really could have loved. Only one man away." She smiled sadly. "I'm sorry if I'm embarrassing you, Billy."

"I'm glad you said it. Even though there's nothing we can do, I'm glad you said it."

Carmela looked at him, her lips trembling. She rose with sudden ferocity and thumped her fists against her forehead. "That bum. That rotten, degenerate bum . . ."

Benson rushed across the room to silence her. "Carmela, for Chrissake."

"This money is small compensation for the years he took away from me."

"Take it for your boy's sake," Benson said. "It'll give him a boost. That's all anybody needs. It'll guarantee nobody shits on him like they did his old man."

Carmela reached out to him. "Stay with me, Billy."

"I got one more thing to take care of. One more thing for Vinnie. Then I'll come back, Carmela. I promise."

Benson hurried out of the house and into the Pinto without bothering to case the street for double-parked cars, dog walkers—any of the obvious signs of a tail. He didn't notice the white van that had slid into a driveway up the street where Sally Fish and Santo sat passing a vial.

"Did you see that satchel that he brought into the house?" Sally asked. "That's the satchel you gotta get."

"Done," Santo said and started out of the car.

Sally laughed and pulled him back by the shoulder. "Not now, the house is full of sleeping people."

"They bother me, they be sleepin' for good."

"Tomorrow there's a funeral," Sally said. "The house'll be empty. You'll probably find it in a closet or under a bed."

"Sure, Mr. Feinstein."

"It's an easy job. Let's keep it that way."

DO YOU BELIEVE IN MIRACLES?

Sal Pescatore is a new player," Lieutenant Paterno said. "He's an up-and-comer."

Paterno had come to Duffy's temporary office in the 19th Precinct with a briefcase full of material about Frankie Carbonaro and the Marino family. He had charts that went back to the mid-fifties, and on one of them he had found the name Benny Pescatore, a.k.a. Benny Fish. From that he had constructed Sal Pescatore's lineage.

"Benny the Fish ran a nothing bookie spot out of a fish store in Sheepshead Bay."

"Was he made?" Duffy asked.

"No, never. He was part of the Marino talent pool in Brooklyn. He was married to Frankie C's sister."

"So this kid is Frankie's nephew."

"Oh, yeah. Well, that's how Benny stayed in the rackets. Frankie C took care of him." Paterno smiled in reminiscence. "Benny was a bigger fish than any fish he ever sold. He was the worst bookie in the world. Guys were always beating him because he couldn't keep his books right. Got so bad old man Marino took the spot away from him and put him to working for Abie Silver in shylocking. That was about the time Sonny DiMaria beat all the shys in Sheepshead Bay for about three hundred Gs, and you're talking 1962 here, that was a lot of money. All the bosses had a sit-down and sent out guys to find him. Meanwhile, Sonny's wife went to Benny and borrowed twenty Gs more. Said she was gonna use the money to find Sonny and bring him back.''

Even Duffy had to smile. "What happened as if I don't know.''

"Nothing happened. Frankie was too big by then to allow anybody in his family to be harmed. Wouldn't even make good on the money. Abie had to write it off as a bad debt. Of course Benny went back to selling fish for real.''

"Is this the first we're hearing of his son?'' Duffy asked.

"He's on the map already. We first heard about him in a wiretap on a hijacking suspect. The guy had taken a truckful of electronic equipment. Pescatore's name came up. He wouldn't talk to the grand jury so he got hit with contempt.''

"So he was sent to Rikers, where he met Arnold Feinstein,'' Duffy said.

"No proof of that connection,'' Paterno said.

"Okay. What do we know about him?''

"He's no jerk like his old man for one thing. He's a real earner for Frankie C. Organized the garment center right under the noses of the other families.

Burglaries, hijacking, fencing, getting safe retail out-
lets, he's been doing it all.''

"Drugs?'' Duffy asked.

Paterno shook his head. ''No information. The guy's
a user, heavy, they say, but so are all the new guys.
You're talking about a five-million-dollar operation.
That involves a big organization, and none of the
informants know anything about it.''

"So he didn't use the Marino people,'' Duffy said.
''He started his own organization. He recruited on the
street. Made his own trips. Does he have a passport?''

"No passport under the name Salvatore Pescatore.''

"He would use a forged one. Set up an operation in
South America. Recruit people to organize the trips so
the mules never met him. He could insulate himself
pretty well. But not from everybody. Somewhere
there's an individual who can tell us a lot about his
operation.''

Paterno shook his head. ''As far as we know, Sally
Fish buttons up the garment center for his Uncle
Frank. He's a very bad guy with a lot of blood on his
hands.''

"I need a piece of real evidence,'' Duffy said.
''Something with probable cause so I can convince a
judge to give me a search warrant. That Locklear from
the DEA knows something about this, but he won't
share it. I get the feeling he's working on Pescatore,
too. I'd like to beat him to the punch.''

"You have a positive identification from that psy-
chologist,'' Paterno said. ''That should be enough.''

"I want to keep her out of this as long as I can. A
smart lawyer could break her testimony down pretty

quick if she were the only witness. I'd rather use her as the icing on the cake."

Paterno shuffled through the papers. "The only hook with Feinstein is the name of the store. Pescatore opened it when he got out of Rikers. There is no Arnold Feinstein connected with it in any way as far as we can ascertain."

"Ascertain," Duffy said. "Nice word."

"I use it in court a lot," Paterno said.

"Doctor Winterman says Feinstein could never be that big a dope dealer," Duffy said.

"She's prejudiced, she was fucking him," Paterno said.

Duffy winced. Paterno noticed the wince and got real busy with his papers again. McKinnon stuck his head in the door.

"I was in the shithouse."

"Go back and wipe your ass," Duffy said irritably.

McKinnon entered with a hurt look. Paterno shrugged in sympathy.

"Johnny boy, you could use a few hours rack time," Paterno said.

Duffy held up his right hand. There were burn marks on his second and third fingers. "I took two butt naps today already. You know the kind that you light up a cigarette while you're reading something and you wake up when the cigarette burns down to your fingers. Two of them today already. I'm very well rested."

"I don't know why you're pushing this. We're making progress."

"Not fast enough for me," Duffy said. "This case

has got a clock on it for me. I keep expecting more homicides, don't ask me why.''

The phone rang. Duffy snapped it up like it was moving.

''Inspector Duffy . . .''

It was Karen Winterman. He couldn't tell if she was laughing or crying.

''Do you believe in miracles, Inspector?''

Duffy called the 20th Squad, Dr. Winterman's local precinct, to cover her building. When he and McKinnon arrived ten minutes later there was still nobody there from the squad. McKinnon laughed softly.

''What's so funny?'' Duffy snapped.

''I'm just thinking of what you're going to do to the guys in the Twentieth Squad.''

''Get 'em over here right now,'' Duffy said. He got out of the car and slammed the door.

Karen Winterman was waiting outside her apartment. ''Thank you for coming so soon, Inspector,'' she said. She seemed abnormally calm, but that was the way some people responded to traumatic situations. After fifteen minutes, Duffy decided she was in deep shock. She told her story in a coherent fashion, but none of it made any sense. Duffy made a mental note to call an ambulance for her and then asked her to repeat what had happened after she regained consciousness.

''That is interesting,'' she said as if she were talking about some experiment she had done. ''I woke up to this weird sound. It was like a cat in pain, you know, when they get something in their paws. It took me a while to realize what had happened. . . .''

McKinnon and some of the precinct detectives were poking around the apartment. There wasn't much to see; it didn't look like anything had been taken. In a burglary like this, the perp usually tosses the joint, throwing everything in the middle of the room.

"Anything missing, Doctor Winterman?" Duffy asked.

"Nothing," she said. "I don't even think he searched the apartment. He obviously was not a burglar."

Duffy winced. The next question was automatic, he'd asked it a thousand times in similar situations. But now, for some reason, he couldn't get the words out.

"Did he . . . ?"

"No," Dr. Winterman said. "He didn't touch me. I guess he thought about it. He tied my hands with a towel and pulled my slacks down around my ankles, but he left my panties on. When I woke up I thought maybe he did it while I was unconscious, but there was no wetness or soreness. . . ."

She was excited, euphoric. People got that way when their lives had been saved. All they could think about was how lucky they were to be alive. Later they sank into a hopeless gloom in which all they could think about was how close they had come to being dead.

"He loosened the knots on the towel," she said. I felt the bed bounce so I knew he was sitting down next to me. And then—" She leaned forward and touched Duffy's arm. She was sitting on the bed where she had been tied, wearing the slacks that had been pulled down to her ankles. Duffy felt a morbid excitement growing in him. "—Then the strangest thing happened. He started speaking to me. Told me about his father, who was a great saxophone player. And one day people would see how great he was when the memorial record album came out and everybody started writing about him in those little jazz magazines. He said his brother had gone to MIT on a scholarship and worked in the space shuttle program, but had shot himself because his white girlfriend had gone for an abortion without telling him."

"It's a psycho rap," Duffy said. "You hear it from addicts and petty criminals. . . ."

"He dealt with that," Dr. Winterman said excitedly. "He said no one could ever believe the kind of family he had because he was such a bum."

Duffy was unshakable. "That's part of it. Even psychos try to be plausible."

"Well, anyway, he went off that and started talking about the city. How he just couldn't understand how people walked around without a gun or a knife. Didn't they know how dangerous it was? Especially old people and women. Women like me. He couldn't understand how women could walk around like everything was okay, because they could be raped and killed ten times a day."

"What did you do while he was talking?"

"Nothing, my God, nothing. Reluctant rapists like that are the most dangerous. They'll kill to cover up their guilt."

McKinnon came out of the kitchen. "That's right," he said.

Duffy looked at him in disbelief.

McKinnon swallowed hard and went back into the kitchen.

Duffy turned back to Karen. "And then . . . ?"

She shook her head. "He left. Without another word. Except I think I heard him crying."

McKinnon came out of the kitchen and stood there, waiting until Duffy looked over at him. "We found something. I don't know what it means."

There were two empty ice trays and a soggy bath towel in the kitchen sink.

"Did you use these, Doctor Winterman?" Duffy asked.

"No."

"Take them in and see if we can raise some prints," Duffy told McKinnon. "Looks like he might have had a headache or an injury."

"He was limping," Karen said. "Quite painfully."

"So he took time out to put a cold compress on his foot. Anything else?" he asked McKinnon.

"Nothing. I don't think he touched anything in the apartment."

"Anything but me," Karen said.

Duffy took Karen back into the bedroom while the technical people went over the kitchen. She seemed unaffected by what had happened to her, almost accepting of it. He'd seen this before, with women especially. They'd get this feeling that maybe they deserved the attack. They even felt gratitude toward their assailant for having spared their lives. Once they were in that frame of mind, it was very hard to get any cooperation out of them.

"After all you've been through, Doctor Winterman, this was really a terrible coincidence," he said.

"Coincidence," she repeated thoughtfully. Then with a mocking look at him she put her hands in her lap and said in a mechanical voice like a good little girl at her catechism: "Coincidence begets mysticism, which begets religion, which begets sin and retribution, which beget repression, guilt, psychosis. . . . By giving significance to random events we impute a hidden logic, which leads to the creation of a hidden power controlling our lives. We then invent strategies to propitiate this power. In other words, we pray. . . ." She broke off suddenly. "Well, Inspector, what do you think?"

"What is that?"

"This is the famous, and I do mean famous, introduction to Professor Karl Auerbach's famous lecture on Freud's *Future of an Illusion,* which he gave every year at the conclusion of his 'Freud as Literature' course. Professor Auerbach believed in coincidence as a determining factor in the development of strategies for social survival. Do you agree?"

"It's a crazy world," Duffy said. "You never know what's going to happen to you from one moment to the next."

"Oh, I suppose so," she said. She threw herself down on the bed, the back of her hand shielding her eyes. Duffy stood over her in confusion. He had the feeling he'd disappointed her. For some reason that was one thing he didn't want to do.

"That man was right," she said. "We really don't know what kind of city this is. . . ."

Outside, Duffy grabbed McKinnon. "Set up a twenty-four-hour surveillance of Karen Winterman. Circulate photos of Pescatore and copies of the sketch of the mugger. If these men are spotted in the vicinity,

I want them tailed, not collared, you understand. You supervise this.''

McKinnon ran his hand through his hair in exasperation. "C'mon, boss, I haven't been off my feet in thirty-six hours."

"So sit down while you're doing it," Duffy snarled. "She's the only eyewitness we've got and I'm not giving them another chance at her."

"What do you mean them? I thought you said this was a coincidence?"

"I don't believe in coincidences . . . or miracles."

A HIT OR A MISS

*T*here were spots all over the city where soldiers in the Marino family congregated. Frank Carbonaro never went near them, but he had a digital beeper with all their numbers programmed onto it. The beeper started going crazy at eight o'clock that evening, and by midnight numbers were still popping up from every spot in the city. Frankie sent Uncle Al to find out what was going on. Uncle Al was back in a half hour.

"This you're not gonna like."

Sally Fish had a beeper programmed to Frankie C's private numbers. He was driving home on Ocean Parkway when it started buzzing. The number was Frankie's safe house in Seagate, at the very end of Coney Island, across the street from the ocean. It was the last house on the block, a very private place. Sally had buried a guy in wet cement in the basement there a few years earlier.

When he pulled up he noticed only one light burning in the living room, but a bunch of cars parked all around. He recognized Frankie's Mercedes and the beat-up old Chevy Caprice of Sammy Calcagno, a head case who collected for shylocks in the neighborhood.

Sammy was sitting in the living room with two guys he didn't know.

"Boss is upstairs," he said with a jerk of his head.

"Where's Uncle Al?" Sally asked.

Sammy didn't answer, and Sally climbed the stairs, enraged at the offhand treatment he had gotten from this nobody.

Frankie C was in a small back bedroom. He had a little desk set up there, a coffee machine, and a cooler. Uncle Al was snoozing on the bed as Sally entered. Frankie shook the bed and Uncle Al got up, stretching painfully.

"You're keepin' everybody awake these days, Sal," he said and left the room, closing the door gently. Sally heard the lock click and turned angrily to Frankie.

"Since when does that douchebag Sammy Calcagno have the right to cold-shoulder me?"

Frankie C shook off the complaint. "The cops have been asking around about you."

"Askin' who?"

"People on the street. Alotta people. Paterno, the OC cop in Queens, thinks he's got reliable stools. He don't know they come back to me. Or maybe he does know and he's sending me a message. We got a little war goin', him and me."

Sally sat on the bed and reached for a cigarette, but Frankie raised a hand to stop him.

"Not in here, Sal, room's too small."

That wasn't the reason and Sally knew it. His Uncle Frank wanted to take away his crutch. His Uncle Frank was mad.

"What are they asking about?"

"You and the garment deals. You and the drug business. You and the cop killings. You're a one-man crime wave these days, Sal."

"They can't touch me, Uncle Frank."

"Yesterday they didn't know you existed. Today they know who you are, who you're related to, and what you do for a living. Tomorrow they'll have a search warrant and a wiretap."

"They don't know where I live."

"You wanna bet your left nut they know by tomorrow? You gotta get over this habit of thinkin' everybody's stupid but you. Everybody in jail is a genius, just ask 'em."

Sally got up with an aggrieved look and paced the tiny room. "I don't know why you're puttin' me through this, Uncle Frank. I do everything you tell me right to the letter. I pulled a move last night that was unprecedented in the annals of crime just to get that stool-pigeon cop his money. It was fuckin' brilliant, that's the only word for it. . . ."

Frankie gestured impatiently. "How many people can slide you into those cop killings?"

Sally stopped and pretended to be thinking hard. "Only two. Benson, the cop, and Edmund, the shooter. They're the only two." Sally stopped pacing and sat down on the bed, looking carefully at his uncle. "Am I in trouble, Uncle Frank?"

"You're in more trouble than you've ever been in your life."

"Is that why you got those three *gavones* downstairs?"

Frankie snarled and came around the desk at him. "You little prick, I'll strangle you with my own hands. I don't need no fuckin' gorillas for you." He slapped Sally hard on the side of the head. "Who else can hook you into these killings?" he shouted loud enough to be heard downstairs.

Sally rubbed his head slowly. He had never heard his uncle raise his voice. "A shrink, a woman. She must be the one who fingered me in the first place."

Frankie C stood over him, arms hanging loosely, staring down with fierce concentration. "Where does a shrink come into this?"

"This kid Arnie Feinstein, she was his shrink."

"Where does he come into this?"

"I used his name, his apartment, phones. I funneled all the goods through him. Then when that thing happened with the cops I figured I had to take him out, so I hotshotted him, slipped him some of this Mexican smack, pure. He was gonna die from an overdose anyway, it was just a matter of time. No big deal. He was a good kid. What are you gonna do? It was either him or me."

"I'm still lookin' for this shrink you're talkin' about."

"He must have called her while I was in the bathroom or something. Because as I was leaving she was just comin' and got a pretty good look at me."

"So . . . ?"

"So I guess she must have fingered me for the cops."

"What did they do, show her a picture of every curly-haired guinea with his shirt open and too much gold around his neck?" Frankie smacked him again. "You lyin' bastard, if you weren't my sister's son you'd be hangin' from a meathook."

Sally shielded his face. "Okay, okay. You can't blame me for holdin' this out on you. They got me on film. . . ."

Frankie backed up and reached for a pack of cigarettes on the desk. "They what?"

"I was in this film, video is what it was, that this kid made. It was like an interview of how he met me on Rikers. I'm in the dark, you know, like a mystery guest. You can't see my face or anything. He showed it to me before he gave it to her."

"Why'd you do this?"

"I'd been up for days with this kid, snortin' coke. You get a little crazy. The kid was doin' this video as part of his treatment. He just asked it as a favor."

Frankie sat back down behind the desk. "This kid blowin' you or what?"

"C'mon, Uncle Frank. I got tight with the guy, that's all. You need somebody to talk to in the joint."

"I was at Sing Sing for three years and never talked to nobody."

"You don't have to talk to people, Uncle Frank. You're better than me in that respect."

"In that respect?"

"Yeah, right, in that respect. Just because you're mad at me don't mean I'm gonna kiss your ass. I'm creative in a way that nobody else in this life ever even thought to be. You see, you're a racketeer, Uncle Frank. I'm a criminal, a master criminal. I do things with a flair. I can spot talent better than anybody. That colored kid, the best. I got a little girl now from Ecuador can do anything. And meanwhile I make more money for you than all these nonentities put together."

Frankie looked at Sally for a long time without saying anything.

"The suspense is killing me, Uncle Frank," Sally finally said. "Is it a hit or a miss?"

Frankie lit another cigarette and sipped his cold coffee. It was another minute or two before he spoke.

"You're smart and you're an earner and you got balls, Sal. But you got a big mouth and that cancels everything else out."

"So . . . ?"

Frankie considered him again for a while. "You got a copy of this video?"

"In my apartment."

"What else you got in the apartment?"

"Expense money. A coupla pieces, clean pieces. Nothin' in writing. I keep everything in my head."

"Got any coke in there?"

"Yeah, I keep some around for consumption purposes."

"That means about a pound." Frankie stood up and glared at Sal, daring him to make a smart remark. But Sal stayed silent. Frankie opened the door. Uncle Al was out in the hall smoking a cigar. "Get Sammy up here," Frankie said. He closed the door and lit another cigarette.

"As long as you're polluting the environment, can I have one too?" Sally asked.

"No." Frankie went back behind the desk. They sat there listening to Sammy huffing up the stairs, taking the steps two at a time. He was flushed when he entered. He gave Sally a quick, gloating look.

"I got a job for you, Sammy," Frankie said.

"Anything, Mr. Carbonaro."

"Give him your keys, Sal."

Sally Fish obeyed. He knew better than to argue with his uncle in front of an underling.

"Go over to Sal's apartment. You're looking for money. How much, Sal?"

"About forty, fifty Gs."

"A gun? Two guns?"

"A Thirty-eight and a nine mil," Sally said.

"Coke. How much, Sal?"

Sally's reply was barely audible.

"How much?" Frankie demanded.

"About a pound," he said louder.

"And there's a videotape. In a box, Sal?"

"Yeah, a black box like what they all come in."

"Tell Sammy where the stuff is, Sal."

Sally cleared his throat. "In a secret compartment under the bar. You slide your hands along the outside rim until you feel a seam in the wood, then you just press down and it'll spring open."

"You got all that?" Frankie asked.

Sammy repeated, "Money, two guns, pound of blow and a videotape. I got it, Mr. Carbonaro."

"If you have a problem, go outside to a pay phone and call the bar. Tell them to beep the boss. Don't use the phone in the apartment."

"Right, Mr. Carbonaro."

"Bring all the stuff back here."

"Right." Sammy turned to go.

"Wait a second," Frankie said. "Give him your car keys, Sal."

Sally winced, but flipped his keys to Sammy.

"Drive the car around the back of the house," Frankie said.

"Right, Mr. Carbonaro."

Sally waited until Sammy's footsteps had receded before turning in agony to his uncle. "Why did you humiliate me in front of this bum? I could have emptied my own pad out."

"Hey, I'm just a dumb racketeer," Frankie said, "but I guarantee there's two cops sittin' outside your building right now waitin' for you to show so they can plant a gun on you and say they noticed a bulge in your pants, which gives them the right to search your apartment. Sammy'll walk right by them."

Sally raised his hands protectively. "Okay, okay, but why'd you take my car? I got some moves to make on this thing."

"You make them from here, Sal. You're not goin' anywhere until everything is squared away."

Sally went pale. Sweat prickled on his forehead. "I gotta have mobility on this, Uncle Frank. I'm doin' something very complex."

"Do it on the phone, Sal." Frankie slapped Sally gently on the cheek. "Be creative."

AN OLD LADY IN BROOKLYN

Around dawn Edmund could feel himself becoming delirious. The pain had been transformed into a rat trapped in his ankle. He didn't know how the rat had gotten inside his body, but there it was, squealing, gnawing, trying to get free. Finally it bit through the bone and broke the skin. Blood flecking its whiskers, it rose in a blue cloud over his head, and there it hovered, a dark shadow in a blue cloud, writhing and clawing. . . .

His mouth was dry, his forehead burned with fever. He had run out of ice and was waiting for a new batch, but he knew he would be out of his mind before it froze up.

"I got an hour, maybe two," he told Karen Winterman, Ph.D. She had been in the house when he got home, sitting on the bed, looking up at him with such gentle reproach that he swore then and there that he'd protect her, that he had a plan. "The fish stinks from the head, you understand," he told her. "If I get the money man there's no contract, and Sally Fish goes away. You understand?"

But she shook her head and gestured hopelessly.

"No, you can't understand any of this, baby, I know. All this shit's too evil for you. And you know what I can't understand? I can't understand how you and me and my mother and my brother and Sally Fish and my father can all be in the same human race. We shouldn't even be on the same planet."

He told her about the dude in Rikers who'd discovered Christ and told him, "We must learn to respect those who are weaker than ourselves . . . for Jesus says the meek shall inherit the earth. . . ." And when somebody stuck him in the neck with a shiv, he screamed, "I'm glad, Jesus, I'm glad," as they carried him out of C block on a stretcher.

He told her about what it was like to be crazy. Because it wasn't like just being out of your mind all the time. It was like going to sleep and waking up, going to sleep and waking up ten, twenty times during the day, and when you wake up you can't remember what you dreamt about while you were sleeping. But slowly, you're not waking up as much as you used to and you know the time's coming when you'll be asleep forever. It makes you so scared you whimper like a little boy and cry for your mother because if she comes and holds you and smooths your forehead with her cool hand, you won't never go to sleep and you'll be alright.

And then the phone rang. Edmund put a finger to his lips. "Don't say nothin', I don't want him to know you're here." But before he picked it up he had a

etter idea. "You better tip. He might have some kind
f electronic way of knowin' that there's more than
ne person in the room. Better go home, I'll catch up
o you later. I'll bring you the key so you can get
vorkin' on my old man's album right away."

The phone was ringing. Karen Winterman, Ph.D.,
at there shaking her head. She didn't want to leave
im.

But Edmund waved her away. "It's okay, baby, I'll
e fine. Don't worry about me."

In a second she was gone. It was safe to pick up the
hone.

"How ya doin', champ? How's your head? Did I
nterrupt anything? You're not humping, are you? That
vould be the day."

"What do you want?" Edmund said, trying to keep
he pain out of his voice.

"Just touchin' base, asshole, what do you think I
vant? There's the matter of a little job that I put some
noney down on. I mean, I know black people ain't
amous for their long memories. . . ."

"What about the job?"

"What about gettin' it done? Tomorrow, you under-
tand. Six P.M. at the latest. You can catch her comin'
1ome from work."

"You gotta tell me who I'm workin' for," Edmund
aid.

"You're workin' for me as usual."

"That ain't good enough."

"You shakin' me down for more bread now at zero
1our? That ain't square business."

"You the wrong guy to be talkin' about square
usiness. Last time I did something for you I almost

got killed. This time I gotta know who and what, you understand.''

There was a long silence. Sally's voice came through muffled like he was cupping his hand over the phone. "Listen, Edmund, I'm in a jackpot here.''

"And don't tell me nothin' about no code of silence motherfucker. You mafia guys is just as big rats as anybody else I ever seen in the joint.''

"There's a reason. . . .''

"Ain't no reason. Ain't no nothin'. Your deposit is not returnable, man, unless you wanna come up here and try to get it.''

Another long silence. Sally was breathing fast like a man running hard. Or running scared. "You wouldn't believe me if I told you, Edmund.''

"You just tell me, I'll check it out.''

"It's an old Jewish woman, eighty years old. It's her contract.''

The woman with the lead-tipped cane. The woman who had attacked Karen outside the funeral home.

"She owns property in Sheepshead Bay, little buildings. Rents to my Uncle Frank for his bookies. She came to him with the contract.''

"Why does she want this bitch killed?" Edmund asked.

"Winterman was her grandson's shrink. The kid OD'd and the old lady blames Winterman for his death.''

"And this Karen Winterman is nothing to you," Edmund said.

"I don't even know the bitch. Hey, man, this old lady's good for the bread if that's what's bothering you.''

"Yeah, yeah, that's it, that's bothering me."

"You gotta take my word for that."

"Your word ain't worth shit," Edmund said.

"Then get off the gig, motherfucker!" Sally shrieked. It was the cocaine clicking in, you could hear it over the phone. "I don't need you, nigger. I got a cop as backup. He'll just walk right up to the bitch, flip her the shield, and take her right up to her apartment."

"You're lyin'," Edmund said. "Ain't nobody but me."

"You think so. Then don't show. Because tomorrow at six Karen Winterman's gonna get clipped, one way or another." And he hung up.

Edmund crawled into the kitchenette and up to the refrigerator where he had put his socks in the freezer. He crawled back to get his shoes and finished dressing sitting on the floor. He pulled the valise out from under the bed. The key was right on top of it. He opened it up and a yellowed fragment of newspaper fluttered out. It was part of an old review of his father's septet: "The plangent tones of Thomas Renard's tenor sax lingered on long after the set was over and we were on the subway heading back downtown. . . ." Edmund put the paper back in the valise and locked it up. He put the key in his pocket. "This is for you, Karen," he said. Then he crawled to the door, grasped the knob and pulled himself up. From now on he would have to stand on his feet. The pain shot to the top of his head and back down again. Okay, that was as bad as it was going to get. He got the .22 out of the false panel in the oven and took a steak knife out of the drawer. Serrated edge, but it didn't matter. She was an old woman.

There was a florist across the street. They didn't have a wreath, but they said they could make one up in ten minutes. He stood there waiting. He saw himself swaying in the mirror, saw the chick who worked there staring at him in disgust. *It's okay, they think I'm a junkie, that's all.* He bought the wreath, stand and all.

It was a long ride to Coney Island. He had to slide over and drive with his left foot, keeping his right foot on the seat. People in other cars stared sullenly at him. A truck driver yelled. He swerved to avoid a guy on a bicycle. The car drifted out from under him. He was driving like a drunk. He aimed the car to get it through the toll booth. Gave the cop a ten-dollar bill.

"Keep the change."

The cop peeked in and started to say something, but Edmund drove away. In the rearview mirror he saw a cop get out of a car and look after him, then walk back, hoisting his pants up.

Edmund drove out to the Seagate Funeral Home. He brought the wreath up the stairs and was met halfway by an old Jew in shirtsleeves shaking with palsy.

"Flowers for the funeral," he said.

"All over," the old Jew said. "Nobody here."

"People who were here yesterday. The old lady . . ."

"Mrs. Krakauer. All over. They buried her grandson already. She's sitting shiva at home. You can take it there."

The old man went inside and came back a moment later with a smudged business card. "Seagate Funeral

Home, Shlomo Fileman, Lic. Funeral Dir." The address was scrawled on the bottom.

The old lady, Mrs. Krakauer, lived at Brighton First, an old building between the El and the beach. It was a dead-end street, cars parked on both sides, a little horseshoe turn at the boardwalk. It would take a U-turn with a couple of moves to get off the block. In case anything went wrong, he was finished. Couldn't park on the avenue. He would faint from the pain if he had to walk more than a block. Couldn't double-park, there wouldn't be enough space for cars to pass. The only solution was to pull into the horseshoe by the boardwalk where there were big "No Parking" signs. It was about a fifty-foot walk back and forth. Couldn't run. It would have to be smooth, no hassles. Ring the bell. If the lady answers, step inside. Has to be a small apartment, you can clock it with a look. If there's nobody around, cut her throat. If there's someone in the pad, step in and check it out. Hand her the flowers, count the house. One or two, they go with her. More than that you wait in the lobby and get her when they leave.

The apartment was on the first floor, right over the street. The outer door was unlocked the way it always was in these old buildings. Edmund leaned on the bell. He heard the cane thumping. The door opened off the chain. Edmund held up the flowers. "Mrs. Krakauer?"

The old woman looked at him without comprehension. Edmund put his shoulder to the door and pushed in, snapping the chain off the latch. He slammed the door and showed the woman the knife. She didn't flinch, just stared at it with fierce dark eyes.

"The deal is off," Edmund said.

The old woman raised her cane, but Edmund was ready and snatched it out of the air.

"I protect my old lady," he said. "I stand between her and the rest of the world."

The old woman looked at him calmly. "You want money?"

Edmund braced himself on her cane and swiped at her with the knife, once, and then backhanded, coming real close to her throat. "You think I won't kill you 'cause you're old?"

The old woman shrugged. "So . . . ?"

Edmund's legs buckled. He put his weight on the cane and tried to keep his balance. His eyes teared with pain. He staggered past the old woman toward the kitchen to get some ice. The mirror on the mantelpiece was covered with a bedspread. Through the open door of the bedroom he could see a mirror over a dressing table covered with a pillow case. He stumbled and clawed at the wall digging his fingers into the flowered paper. There was a photo of a little white boy in a sailor suit. It shook and fell off the wall.

The old woman held some crumpled bills out to him. There were tattoo marks on her outstretched wrist. Looked like the kind of tattoo kids gave each other in the joint.

"Lyin' old bitch," Edmund said. "I'm gonna kill you."

She thrust the money at him. "Go. I am already dead. *Ich bin shoyn toyt*. Go!"

The old woman seemed to dissolve in a hot blur. Like a ghost. Edmund waved the cane to fend her off.

She came out of the mists waving something. "I know more about killing than you."

Edmund tried to move around her. His ankle went out from under him and he went down hard. He rolled over and pulled himself up on the arm of a chair. He was throbbing right up to the small of his back.

"I gotta get things straight," he said.

The old woman was gone. He heard her voice as if from a great distance. She was across the room. Too far away. "I will call the police," she was saying.

The *police*. The police were going to kill Karen. They were going to knock on her door and hold up their badges to the peephole. Then go in and kill her.

Leaning on the cane, Edmund limped to the door.

"I gotta get things straight," he said.

NOBODY EVER GETS EVEN

After leaving Carmela, Benson had driven out to Baldwin. He sat in the car outside his house until all the lights went out. Then he waited another hour until he was sure the Valium had hit and Doreen was unconscious for the evening. She was snorting like a starving hippo when he slid into bed next to her. Careful not to touch her, he eased the covers over his chest and lay there staring up at the ceiling until sunrise.

He awoke with the sun burning through the slats of the venetian blinds. It was almost two o'clock. Doreen had let him sleep all this time. As he shaved he heard her poking around in the kitchen. He took a shower and took his time about getting dressed, hoping she'd be out by the time he got downstairs. But she was waiting for him. She'd stay there until Easter if she had to.

There was an empty jar of Folger's Instant on the

counter in the kitchen. Doreen had really been stock-piling the caffeine since morning, he could see that. She was all dressed up, lipstick, makeup . . . and she was spoiling for a fight.

"Where were you last night?"

"Carmela was in pretty bad shape, so I sat with her."

"Until six o'clock in the morning?"

"You wanna let me finish?"

"Carmela went home to bed at seven o'clock last night. I called the funeral parlor."

"What are you, a detective all of a sudden?"

"We're through, Billy."

Benson slumped over the table, head in hands. "For Chrissake, Doreen, put it on hold for a coupla days."

"This is something I should have done a long time ago. We have no life together. While I'm still young enough I want to try for something else."

"Doreen . . ."

"I'm going to a lawyer right now, Billy. Don't try to stop me."

"I don't want to stop you, just slow you down. Your new life can wait a coupla weeks, can't he?"

"You would think that," Doreen said. She stormed out, slamming a cabinet shut. A moment later she was back. "Just because you're a liar and a cheat, you think everybody else is."

"I don't think, I don't care."

"I'd appreciate if you weren't here when I get back." She stormed out again. And came back again a moment later. "Your Spanish girlfriend called."

"Look, Doreen, I don't have a . . ."

"You must have gotten this one right off the banana boat, I could hardly understand a word she said."

She threw a crumpled piece of paper on the table. "Tell her she's in America now, she'd better make up a better code."

Benson unfolded the paper and read: "The black man will be at 310 West 89th Street at five o'clock. Your only chance."

McKinnon was nervous. He had too many men on this detail. All the years of begging his bosses for more backup on undercover operations, more bodies on stakeouts, he had never thought he would come to a point where he would look around and say to himself: *Too much backup, too many bodies, we're gonna end up bunkin' into each other.*

Duffy had gotten him eight guys from Anti-Crime. He had two guys from Major Case following Karen Winterman wherever she went. Right now, according to their last report, she was walking through Central Park on her way home from work. He had put a punked-out Anti-Crime guy with an earring and a guitar in front of her building. There were three guys in a phony N.Y. Telephone van across the street. Two guys at one end of the block, two guys in the car with him. Karen Winterman was covered just like Duffy had wanted.

Still, McKinnon had that incomplete feeling. With Duffy you always felt you were being tested. So now it was like Duffy had said, *I'm giving you more man-power than you ever had. I dare you to blow this.*

It was all too good to be true. Something had to go wrong. Like one of those deals where four guys sit in front of a building and the target sneaks out the back window because you forgot to cover the rear of the building. Or where the target goes into a bar and the undercover can't tail him in because he doesn't have enough petty cash to order a drink. It was one of those deals. Something had been overlooked, McKinnon was sure of it.

The block was calm enough. Nobody around except an old black guy, all hunched over with a cane and a Yankee cap, limping in and out of the building. That was probably the super. Across the street a cute little Spanish broad—mother's helper or something—was sitting on the stoop of a brownstone rocking a baby carriage. Hanging out on the block because she was too lazy to go to the park, probably. No problem there.

No problem anywhere, actually, except in McKinnon's head. A lot of that was the paranoia you got working for Duffy. McKinnon felt his eyes twenty-four hours a day. He would lay awake nights with the nagging feeling that there was some little thing he had left undone, something that Duffy would ream him on the next morning.

So now he sat in the car lighting one cigarette off another and telling himself, *Everything's cool.* This broad'll come home. We'll tuck her in and take off for the night. Once she's behind closed doors, it's Duffy's problem.

Then he saw the Pinto drive by for the third time. One of his guys nudged him. "This hoople's lookin' for a parkin' space and we got the whole block booked."

"That's Billy Benson," McKinnon said. He jumped

out of the car like it was on fire. "I gotta call the boss." He started down the street and stopped dead.

Karen Winterman was turning the corner.

Benson had been double-parked on West End Avenue. At 4:45 he pulled onto Eighty-ninth Street and drove by the building. He was looking for a light-skinned black guy. His first pass around the block he came up empty. Second time around he saw an old black dude with a cane puttering around by the service stairs. Third time around the old black dude was standing in the middle of the sidewalk staring down the block at something. As Benson drove by, he checked the guy out in the rearview mirror. He wasn't old at all, he was a kid. And there was something so hard in his face that you could spot it in a rearview mirror thirty feet away.

Benson pulled over in front of a hydrant. He slid out of the car. The guy had both hands on the cane, no weapon in sight. *I'll be able to get my hands around his throat*, Benson thought.

He walked slowly, trying to keep things casual until he got within arm's length. The guy stood rooted to the spot. He was looking at something behind Benson. Then his eyes flicked over and he met Benson's gaze. For a moment they stared at each other. The guy seemed to recognize him. He raised the cane over his head.

"Get back, Karen," he shouted. "Karen Winterman, Ph.D. . . ."

Benson turned, following the direction of his eyes. A dark-haired girl was coming up the block. She stopped and looked around in a panic.

"Benson, watch out!"

Benson turned again. McKinnon from Duffy's office was running across the street, his gun drawn.

He felt a sudden sharp pain in his gut and reached out instinctively. A blade scraped against his palm. The black dude was breathing in his face, his features twisted, his red eyes popping. "Deal's off, motherfucker," he said. He stepped back, waving a bloody knife, and came at Benson again. Benson lunged at the blade, wrapping his hands around the serrated edge and kicked out at the dude's bad leg, catching him in the shin. The guy shrieked and let go of the knife.

Somebody shouted, "Benson, get down!" Benson heard shots coming from behind his ear. The black dude went down, rolled over and then came up with a gun.

Benson dropped down, pulling at his ankle holster. He shot twice from the ground. The black dude doubled over, holding his gut. Shots were coming from all directions. The black dude did a three-sixty, firing wildly, then went down hard on his face, his gun skidding into the gutter.

Benson crawled along the cold, pebbled pavement. It felt cool and soothing like the bathroom floor when you're really shitfaced and you want someplace nice to lie down. Had to find a nice cool spot close to the toilet, in case he wanted to spit up some of this blood. Had to be careful not to lie on his stomach. The knife was in there. Had to roll over onto his back. Benson's head lolled back off the curb. He looked up into the quiet rustling leaves of a tree. For a moment the branches parted and he saw the sky.

*　　*　　*

McKinnon had a wounded cop, a dying perp, and a block full of hysterical people. But he knew what his first order of business had to be. He ran down the street to where Karen Winterman was gasping and writhing in a detective's grasp. It looked like she was having convulsions.

"Is this ever going to end?" she was saying. "Is this ever going to end?" She kept repeating it.

McKinnon drew one of the cops aside. "What happened?"

"I tackled her when the shooting started," he said. "She got a little hysterical. I guess she figured I was after her." The guy took off his snap cap with an apologetic smile. He was a black Anti-Crime guy and looked more like the people he was supposed to arrest than they did. "I guess I scared her," he said.

McKinnon walked up the block. Guys were yelling into their walkie-talkies as they tried to keep the rubberneckers away from the scene. The black guy had been hit at least five times, but he was up on one knee, forehead scraping the ground, crawling around in circles. Benson was on his back, his head in the gutter, his belly heaving, a kitchen knife buried up to the hilt in his side. The Anti-Crime kid with the guitar hadn't had time to take cover and had been hit in the shoulder. There was blood everywhere and more coming.

McKinnon bent down to Benson. "Hang on, Benson, we got an ambulance coming."

Benson screwed up his face and clenched his teeth. He looked like he was trying to push the knife out. "Payback is a bitch," he said.

McKinnon got his men to form a circle around the

scene until the uniform guys showed up. They stood there detouring pedestrians, but nobody left the area, and in two minutes the radio cars had to scream threats over the P.A. to get through. By the time the ambulance came there were at least a thousand people on the block. A brown Plymouth nosed through on the sidewalk and Duffy jumped out. As McKinnon ran to meet him he went over the series of events, hoping he had done the right thing. *The prick'll figure out a way to blame me for this.*

Duffy pointed down at Karen Winterman, who was on a stoop, talking to a paramedic. "How's she?"

"She freaked out when the shooting started, but she's okay."

Duffy pointed up the block toward the two stretchers that lay side by side at the curb. "What happened?"

"They went after each other, that's all I can tell you. The black kid stabbed Benson with a steak knife. Then he fired on us. We shot him."

"Any idea what Benson was doing here?"

"He said something about payback."

Duffy nodded and went over to the stoop where Karen Winterman sat with her head in her hand as the paramedic took her blood pressure.

"Doctor Winterman . . ."

She blinked and grimaced like a little girl. To McKinnon she looked like his seven-year-old when he said he had to work and couldn't take her to the circus.

"Why is all this happening to me?" she asked in a quavery little-girl's voice.

Duffy bent over and took her hand like he was asking her to dance. "It's almost over," he said.

"I tried to help Arnie. I swear I did. I wanted him to get better. I didn't want him to die."

"We know now that you were right," Duffy said. "Arnold Feinstein was not a drug dealer. He was being used as a cover by this other man, the man you saw outside his apartment."

But Karen Winterman wasn't consoled. "I wanted to help Arnie, Inspector," she said. Sobbing, she fell forward onto his chest. "Why am I being punished?"

With an awkward look at his men, Duffy put his arm around Karen Winterman's shoulder. "If you can just come over and take a look at this man."

He walked through the crowd of cops and paramedics to the two stretchers where Benson and Edmund lay side by side hooked up to IVs, oxygen tubes in their noses and mouths.

Benson looked up at her without interest, then turned his head.

"Is this the man who saved me?" Karen asked.

Duffy nodded solemnly and moved her over to Edmund, who was strapped down and still bucking violently. "We had to restrain him," the paramedic said. "He kept yanking the IV loose."

Karen recognized him instantly and turned away with revulsion.

"That's him," she said.

At the sight of Karen, Edmund's struggles increased. A ribbon of blood trickled out of his nose. He was trying to talk, but they had put a piece of plastic in his mouth so he wouldn't bite his tongue. The veins popped in his temples. He threw his head back and managed to free his hand. The fist was clenched so tightly that his arm trembled. He slowly unclenched it. There was a bloody key in the palm of his hand, the kind that opened suitcases.

"I think he wants you to have it," Duffy said.

"No!" She turned away and buried her head in his shoulder. "Please, can I go now? Please take me away from this."

Duffy patted her hair. "It's alright, it's all over. I'll take you upstairs." He put his arm around Karen, whispering reassuringly. The crowd parted as he walked her toward her building.

Edmund's arm went limp. The key dropped onto the sidewalk where it was retrieved by a detective, who wrapped a cellophane bag around his hand to pick it up, then dropped it in another bag and into his pocket, where he forgot about it for a week until he brought the suit in to be cleaned.

Edmund died a few moments later. Benson watched as they slid the sheet over his head and buckled the corpse at the knees to keep it from falling off the stretcher as they lifted it on the ambulance.

He turned to McKinnon, who was crouching by him. "You gonna put a sheet over my head, too?"

McKinnon squeezed his hand. "Hold on, pal."

Duffy came over as they were getting ready to move Benson into the ambulance. "Can he talk?" he asked McKinnon without waiting for an answer, bent down and asked, "What was this all about, Benson?"

"That's the guy who killed Vinnie," Benson whispered.

"You got even."

"Nobody gets even. You gonna take my shield?"

"Give me Sally Fish."

"And . . ."

"You're a hero. You saved my star witness. You killed the man who murdered four policemen. You'll retire on three-quarters pension for disability."

"I'll give you Sally Fish on a silver platter," Benson closed his eyes. A pulse flickered in his neck. Duffy looked over at the paramedic. "He'll make it," the paramedic said.

"Did you hear that?" Duffy said. He raised the sheet and looked at Benson's gaping wound. "This is your lucky day, Billy the Kid."

DOUBLE BANG

*T*he little Spanish nursemaid pushed her carriage down the block away from the scene. Anyone passing would have been amazed that her charge could sleep through this racket. But there was no baby in this carriage.

The nursemaid walked a few blocks to a pay phone on West End Avenue. As she dialed her number, two ambulances speeded by followed by a convoy of screaming police cars. She couldn't hear the person on the other end until all the cars had passed. When it was quiet again she heard that familiar chuckle.

"Something big must have happened," he said. "Tell me, Ida."

She told him everything she had seen. The black man and the white man fighting. The police shooting the black man. In the crowd she had overheard people talking in Spanish about how both men were dying. She told him that, too.

"You're the best, *muñeca*," Mr. Feinstein said. "You're better than any man. Now, did you see the woman?"

Ida told him about the woman who had been brought to look at the two men.

"You recognize her from the photo I showed you?"

"Yes, it is the same woman."

"Ida, I am full of emotion. You have given me the gift of life today. I would have been with you, but there are men in my business who made me stay here until certain things were done. Now because of you I am free. I can work day and night to bring Prudencio home to you. You understand?"

"Yes."

"Now this woman. You would know her if you saw her again."

"Yes."

"Now you have that pistol I gave you."

"Yes."

"Good. Now listen to me, *muñeca*. I have one more job for you."

Sally Fish hung up the phone and patted his shirt pocket. He needed a one and one, a cigarette. After pulling off a double bang by remote control he deserved a blow, and he was going to get it. That and his guns and his money. And no remarks about his cocaine habit.

Sally tried the bedroom door. It was locked. He rattled the knob. "Open the fuckin' door!"

The lock clicked and the door creaked back on its hinges. Sammy Calcagno was standing in the darkened hallway with two oversized mamelukes behind him.

"Hiya, Sal."

Sally walked out so quickly that Sammy tripped over his own feet backing up in the narrow hallway and almost went over the banister.

"I want my Uncle Frank," Sally said.

"He's in his room, Sal." Sammy came at him, blinking, shrugging, holding his palms in the air, making every submissive gesture in the book. "Look, Sal, I'm sorry about this, you know, but I had to do what I was told. You know how it is. If it had been up to me . . ."

Sally smacked him hard on the side of the head. "Apologize with your feet, asshole. And take these fuckin' ballerinas with you."

"Okay, Sal. Anything you say, Sal." Sammy waddled down the stairs. The two mamelukes made themselves real small, easing by Sally, eyes averted.

Sally walked down the hall to Frankie's door. He knocked softly, then pushed the door open without waiting for an invitation. Frankie was on the phone. He waved and pointed to the bed. Sally stacked the pillows and lay back against the headboard, his shoes on the sheets.

"Yeah," Frankie said into the phone. He listened for a few minutes, staring impassively at Sally. "Uh huh," he said. Then he hung up.

"You're sure you didn't tell this guy too much, Uncle Frank," Sally said, smiling broadly so his uncle would know he was kidding.

Frankie fished out a cigarette and lit it. He slid an ashtray close, picked a shred of tobacco out of his teeth and brushed a little gray ash off his sleeve without taking his eyes off Sally.

"Remind me never to book you on the Johnny Carson show," Sally said. He got up and slipped a cigarette out of his uncle's pack, grabbing his uncle's lighter to light it.

Frankie's lower lip twitched, which for him was the equivalent of a belly laugh. "You act like a guy who just hit the lottery," he said.

"Any shmuck can hit it, I fixed it," Sally said. "Benson's dead, Edmund's dead and the shrink will be dead by tomorrow night. All this accomplished in a locked room against all odds by your much maligned nephew Salvatore."

"Gonna handle Karen Winterman yourself?" Frankie asked.

"No." Sally wondered how his uncle knew her name. Had he told him? Didn't think he had, but there had been so much frantic rapping in the last forty-eight hours. "I got my little Ecuadoran set up for that one. Just gotta get with her to work out the details."

"Then you'll clip the little Ecuadoran, that the plan?"

Sally's neck stiffened suddenly. This thing wasn't going right at all. "She's with me, Uncle Frank. You clip everybody who does things for you, there'll be nobody left to do anything for you."

"She's with you?" Frankie said as if he didn't understand. "A little broad who can't speak English?"

"Excuse me, Uncle Frank, but she's got bigger balls than anybody you got in this whole family."

Frankie's lower lip twitched again. "Present company included?"

This was too much. Sally jumped up. He raised his hand but turned quickly to avoid jabbing his finger in his uncle's face. "Not for nothin', Uncle Frank, but you got more deadwood in this family than a fuckin' lumberyard. Why do you think they're crackin' down on the rackets? Why do you think they're closin' down all of our operations? No talent, that's why. No fresh air, no new faces. The world's changing, and we have to change with it."

Frankie looked thoughtful as if maybe Sally was getting through his thick Sicilian head. "So how do we do that, Sal?"

"First we modernize, we streamline. There's a coupla four-hundred-pound *gavones* we don't need. There's a buncha drunks and degenerate gamblers—you know who I'm talkin' about."

"What do we do about them, Sal?" Frankie asked.

"Gee, I don't know," Sally said. But the sarcastic approach didn't work with his uncle, so Sally switched to sincerity. "Gimme some real clout in this crew, and I'll show you the difference inside of three months. Let me make some moves. I got alotta fresh ideas, new ways to do the same old business. Haven't I proved myself already?"

Frankie rose slowly. For a second Sally didn't know if his uncle was going to shake his hand or smack him. Then Frankie came around and grabbed him by the shoulders. "My little nephew Sally boy, you grew up so fast." He squeezed Sally in a bear hug—he had long arms for a short guy. "Remember we used to watch you play basketball in the schoolyard? Always bet on any team you were on."

"I always found a way to win, Uncle Frank," Sally said. "I still do."

Frankie pulled back with a stern look. "No more drugs, Sal."

"No more drugs, Uncle Frank. I promise."

"Go take care of your business." Frankie gave him a little shove. "I'll talk to you tomorrow."

"This is the best move you ever made, Uncle Frank. Believe me."

Sally ran downstairs looking for that mook Sammy Calcagno. But the house was empty, nobody around. His Targa was in the driveway, the key in the ignition.

"Sally boy."

Al Lucito came around the side of the house, his knees buckling, booze reeking off him.

"Little early for you," Sally said.

"Sometimes a drink is the only thing that'll do it," Al said. He handed Sally an envelope. "Here's your money. I guess it's all there, but I wouldn't have a heart attack if I found out a few bills had blown away in the breeze."

Sally pocketed the envelope. "I know where to find that breeze any time I want to, anyway."

"Your guns are in the glove compartment," Al said. "I pulled through a few times on the Thirty-eight." Al shook his head in sad reproof. "You gotta keep guns clean, Sal. You want 'em to work when they have to. You only get one chance with a gun."

"That's why I don't use them," Sally said. "I like to stretch the odds out a little. Guns are okay for mechanics like you."

"Shouldn't talk down to people, Sal," Al said. "Even runts like me who deserve it."

Sally got in the Targa. "You just comin' from confession or what?"

"You gotta bring a sleepin' bag if I go into confession. No point anyway, I'll burn in hell for what I've done and I know it."

Sally adjusted the front seat. "That fat slob Sammy Calcagno probably fucked up the transmission." He turned the key. The Targa roared up underneath him. Sally pulled on his driving gloves. He floored the pedal just for the pleasure of hearing the engine sing. "This is better than sex, you know that, Al?"

"Yeah, look." Al squinted up at Frankie's window. "He'll kill me for this." He slipped a cellophane bag out of the pocket of his windbreaker.

Sally grabbed the bag and hefted it. It was his stash, untouched.

"Frankie's like a priest," Al said. "He don't have no vices and don't understand anyone who does. The rest of us need a little consolation, you know what I mean?" Al patted Sally on the shoulder. "Wait'll you get home, alright, Sally boy?"

"Sure. Thanks."

Sally revved the Targa and peeled out of the driveway in reverse. He drove along for a minute or two, the cellophane bag warm against his leg. When he turned onto Surf Avenue he couldn't take it anymore. He pulled over near the Cyclone. No time for a spoon—he dipped his pinky into the bag and took a woof. Then another one. The coke scorched going up. It was amazing. You laid off one day and it was like doing it for the first time. Sally dipped again. Again. And again, until the air-conditioner went on in his brain. *What a day,* he thought. The blow was pounding behind his eyes. He pulled to a light and tried to shift into neutral, but he couldn't close his hand around the knob. He laughed. "Good blow." Horns honked behind him. "Wait a second, asshole, where ya goin'?" A bolt of lightning lit up in his head. For a split second he thought he'd been shot. The gears screamed. The Targa bucked out from under him. His eyes were boiling. He couldn't see. All he could hear was gears clashing, clashing. He pounded his head against the steering wheel. "Shmuck, they poisoned you. They took the easy way!"

The Targa jumped the curb, then stalled and rolled a few feet coming to rest up against the boarded-up facade of a shooting gallery. A group of homeless men wandered out from under the boardwalk to within a few feet of the car, but hung back, put off by the unearthly shrieks coming from inside. When the shrieking stopped, they approached and saw Sally Fish writhing in silence, his larynx having been burnt to the point where it could only emit the hiss of departing breath, like air leaking from a tire until it is finally flat.

A week later Inspector Duffy called Karen Winterman at the hospital. The corpse in the car had finally been positively identified as Sal Pescatore, and Duffy thought she should know. He was surprised to find that Dr. Winterman was no longer affiliated with the hospital. A call to the head of the psychology department confirmed this. Dr. Winterman had resigned. She had told friends she was leaving New York City for good, and although many people often make this declaration, Dr. Winterman had proven her resolve by giving up her rent-controlled apartment.

She had taken a job as an assistant professor on the psychology faculty of an undistinguished regional branch of the State University, Duffy was told. This had surprised her colleagues, who had always predicted a brilliant and significant career for her. Offprints of her article on charming sociopaths had been circulated in the community and had provoked an astonishing response. At the time of her departure her office had been flooded with referrals and offers of grants from the NIH, the Defense Department, the Bureau of Prisons. Her work had been accepted. Her future was assured.

Dr. Winterman had gone back to her home town, a small city in northwestern New York near the Canadian border. Her father was retiring after forty-five years of medical practice in that rural area. He faced a very trying period of transition, Dr. Winterman had said in her letter of resignation. She expressed a strong desire to be with him in his hour of emotional need. Her father's happiness was the only thing that mattered to her now.